No Chance in Spell

FATE WEAVER
BOOK FOUR

REGINA WELLING

No Chance in Spell

ISBN- 978-1-953044-03-7

Cover design by: L. Vryhof
Interior design by: L. Vryhof

http://reginawelling.com
http://erinlynnwrites.com

First Edition
Printed in the U.S.A.

Contents

Chapter 1

Clara

People—even witches—find great comfort in telling their secrets to the dead. Or, in my case, the not-quite-but-assumed dead.

Not that I could fault the theory. I had, after all, been turned to stone. Most people wouldn't survive the experience.

Why confess their hearts to a witch with a heart of stone? Because no matter how petty were the crimes of my sister witches, they paled in comparison to mine—to the worst sin imaginable. I stand (because I cannot do otherwise) accused of killing my own daughter. A gravely-mistaken assumption, but who could blame them for jumping to the conclusion? The punishment for killing another witch is being turned to stone.

No one knows by whose hand the sentence is served, only that it is swift and irrevocable. Kill a witch, become a living monument: an effective warning against falling prey to the destructive side of the power that runs through the blood of our kind. All the evidence was against me.

Not having murdered anyone before, I'd had no idea if stoned witches remained awake inside their prison for all eternity. In the middle of a heated discussion with my daughter—a fight, if you want to be technical about it—my binding spell crossed with Sylvana's ball of dark magic, picked up some of her intent, mixed it with mine and slammed us both with the result.

Nothing remained but a burnt scar on the earth and me, fearful I'd destroyed my own flesh and blood, forced to stand watch over the scene of my own destruction. Wanting to cry and not being able to shed a tear is the worst feeling in the world.

I'd resigned myself to an eternity of listening to the transgressions of others while wishing I'd eventually die inside my cocoon—that is, until sly Sylvana showed up very much alive and well. And with no intention of releasing me from stasis.

When word of her miraculous resurrection spread, the number of huddled confessors decreased dramatically.

Since then, witches pass me by with a look that

says they hope I never heard a word of their transgressions and if I did, that I never have the chance to speak of them out loud. But I've smelled the dirty laundry flung around my feet, and I remember the stench of every tiny tidbit.

Lexi stands before me now with fierce determination in her eyes and a longing to set me free so strong I can feel it in my granite bones. She's tried before and failed, but third time's the charm. So they say, anyway. A pot of Balefire sits at her feet; the Bow of Destiny rides her hand with an arrow aimed at my heart. It's a good thing I'm virtually frozen, because my instincts are screaming for me to duck.

I can't duck. I can't look away. Nothing is left but to stand (as if I had any other choice) and listen for the twang of the string, wait for the burning sting of the barb, and hope that her aim is true.

Lexi

Shooting my stoned grandmother with Cupid's bow and a flaming arrow. What was I thinking? There are a hundred ways this could go wrong.

Determined, I pulled the bowstring back, forced trembling nerves to rock steadiness. Hushed calm flowed like water to fill me from the bottom up, pushing out my breath on a sigh. There would never be a better moment than now.

I let the arrow fly.

Time slowed to a crawl, and crystalline clear vision focused on the burning arrow crawling through the air toward its target. The golden barb picked up light and magic until it passed the halfway mark and time fell back to normal speed.

Pink flame arced straight and true, pierced stone, and lanced into Clara's heart. For half a second, nothing happened, and it was as if the whole world held its breath.

My heart tried to punch a hole in my throat.

A lifetime of longing for blood family—for the mother of my dreams—hadn't come to much once Sylvana finally appeared. Wicked witches make lousy parents, and you can't trust them as far as you can throw a unicorn. Don't try that, by the way, unicorns get stabby when you pick them up. Especially the purple ones.

The pressure popped my ears, my stomach plummeted into my shoes, and the Bow of Destiny slipped to the ground. Nothing else moved in the cotton-heavy silence—not a bird, not a bee, not even me.

Failure.

I'd been so sure my plan would work. Turned to stone in a freak accident involving wicked witchery, my grandmother's statue guarded the clearing near my house for as long as I could remember. Once I'd learned her stoning wasn't a lifetime sentence for killing another witch, I'd searched high and low for a means to set her free.

Salem and I had put our heads together—my familiar used his human head, not his cat one—and hatched a plan to use my newfound Fate Weaver abilities and my father's bow to infuse Clara's heart with the mighty power of the Balefire. It's a good thing tending the magical flame is only one of my legacies, because Cupid's bow—technically mine at the moment—turned out to be the pivotal part of the plan.

It would propel an arrow made from living gold and the essence of myself—don't ask how that works because I'm a little hazy on the details—through the stone encasing Clara's body and into her heart. Dipping the arrow in the Balefire would, if all went as planned, inject enough of the fire's healing energy to bring her back to life.

Sounds like a long shot, I know (no pun intended), but it made sense when we came up with the idea. I am Lexi Balefire: Keeper of the sacred fire; maker of matches; weaver of fates. Shouldn't I be able to weave one for my grandmother that didn't involve eternal punishment for a crime she didn't commit?

Sound rushed back to a world I'd already forgotten had gone silent. The first thing I heard was the sound of my breath hitching as I cried. I glanced behind me at the grave faces of my companions and tried to accept my failure.

A sharp crack rent the air.

Then another, and another.

Stone slid off my grandmother like snow off a roof—one slow ripple that revealed her by inches and raced my tears of happiness to the ground. Like mist, the arrow infused with living gold faded from her chest without leaving a mark. I felt its weight return to the quiver slung across my back.

"It worked." A whoop went up from dear Aunt Mag, the newest member of my ragtag family.

I walked forward until I was standing close enough to touch my grandmother, but too shy to actually lay so much as the tip of one finger on her skin.

"Nice shot." A warm smile brightened her first words to me as I launched into the waiting arms of a woman who could have been my double save a wrinkle or two around the corners of her emerald green eyes. I know witches aren't supposed to cry, but whoever put that nonsense out into the world was an idiot. We're human. Fancy extras and all.

Most of my body shook from the relief of pent-up tension, and I buried my face in a neck that still smelled of sun-warmed stone.

"It's Lexi. I mean, I'm Lexi Balefire. You're my…you're Clara." Nonsense tumbled out of my mouth like I thought she had been in a coma or something. Perhaps she had—I'd no idea whether she'd been cognizant all this time, and I desperately hoped she hadn't.

"I know, dear girl. I know." Gentle hands nudged me to arm's length so she could get a better look at me. The abandoned child who lived in the corners of my soul crept out from the shadows and into my grandmother's light. That child had taken a beating, poor thing, when my mother came back, and I knew she represented the part of me that feared another devastating fiasco.

My smile so wide it hurt, I turned to my made-from-the-scraps family and saw there wasn't a dry eye in the bunch. Salem stood next to my four faerie godmothers and my boyfriend, Mackintosh Clark—also known as Kin since Mackintosh is kind of a mouthful. The only thing missing from the list was a partridge in a pear tree, but I wouldn't be surprised if we had one of those perching somewhere in the backyard.

Even Salem's cat-like emotions suffered from a touch of sentiment. I'd save the teasing for later. If I had a bad case of jelly legs after this experience, I could only imagine how Clara's must feel given the number of years she'd been immobilized.

"Can you walk?" I whispered, instinctively knowing she wouldn't want anyone to see her at a disadvantage.

"I think so." My grandmother's arm went around my waist and mine around hers for added support. Plus, I relished the safe sensation of being snuggled against her side. We took a tentative step or two away from the site where her feet had rested for all those long years, and she stopped for one brief look back. Petals drooped until nothing more than brambles remained of the roses that had twined around her skirts mere moments before, and while we watched, even those turned to mulch. Maybe the force of her displeasure killed the delicate flowers, or perhaps they couldn't survive the loss of her essence. Either way, petals fell to dust and rode away on the breeze.

A satisfied smile that was just this side of a smirk crossed Clara's lips as she turned her attention toward the waiting group. "Mag, you haven't changed a bit. It's good to see you." Stepping out of the shelter of my embrace, she moved forward on her own. Never let it be said the Balefire women lack resilience.

If there was any animosity between the two sisters, they hid it well. I caught myself staring and wondering again at the visible difference in their ages. Maybe now I'd get to hear Mag's story. But first, I made introductions.

"These are my…"

Clara pointed to the faeries in turn. "Evian, Terra, Soleil, and Vaeta. You have my undying gratitude for the way you've cared for Alexis over the years."

"Lexi. Everyone calls me Lexi."

"We love her." Terra's simple statement—truth, because the Fae don't lie—warmed me to my toes. Welcoming Clara back into our—her—home was sure to beckon complicated emotions into the mix and with the Fae, emotions sometimes turned tangible. Not only had I opened a can of worms, but they were also enchanted worms with the power to multiply until they cluttered the entire house.

I wouldn't have it any other way.

"Mrs…Miss…" Kin shot me a desperate look as he tried to figure out how to address this new person in my life.

"Call me Clara. You'd be Kin." Clara gave him a mock measuring look, but Kin didn't pick up on the nuance.

"Yes, ma'am. Good to meet you. You're not…I mean…Lexi's mother was…" Poor thing. I'd give him props for standing up for me, but asking my grandmother if she was wicked might not be the best way to make a first impression.

"My daughter and I share many things: our face, the Balefire blood, a regular craving for butter pecan ice cream. But we operate off an entirely different set of values and perspectives. She's not entirely bad, my Sylvana." A sigh gusted from Clara's lips and she gave Aunt Mag a warning look. "I made a great many mistakes with her. Mistakes that shaped her into a…"

Mag chimed in, "Selfish brat with way too much power and almost no impulse control." Nail, meet the hammer that's about to hit you on the head.

Letting the conversation go before it turned ugly,

Clara singled out the last member of her welcoming party. "Salem, how nice to see you again." She reached out to grasp his hand in hers and gave his arm a little rub that made him preen.

"Clara, always a pleasure."

"You two know each other?" How was that possible? Clara had been stoned long before he'd shown up on my doorstep.

"Of course we do. We met during my job interview. While I was between witches."

I made an effort to yank my jaw back off my chest. Obviously, there was more to certain witch-related processes than I'd been led to believe. Since Salem's life—his ninth and final one, no less—will end the moment I die, I'd assumed we'd also been born simultaneously. Familiars competing for placement in a family seemed mundane by comparison. Job interviews, though? Really? Did they have to provide references? A resume?

"Speaking of food cravings, you wouldn't happen to have any butter pecan ice cream in the freezer would you?"

If we didn't, there would be some in there by the time we hit the kitchen. My faerie godmothers rock it out when it comes to conjuring yummy snackage.

Walking past the Bow of Destiny, I bent down to retrieve it before one of the fairies accidentally touched it again. Repairing the bow after its first devastating Fae encounter had been enough of an ordeal to last me a lifetime. Now all I had to do was figure out how to use it for its intended purpose, and not as a method for pelting my relatives with flaming arrows.

Objects of great power always come with rules. Complicated rules designed to create problems for anyone who tries to use them and complex enough not to be parsed with ease. Forged by my father, the Bow of Destiny was sure to come with a set worthy of his station.

The bow was meant to help me match souls, and there was a distinct possibility I could be held accountable for using it to my own advantage with Clara, even if it was for a good cause. Whatever you put out into the world comes back to you threefold, and depending on your intent could either lift you up or tear you down. I'd picked up the bow knowing all of that, and had chosen to accept whatever consequences came from my decision.

But I wasn't thinking about any of those things at the moment my fingers closed over the section of the riser just above the handle—and then I wasn't thinking anything at all.

You can't think when your mind has been taken over by something with a consciousness deeper than you ever imagined. Take it from me, I've been there.

Overpowered by it all, I hit the ground like a marionette with clipped strings. That's what they tell me, anyway.

Wild energy swelled and swept through my head like a whirlwind of echoing vastness with only one goal: to make room for itself within the confines of my puny existence. My hand gripped the bow as though it were an electric fence and while the current jolted through me, I was helpless to let go.

Puffy pink clouds floated across my vision while words boomed through my head in a language made up of sounds resembling music—if music itself were a god. Full and round and more real than anything I could touch with my hands, the sound carried me as if I weighed less than a windborne seed. A tiny parachute of dandelion fluff to be buffeted in any direction the breeze deemed to blow.

A single conviction burned itself into my soul. This was no toy and the matches I made using the bow would never, could never be broken. I needed to choose wisely before pointing my arrows.

My throat swelled with the depth of emotion being transferred to me from the living weapon as it made itself mine. Or took me for its own. To this day I'm unsure whether I became the carrier of the bow or its pawn.

The bow carried an electric energy that knocked me out cold. For the second time in less than an hour. I came to with the sound of my name ringing in my ears and Kin's face just inches from mine.

"Lexi, can you hear me? How do you feel?"

The answers I meant to give were *yes*, and *I feel amazing*. I think I said something like, "Gah."

Eloquence is me.

"I'm calling 911." Kin pulled out his phone. "You fainting twice in one day is more than I can take."

My focus snapped fully back to the present.

"Fainting sounds so wimpy. I'm fine." Kin's eyes widened doubtfully. "Better than, actually." If I could bottle this feeling and sell it, I'd be a millionaire inside of a week. Probably a gazillionaire. "I feel incredible." Like I could move mountains.

The only thing I moved was myself—off the ground. Then I remembered how I ended up down there in the first place and reached again for the bow.

"Where is it?" Swiveling my head left and right, I searched the area around where I'd fallen. "Don't tell me it's broken again."

Kin's face turned a shade paler, but his voice stayed steady as he answered, "It's gone."

"Gone? What? Where?"

"Inside you." Helpful answer. Not.

"Excuse me?"

"It…I don't even know how to describe it, but you absorbed it. Or it melted into you. Quiver and all." Kin brushed a few errant blades of grass off my legs and gave me time to formulate a response. Nothing reasonable came to mind, so I chose to accept the weirdness for the time being and think about the repercussions later. I finally knew why Scarlett O'Hara preferred to put things off until tomorrow. I had enough on my plate for today.

My gaze traveled to Clara's face. It had gone all grandmotherly and concerned. I lifted my chin and dared her to push the issue. "Why don't we go inside and raid the fridge?" After an epic day, all I wanted was something mundane to bring me back to earth. Parts of me still felt like they were jetting through the clouds.

As it turned out, there was a final surprise or two still in store.

"It all looks so different." Clara rubbernecked to take in the changes to her home. I'll confess my knees felt a little shaky in anticipation of her reaction to the lighter, more airy color scheme we'd selected during the big renovation.

Twenty-five years is a short time in the lifespan of a witch, but a long one when it comes to technological advances. What would Clara think about the 55-inch flatscreen that had replaced her bulky 19-inch television set? Or the shabby chic feel of the whitewashing technique on the wainscoting in the hall. The kitchen had doubled in size when we added the faerie's wing, but Clara's bedroom remained untouched. She would have one familiar space at least.

"We can put it all back if you hate it." As offers go, this one was half-hearted at best. Restoring this house to its former state would be about as easy as unscrambling an egg. I appealed to Terra, begging her with my eyes to say something. Anything. The only time the four of my godmothers are ever this quiet is when they're getting ready to launch of one of their epic battles, so what was up with that?

Terra winked and then tossed me under the bus without a second thought. "We have some work to do, so we'll just leave you to get acquainted again. Clara, it's good to have you back." She said it, so I had to believe she meant it, no matter what the repercussions. Kin received a pointed stare from Terra on her way out and took the hint.

His kiss carried the perfunctory awkwardness of feeling watched by a gun-toting father. I was pretty sure my grandmother wouldn't need a firearm if she decided she didn't like my boyfriend. Not that she would, he was a likeable sort. "I'll see you tomorrow, babe."

Suddenly the room felt empty, and I wasn't sure what to say to the veritable stranger wolfing down ice cream like it was made from honey and nectar. Apparently, twenty-five years spent frozen in the front yard wasn't as big a deal to the witches in my family as it was to me.

A whole new world was opening up right in front of me, but my grandmother and great-aunt acted as though Clara had simply been on an extended holiday. Mag filled in the awkward silence with fodder about witches I might have met but couldn't put a face to any of the names.

"Matilda Backwater mixed up marigold with mandrake in a batch of that cough syrup she's always bragging about. It reacted with one of the other ingredients and produced a series of interesting side effects. That was a good one." Mag dished up gossip.

"What happened?" Spoon pinging against the bowl, Clara scraped the last bit of ice cream from the bottom.

"Lost her mind, that's what. Went on what amounted to a week-long acid trip. Don't mention dragons in front of her unless you want to hear the tale of how she brought down an albino Wyvern using an enchanted golden lasso. I guess she thought she was Wonder Woman or something."

Gran's laugh burst out, "Thanks for the mental image of Matilda all kitted out in a patriotic bathing…"

A whooshing noise pushed against our eardrums.

"My heavens!" Clara exclaimed as the room filled with billows of blue smoke and interrupted the conversation before Mag went off on a diatribe about the proper methods of potion making. Through a wide set of doors leading from the kitchen to the parlor, I glanced toward the ever-burning hearth and saw the Balefire sneeze and emit another belch of smoke. Tongues of flame burst out into the room in a flash of light and fury, then retreated just as quickly.

"Does this happen often?" Clara's mild tone

infused the question with deeper meaning.

"Never." Embarrassed that on my first day with my grandmother I'd already come off looking like an incompetent, I rushed toward the fireplace to see if I could find a reason for the outburst. "Have you seen anything like it before?" Thrusting my hands into the fire, I picked and prodded my way through the flames feeling for inconsistencies or anomalies that would give me a clue. Soot darker than night stained a trail up the overmantel and across the ceiling.

"Here, let me." Clara gently nudged me aside and did essentially the same thing I had just done. Evidently, she came to the same conclusions, too, because after a minute she dusted her hands off on her dress and shrugged.

"Probably just flustered," she proclaimed. "By having two keepers in the house."

The Balefire formed itself into a shape that reminded me of a person holding hands to either side in confusion before retreating to the back of the fireplace where it turned sullen and banked itself low save for the occasional spark. One fire, two masters. Oh, goody. Why is it that every time I take a step forward, I'm shoved two steps back?

Chapter 2

"You painted the brickwork around the chimney. I think I like the lighter colors." The warmth and reassurance failed to quell the jump of nerves in my belly as my grandmother's sharp gaze scanned the parlor before landing again on the fireplace. She reached toward the handle resting inside the flame, then asked, "Do you mind?"

"Of course not. It's your house, and you should feel free to go anywhere. Though, I'd knock before walking into the faerie's wing. They have a tendency to react first and think later. It's their nature."

The last thing I needed was Faerie Armageddon with a side of Witchfest.

"Noted." Straightening back to standing, my grandmother leaned sideways to look past me at the rest of the parlor. "I take it the party planning business is going well." If there was a hint of dryness in her tone, she hid it behind a quick smile.

My glance strayed toward the far end of the room where a dozen potted palm trees awaited their debut at Saturday's beach-themed, sweet sixteen party. The faeries had a habit of leaving more business lying around than the house could handle. Dodging around bins, boxes, and elaborate floral arrangements was becoming the norm rather than the exception.

"Too well." I nodded. "But it makes them happy, so I don't like to complain." Happy faeries were merry faeries. I preferred them to the cranky versions. "But I'll speak to them about keeping the common spaces clear. There's plenty of room in the garage these days."

Forgoing a comment, Clara bent again and reached into the Balefire for the handle that would unlock the room behind the fireplace. Even though I knew the flames wouldn't penetrate her skin, it's still strange to see someone willingly reach into a fire.

Maybe it was just bad timing, or maybe the spirit of the flame chose that moment to descend into pettiness, but whichever it was, Gran's face hovered inches away from another sneeze-like eruption.

Her head disappeared in fiery gout, and despite what I just said about the Balefire witches' affinity with the flame, I indulged in a momentary freakout. A great cloud of ash and smoke blasted the fronds off several of Terra's palm trees and rolled Clara away from the hearth like a bundle of rags. She fetched up against the couch and lay in a shaking huddle while I let out a strangled scream.

"No!" I'd only just met her, it was too soon to lose my grandmother again.

Mag, spry despite all evidence of advanced age, got there first.

"Help me roll her over," Mag ordered, and together, we gently eased Clara onto her back. A swath of ash-strewn hair hid my grandmother's face, and I dreaded the sight of whatever injury lay below the white-brown strands. Burns are the worst. Before either of us could brush away the tangles, Clara did the deed and revealed a face untouched by anything other than mirth.

Laughing. The crazy witch found this funny. Fall on the floor, laugh yourself silly funny. Really?

Relief spread through me at about the same rate as pique over needlessly being frightened. But it's hard keeping a fierce face on when someone else is dissolving into unladylike giggles.

"It's not funny." I knew it sounded shrewish.

Clara pointed at me and laughed hard enough that I wondered if she'd been hit with a goofy spell or something.

"It sneezed," she finally wheezed out. "Get it? The Balefire has a cold."

The corner of Mag's mouth twitched. Just a little. She tried to pull it back, but like yawns, giggles are contagious. I caught them next but was the first one to sober up.

"This is serious." Everything in my life was serious these days, or had the potential to become a headache at any given moment. Take Clara, for instance. I'd wanted to save her, needed to make up for my mother's deceit, and yet, having her in the house altered everything. I'd had my own private wing—okay, so maybe it was more like a wingtip, but still, it had been mine alone.

No longer.

A pair of sharp-eyed elders would put a crimp in my alone time with Kin. I wasn't sure I could have my boyfriend sleeping—or not sleeping, if you know what I mean—over with the two of them down the hall. Not even with a silencing charm.

And now this effect we were having on the Balefire put another butt-shaped wrinkle in the linen pants of my life. The parlor was in shambles and they'd only been here for a few hours. What would happen in another month, another year? Was I supposed to give the Balefire back to Gran now that she was capable of taking care of it again? Was that even a possibility? None of the Balefire lore covered this contingency.

The duty of Keeper, as far as my research could tell me, passed to the next in line at the time of death. That Clara's death hadn't been exactly permanent was a problem.

"Of course it's serious, dear."

Giggles subsiding, for now, Clara scrambled to her feet and placated me with one of those pats on the arm that adults give a hysterical child. I retreated toward the fireplace while she reached down to give her sister a hand up. "I'd like to see the workshop, but I think maybe you should be the one to open the door. The Balefire seems to like you best."

How did she figure that? My puzzlement must have shown on my face because she pointed toward my feet. Flaming tendrils had snaked across the hearth to twine around my ankles like chubby puppies at play.

"Shoo," I slapped at the questing flames and reached for the handle. Best to get this over with and once our business was concluded, I might try and talk the godmothers into setting up one of their famous hot tubs on the patio.

The Balefire flickered a series of shadows against the chimney, and I swear I saw the outline of a hand holding up the middle finger. Witch or not, inanimate objects taking on a life of their own was getting a bit tedious for my tastes. I stuck my tongue out at absolutely nothing and gestured for Gran and Auntie to go first.

On the one occasion when Aunt Mag had joined me in the Balefire witch workshop I'd come to think of as my sanctum, I'd been shocked by the way the room reacted to her presence. The furniture had practically danced as it reconfigured from my preferred arrangement to hers. A less-than-subtle way of letting me know which witch was the alpha.

It wasn't me, in case you're wondering.

The experience had been humbling, but walking in after the sanctum recognized Clara's energy made me feel about *this* big.

Bracing myself for an entirely different aesthetic than I was used to, I took in my surroundings and would have let out a low whistle if I wasn't hopelessly miserable at whistling.

The large, circular dais still sat in a place of honor, just below a gigantic domed glass ceiling framed in intricate wrought iron. I'd recently learned my great-grandmother had forged and inlaid the living gold pentagram design around the perimeter shortly after the house was built, and of course that hadn't moved either. The rest of the room, however, had undergone a drastic transformation.

"Is that my second best cauldron stand? I knew you borrowed it and never gave it back." Mag went on the prowl for more of her purloined items. Grumbles of disgust and the sound of things being shoved aside followed her progress throughout the room.

Brighter lighting sparkled over a space organized to the nth degree. Double the usual number of shelves pressed themselves against the exterior walls, leaving a single, circular workstation dominating the otherwise open space.

Ingredients, utensils, and potion bottles marched along the shelves and formed into groups related to their intended use so anything she might need would be close at hand. It made sense, even if I prefer separate work zones because I tend to compartmentalize my magic. Obviously, Clara's view of the craft was more holistic in nature, and I hoped I'd one day see things the same way.

A solid library ladder replaced the rickety one, enticing me to climb its rungs and choose one of a thousand tomes with titles like *Burns and Boils, Volume 3*.

"I wasn't sure I'd ever get a chance to see this place again. It feels good. Like home."

Emotions crawled up my throat to form a lump that wouldn't go down no matter how many times I tried to swallow it away. My grandmother was home. Here. In the flesh. Trading my privacy for her presence? Total no-brainer. I'd do it all again—a hundred times over—if it meant I could watch Clara's hungry face absorb every detail of her domain.

She tossed a glance at Mag that spoke of private things and received a slight head shake in return.

Clara announced she would love a hot shower and a change of clothes and I got the impression the sisters had decided their business could wait.

To cover up that I knew they were hiding something, I did what I always do and babbled. "We kept your room just the way you left it, and I know it's small, but we can clear the boxes out of the dormer room." I turned to Mag, "I don't know where you've been staying since your place is gone, but you're welcome to stay here. You could have my room if you need more space."

"Don't be worrying, child. I'm not exactly burdened down with possessions. The dormer room suits me fine." Aunt Mag offered no explanation of her current living arrangements, and I didn't press her on the subject.

Midnight snack time is sort of like second breakfast in my house—completely unnecessary, but an institution we're not willing to abandon. It's a good thing we live just on the outskirts of Port Harbor because I don't like cars and walking almost everywhere burns off Terra's late-night monkey bread obsession.

I'll always have curves, though, if Clara's hourglass figure is any indication. We both have flowing, healthy chestnut-colored hair, and heart-shaped faces. We both have full, berry-stained lips and thick eyelashes. It stands to reason that unless I decide to let myself go entirely, I'll look almost exactly like she does when I get old. We witches age well, but I'll still pass up a taxi if it means fitting a little cardio into my day.

Gran's reintroduction to the household didn't stop me joining the godmothers, who assembled in the kitchen around the witching hour, and the scent of cinnamon and sugar had drawn more Balefire women than just me from their beds.

"What is that heavenly smell?" Gran asked, rubbing her eyes as she pulled a chair up to the island counter and smoothed a wild lock of hair behind one ear.

Just as I opened my mouth to respond, a peculiar wind began to gust outside. Hinges rattled in the doors, the floors began to creak, and a great, animalistic howl pierced the relative darkness that settled around us as the storm raged above.

Clara's eyes lit up, though for what reason I couldn't possibly imagine, and she looked to Aunt Mag with excitement, "Could it be?"

"Could it be what?" I asked with curiosity and a smidgen of concern.

"I can't think of any other alternative, so my guess is yes," Mag looked positively giddy with excitement.

"What's going on?" I asked again, looking helplessly toward the faeries, who merely shrugged and continued to sip coffee while feigning disinterest. Utter hogwash, that.

Apparently, I'd turned invisible, because nobody seemed to have any intention of answering my questions. Another bang drew my attention to the ceiling, where I could hear Salem's footsteps turn from the light pitter-patter of kitty paws to the heavy thump of a man's gait.

When he rounded the corner with ears perked—yeah, even in human form, I can tell—I assumed he was just as curious as I was, but of course, Salem had an inkling of what was to come.

At the sound of a sharp rap on the door, I jumped up from my seat alongside Clara and a surprisingly spry Mag. I opened my mouth to ask for information one last time and then promptly shut it as Gran opened the door and the answer hit me in the face like a ton of bricks.

The most quintessentially beautiful Siamese cat sat perched on the top step, glittering blue eyes peeking out from a mask of dark brown fur.

"Pyewacket!" Gran exclaimed, tears of joy jetting down her face as a miniature, purring tornado engulfed the cat in a swirl of fur. The woman left standing in the wake was just as gorgeous as her feline form. Sleek and perfectly put together, she all but oozed into the room.

Gran stepped forward to envelop her familiar in a warm hug, but Pyewacket took a step backward and raised a haughty chin. Ice blue eyes rode slanted cheekbones set high above lips that were probably lush and full when they weren't pressed into a firm line. We all watched in fascination as Gran's back went ramrod straight and all the tension in her body traveled north to square her shoulders in anticipation.

"Clara, what happened? Why was I stuck in Mrs. Chatterly's yard? What sorcery confined me into the form of a garden gnome? Do you have any idea how boring it is watching chipmunks and squirrels frolic around without a care in the world? There are no words to describe how insufferable that woman can be. She complains non-stop about her weight and then stashes Milky Ways in the potting shed. Twenty-five years! Explain yourself, please."

Pyewacket kept her gaze trained on Gran's eyes, and it occurred to me that perhaps insubordination and general disdain were traits all familiars shared. I could only imagine the diatribe I'd have to endure if Salem had been put in that situation. He'd only been stuck in his cat form while awaiting my Awakening as a witch, and my penance included a glut of seafood in exchange for forgiveness.

"Oh, Pye, I had no idea!" Gran explained the general gist of how she and my mother had waged magical war against one another and landed them both on karma's naughty list.

"I was in the same situation as you, and I had to watch Lexi grow up without a grandmother or a mother. I mean, of course, she had her godmothers," Gran shot an apologetic look toward the faeries, "but it wasn't exactly a picnic for me either. I'm so sorry!"

Pye finally conceded, allowed herself to be hugged

while she rubbed the top of her head against Gran's chin. The rest of us retreated to the kitchen to afford the pair a bit of privacy. I had to drag Salem by the scruff of his neck. Judging by the look on his face, I'd say he was about as smitten as a kitten can be. And who could blame him?

Chapter 3

An inch away from the sturdy six-panel door, my loosely-clenched fist froze before I could knock. Doubts crept from hidden alcoves of my psyche, whispered dire predictions in my ears, and then slithered back into the shadows to seethe. In happy TV families, young women sought heart-to-heart talks with their mothers and grandmothers without fear or whatever nebulous dread was settling over me. Surely I could do the same.

This would be easy. A piece of cake. What's so easy about a piece of cake, anyway? I've tried baking, and there's nothing easy about it. People say the weirdest things and standing in the hallway contemplating cake-related cliches smacked of escapism.

I had questions. Clara had answers. All I had to do was knock.

"Stop dithering around out there and come in." No

hint of displeasure tinted the command, but I blushed at being caught in a bout of fearful skulking.

Summoning my courage, I did as my grandmother ordered. Her smile, warm and inviting, chased away most of the nerves. Her hug banished the rest. I relaxed into it for the first few seconds and rested my head on her shoulder before living out one of my childhood dreams and cuddling next to Clara on the bed.

Missing pieces of my soul settled into the gaping holes my inner child had spent a lifetime skirting, and yet, I had trouble trusting the feeling of wholeness. After a shining moment at the base of a rainbow-hued waterfall with Sylvana—a moment that had, unfortunately, been rife with hidden betrayal—I had trust issues. Who wouldn't?

Blood calls to blood. Clara certainly called to me. A siren's song luring the shy waif who spent too much time alone and abandoned, even when in the presence of friends and a caring group of makeshift family.

Droves of people in this world grew up with far less than I was blessed with, but self-pity is just as hard to banish as it is easy to let in.

"Can I ask you something?" My breath hitched and caught in case the answer was no. Or yes. Either alternative might bring devastation.

"Anything." Such warmth, such gentleness. I basked.

"Did my…Sylvana, did she mean to kill you?" I

would not, could not, use the term *mother* out loud; and I hadn't uttered it once since Sylvana proved for the second time in my life that my happiness and well-being fell below the bottom of her priorities list.

Through the magic of…well, *magic,* a time traveling ring let me witness the fight that left me orphaned.

Seeing it play out first hand answered a lifetime's worth of questions while raising one more.

With witches, intention during the casting of a spell is everything. Intention and the traits that come down through the blood. That fateful day, Sylvana's ball of black witchfire crossed with Clara's binding spell. The collision of wild magics resulted in a blended mess that backfired on both of them and turned me into a motherless child who would grow up wondering how much evil ran in her blood.

Now was my chance to find out.

As if searching for the right words, Clara paused briefly.

"Anger clouds even the wisest woman's judgment." The memory of the worst time my temper raged out of control pinked my face with a shameful blush, and I nodded my understanding.

"Too clever for her own good, Sylvana never aspired to wisdom—only power—and when she didn't get what she wanted, she lashed out without thinking about the consequences. Trust my daughter to miss the obvious." A trace of bitterness spiced the truth. "However, as selfish as she could be at times, I doubt Sylvana would have traded her own soul for the death of mine. Does that answer your question?"

Did it? During the few weeks I'd known her, my mother had tried but failed to hide a mile-wide self-centered streak behind a set of blinders. Pushed to the brink, I wasn't sure what she might be capable of doing, and she hadn't spared a second thought for Kin when she chose the Bow of Destiny over saving the man I loved. My happiness never entered into the picture, and yet, I didn't think she would chance an eternity in granite over a fit of pique unless she'd gone over the ragged edge of reason.

"If she comes back…" Unlikely, since I'd laid out the unwelcome mat and booted her backside across it without ceremony.

"We'll remain cautious, but hopeful."

"Hopeful? Are you saying you could forgive her after everything she's done?" I gave my grandmother the rundown on what happened during the bow-retrieval fiasco. "She would have let Kin die. I saw it in her eyes." My throat swelled with a painful lump as I relived the moment he'd teetered on the edge of an ebony-shadowed abyss and my mother had done nothing to save him. Some people are redeemable while others carry a stain so deep it blackens their bones. Sylvana would have to move more than a mountain to prove herself to me—providing she cared enough to try.

"Hate hardens the heart of the hater," Clara chided gently. "A second chance is a blessing we can give to even the most undeserving souls—one that will come back to you a hundredfold. I'll be asking for my own second chance should she decide to return, since I wasn't an unwilling participant in what happened." A sigh gusted from her lips and my grandmother's shoulders rounded from the emotional burden she carried.

"All you did was try to bind her powers temporarily. I saw the spell, and that's what it looked like to me. Completely justified, in my opinion."

"Exactly how many binding spells have you witnessed?"

"Er…One."

"And that makes you an expert?"

"No, I guess not."

"It's easy to see people in black and white. Your mother hurt you, so she's the bad guy. But you don't know me, Lexi. Not yet. Are you so certain I'm the good guy?"

Was I? Did fifteen minutes of observing her at one of the worst moments in her life really give me a perfect picture of my grandmother? Or did I need so badly to believe I came from good people?

Leaning back against the headboard, I fell silent while I played the whole thing through my head for the hundredth time. Only this time I tried to judge the event without emotion and with a clear head.

"You thought you killed her. That whole time." Grannie was a stone cold witch—not literally. Well, not anymore.

Clara's face reddened.

"My emotions clouded my intentions." And that was the last she would say on the subject. We sat quietly for a few moments, then I hugged her and left the room.

Clara

What a mess I'd made of things.

No, I hadn't gotten here alone, but I certainly wasn't an innocent bystander. I'd had an inordinate amount of time to think about what I'd long-considered my last moments of living, and I wouldn't—couldn't—pretend otherwise. Sylvana was what she was, but I'd played a role by allowing her too much freedom and offering too much information that would have been better kept under wraps.

Much like my sister, my daughter was a force of nature. Unlike Mag, Sylvana carried a nasty streak. One she'd taken out on poor Endora, for instance. A more beleaguered familiar never existed, and I was just as guilty for not doing more to stop the abuse.

Sylvana burned bridges with the children her age. Never seeming to regret being left out of everything. she spent most of her time studying the craft, searching through dusty tomes for ways to build more power.

I saw the darkness rising in her, but had I done anything about it, really? Besides curse the stars for blessing me with such a handful—the answer was a decided *no*.

Now, Lexi had doubts about the moral rectitude of the Balefire women, and I couldn't blame her. How many years had she huddled near my feet to fret and fuss over becoming a wicked witch? I'd witnessed the tug of war she'd been forced into; alternately wishing to gain her power and fearing what type of witch she'd become if she did.

And I couldn't move a muscle; much less do anything to soothe her weary nerves.

Well, I'd make up for it now, with interest. I'd do whatever I could to make her feel happy and secure. *Sure, now that she's grown and can take care of herself,* a little voice goaded me.

Lexi has more power and prowess than any Balefire I've ever known, but she still doesn't know how to fully use her gifts, I whispered back. *I'm here now, to teach her.*

Shame, I could deal with. Self-pity was easy to cultivate, and anger could pull you into its undertow as easily as a summer breeze plucks petals from a flower. But regret? That was the worst kind of curse.

I might not be able to change the past, but I

certainly wasn't going to allow myself to repeat it.

I would be better for Lexi than I had been for Sylvana.

I'd give her all the things she'd longed for, and all the things she'd never thought to want.

I would.

Chapter 4

Lexi

You know what they say about death and taxes, right? Well, the same adage applies to work, especially when you run your own business.

Clients needed me back in the office, and didn't care what I might miss while I was gone. Sure, things were hectic, considering how many people now lived in my house. Four elemental faeries and three witches made for seven of us crammed into the place.

Two familiars brought the total to nine, and when I could talk him into staying, Kin rounded the count to ten. Until Mag's familiar finally toddled up to the door and then we were eleven.

Salem happily indulged in a massive amount of shop talk with not one, but two full-fledged, highly-trained witches in the house. Add a hot familiar to the mix, and he could barely contain his glee.

Or the constant snarky remarks on my lack of knowledge.

"You're not leaving. We have a full roster of witch training today." He said when I passed him on my way to the coffee pot.

"I have a few work-related things on the books for this morning. I'll be home in the afternoon."

"Don't be late," he sing-songed.

I matched his tone. "Don't be annoying."

With my mind occupied elsewhere, my official training in the witchly arts ran at a pace that made a snail look like a sprinter. As my familiar, it was Salem's job to teach and assist me. Not to clean up my messes or serve as an errand boy.

To heap irritation on top of annoyance, Salem didn't seem to think my street smarts held as much weight as a formal education, so he often treated me like a child.

Coffee in hand, I snagged a still-warm pastry from the tray Soleil had left in the oven. Singeing my fingers was little enough to pay for the faerie version of a Pop Tart. Flaky crust filled with mixed berry preserves. Delicious.

"Tansy Blankenship. Why does that name sound familiar?" Clara, I learned, liked to watch the morning news over breakfast. A habit none of the rest of us appreciated. The godmothers had little interest in current events, and I just wanted coffee and peace—not that I usually sampled both at the same time. Speaking of less-than-peaceful things, where were the godmothers? It wasn't like them to cook and run.

Having picked up on the new technology faster than I'd expected, My grandmother paused and reversed the live news feed.

"…Identified as Tansy Blankenship, age twenty-six, who was last seen on Friday the 13th. Port Harbor police are asking anyone who might have seen or heard from Ms. Blankenship in the days before she went missing to come forward. The investigation is ongoing." A photo of a woman with dark hair and pretty eyes flashed on the screen. When the announcer moved on to the next bit of news, Clara lowered the volume and turned to me.

"You must have known her, she was about your age."

Rifling through my sleep-addled brain failed to produce anything more than the niggling sense I'd heard the name before, so she must be part of the witch community. "Sounds familiar, but I'm not sure why. I might have heard the name somewhere, but I'd need another cup of coffee to come up with the context."

"Where's the phone book? I'll look it up, maybe that will jog my memory." Clara seemed a little uncomfortable asking where to find things in her own home. This must be a strange transition for her.

"We stopped getting them a couple of years ago. Easier to look up numbers on my cell. "Here," I handed her the device I carried practically everywhere. "You just touch the search box and type in her last name using the on-screen keyboard." I showed her by typing the first couple letters and let her do the rest. "Add Port Harbor after Blankenship, press the go button, and that should bring up a list for you."

Clara had all but missed the onset of the computer age. Those twenty-five years ushered a lot of changes into the world, many for the better, but not all.

Frowning with concentration, she tapped the name in slowly and grinned at me when the list popped up. I had a feeling Clara would enjoy certain aspects of being a modern witch. I should introduce her Flix. My best friend and business partner loved all things digital.

"That's it. Tansy is Letitia Blankenship's little girl," she mused. "Not so little now, I guess. I've missed so much. I wonder why Letitia never brought Tansy over to play when you girls were younger."

I had a theory about that, "Probably thought the wickedness would rub off. This wasn't a popular hangout for the Port Harbor witchy crowd between one Beltane and the next." I hadn't been shunned outright, but neither had I been welcomed into the flock.

"Me not having magic and all." My eyes narrowed, and the corners of my lips curled into a scowl at the memory. "Something tells me things will be different with you in the house."

"My friends have a lot to answer for," Clara said darkly.

"Please don't fight with anyone on my account. I made out just fine and other than losing so much of the time I could have spent with you, I had a happy life."

Terra chose that moment to walk through the door, and I caught the pride on her face, followed by a hint of sadness before she smoothed away the expression. Everything could change. As much as I wanted to simply add my grandmother into the household and go on as one big, happy family, there would be a lot of adjustments to make. Not all of them by me.

Clara clicked the remote, and the TV went silent while Evian, who'd been just a few seconds behind her sister, glared at it in horror. I remembered that look from the day I'd brought the little flatscreen television home.

I'd had the bright idea that if I had access to cooking shows in the kitchen, I might learn how to do more than boil water. Amid vociferous protest, I'd hung it on the wall and then taken so much flak for it being there, I'd never once turned it on. The faeries would cook, I would eat. That was the natural order of things, and there would be no further attempt to flout the status quo.

"What's wrong? You look like someone burned down the barn around your prize cow."

I raised an eyebrow at Evian's choice of metaphors

but answered anyway. "A young witch turned up dead last night, and grandmother knows the family."

"Someone's dead? Who?" Mag walked faster than a woman her age ought to be able to move. She listened intently as Clara provided what little information she had learned from the news broadcast. "Letitia Blankenship's girl. She'd be just a year or two older than Lexi. Reading between the lines, I'd say foul play is a distinct possibility."

A look passed between Clara and Mag that I assumed had to do with being glad someone else's family had experienced tragedy and then feeling bad about feeling glad; a typical response to this kind of news.

Resolving to push the sad event from my mind, I walked to work and thought of nothing else the entire way.

I live on the outskirts of a quaint northeastern coastal city traditionally known for its lobster and fish trade, but which, in recent years, has become a mecca for modern-day hippies. Personally, I like it better this way.

Parks and community gardens grace nearly every empty lot, flowers and vegetables flourish in the spaces between buildings, and on almost every street corner and rooftop in the city. Each weekend sees a festival winding its way through the already-cramped historic district, and nary a day passes where I don't hear the sounds of street-side musicians wafting through my office windows.

Port Harbor enjoys a reputation for being one of the safest cities in the country, and I hated to imagine a murderer haunting her streets.

What if Tansy was a target *because* she was a witch? Did that make me a target, too? Scenes right out of Buffy the Vampire Slayer played through my head, each one with Tansy as the victim. Demons, and faeries, and shifters. Oh, My.

While thoughts of murder ran through my head, I scanned faces for evidence it was time to pull out the Bow of Destiny and take a pot shot in the middle of the street. That I had no idea how to access the weapon, no clue who I was supposed to use it on, or how to hide my actions so I didn't end up in jail were just details in the landscape.

Love in the midst of death.

I trudged the last few blocks and opened the door to my office. Long before I understood there was a reason for it, my innate power fueled my working life. Touched by Cupid in a very literal way, I'd managed just fine without any fancy tools or tricks.

There were no bells and whistles at FootSwept—my partner, Flix, finally got me to agree to schedule appointments using a notebook computer, but I didn't touch it unless I had to. We didn't videotape our clients, and we didn't set them up with dozens of potential matches or send them on cringe-worthy blind dates.

Who wants to tell their grandkids they got together because a computer told them they had points of compatibility? Okay, plenty of people, and good for them because love is love, after all. As for me, I try to give my clients a really good story, and most of the time, I make it work.

Flix mans a high-end hair styling salon out back where we pamper the lovelorn.

Or he used to, anyway.

Flix and I had been on the outs ever since his boyfriend, Carl, got tangled up with my arch-nemesis, Serena Snodgrass—daughter of Calypso, Gran's replacement as coven high priestess, no less—and I'd refused to let him unleash a can of Faerie-brand whoop-ass on the pregnant witch.

I'm not saying she didn't deserve it, but she happened to be carrying my half-niece or nephew in her belly. My conscience wouldn't allow any harm to come to the babe just because its mother was dumb enough to get involved with a jerk like my half-brother, Jett.

And thank the Goddess I hadn't. The chances of Calypso welcoming Gran back into the fold with open arms were about the size of a flea, and if I'd let Flix loose on Serena, they'd shrink to where you'd need a microscope to see them.

Knowing what I would find, I opened the

connecting door leading into the darkened salon where a fine layer of dust showed it had been several days since he'd come to work. I avoided making eye contact with the oversized glamor shot of Flix mounted above his chrome barber's chair and retreated to the front office.

If this kept up, he'd break our record for staying mad. I was the current holder of the BFF belt for bitchy behavior with a solid three weeks of cold shoulder action following a stupid argument over a board game. We'd be fine. Eventually. I hoped.

Finished with my final appointment of the day, I was squaring up a pile of papers when I noticed the edge of a hot pink sheet of card stock sticking out from underneath. A stray flier for the event that happened on the last night I'd seen Flix gave me a pang when I saw it.

Worse than the pang, it served as a reminder of some unfinished business. The matter of the most annoying client in the history of ever: one Joshua Owen. I'm ashamed to admit my heart had skipped a beat the day that gorgeous hunk of a man walked into the office. Turns out I'm shallow sometimes.

Hey, I might have a boyfriend, but I'm not blind, and even if what was inside turned into letdown, the package had been especially impressive. Appreciation had almost immediately given way to irritation when he opened his mouth and essentially made a mockery of my life's work. The man had the gall to offer me a bonus for setting him up on dates with an even dozen women.

What did he think I was, some kind of matchmaking madam pimping out my clients?

Given my distaste for the man, I hadn't considered him a top priority client despite feeling the tingle that signaled he had a soul mate nearby. But the bow—which at that point had still been broken and could only whine plaintive tunes in my ear—seemed to think differently.

Now that the bow was fixed, I was dying to finally shoot someone with it. What's more, the ick factor had somewhat dissipated once I knew I wasn't actually going to messily pierce anyone's heart with a pointy arrow.

Clara seemed no worse for the wear, and the one she'd been struck with had been tipped with flaming Balefire. Joshua's physical well-being wasn't high on my priority list, so he'd make a perfect test subject even if it would be difficult to resist shooting him in the backside instead of the heart.

Centering him in my thoughts, and taking a moment to tune in, my internal LPS—Love Positioning System, as I'd taken to calling it—extended its reach from a spot behind my navel and pinpointed Mr. Owen's exact location. Ten blocks east of the office, at a pub in the financial district. The fourth booth from the left, to be exact. I checked my watch. It was half past noon and assuming Joshua took long lunches, I might catch him if I hurried.

Trekking it on foot, I contemplated getting myself

one of those little fitness tracking devices everyone raves about. The kind that tells you how many miles you've walked throughout the course of the day. With Pinky, my beloved scooter, reduced to a pile of rubble (thanks again to Serena Snodgrass), I'd probably max out the display. With lunch time traffic, a cab would take longer than walking, so I hoofed it until quaint period architecture gave way to the clean, modern lines of the section of town that held Port Harbor's few skyscrapers.

I fished a pair of dark sunglasses out of my purse and began twisting my hair into a bun before it occurred to me to cast a glamour over my face if I didn't want to be recognized.

A glamour was one of the spells I'd worked hard to perfect. Even witches have the occasional bad hair day.

Disguised to my satisfaction, I settled myself onto a bench across the street from where Joshua lunched. It wasn't the first time I'd had to pull a similar stunt, and I chose my position carefully, half-obscured by a large concrete planter filled with cigarette butts and situated catty-corner from the restaurant door.

Then I waited. And waited. And waited some more. Apparently, there had been no need to rush, because what I'd taken for a leisurely lunch turned out to be a business meeting slated to last half the day. Nearly two hours later, I'd counted the bricks on every surrounding building, cataloged how many foreign versus domestic cars lined the streets, and completed three extremely frustrating levels on Candy Crush Saga.

When Joshua finally pushed through the glass double doors surrounded by several men in nearly identical black business suits, the bow began to sing a tune that signified, I assumed, something about the target's psyche. I wouldn't have guessed that under all that yuppie attitude Joshua was actually a heavy metal kind of guy. Drums and bass vied for attention, pounding through my skull like a sledgehammer.

Distracted by the sudden pain, I almost missed it when the restaurant door opened and two women stepped out. Even without the bow stepping up the tempo, my LPS homed in on the pair. One of them was Joshua's perfect match, I was sure of it.

Was it the gorgeous blond dressed in a Vogue-worthy silk jumpsuit the color of heavy cream paired with dangerously high stiletto heels, and a wide belt with a gleaming gold buckle? Given his proclivities, it wouldn't be a stretch to assume Miss Business Suit was the one.

Or was it the other woman? Quietly attractive, well-dressed but not flashy. Nope, way too tame for Mr. Hook-Me-Up. My money was on the first one, but I had to know for sure.

Nothing for it but to apply the touch test, so I double-checked my glamour and hauled off down the sidewalk. Pretending to be preoccupied with a phone call, I managed to pinball my way into all three of them.

Miss B.S. never even raised a tingle of a vision. She impolitely called me a dog's mother before she blew past Joshua with barely a nod. All of this registered only faintly with me because I was having a vision of Joshua staring at the more understated woman with stars in his eyes.

When their entire future unfolded before me, I knew I'd squarely hit my mark. Justine was her name, and under Joshua's shockingly tender care, she blossomed into a woman lit from the inside by the beauty that comes from being truly loved.

It was so sweetly romantic, I closed my eyes to savor the moment.

When I opened them again, I found myself holding an intangible, glowing representation of the bow I sure hoped nobody else could see. I bit my lip and waited for passersby to start pointing and screaming at the freak with the cocked weapon on the corner of a busy street. When nobody batted an eyelash, I shrugged off the worry.

A gust of wind blew my hair into my face as I lowered my eye to the sight, and what I saw through it made me jump out of my skin. Actually, that's not a half-bad analogy, considering the way it all went down. Slack-jawed, I watched as part of myself detached from the rest and stood, surrounded by pink smoke that curled up into hearts all around it—her—me.

My astral self turned her head to face me, the hair

of her chin-length bob obscuring one blazing pink eye, and winked at me with the other before fitting arrow to string.

If you ever tell anyone I said this, I'll deny it, but I envied her cool stance, the way she stood hipshod and ready to let the arrow fly. It takes a brave woman to break up a faerie fight, so it's not like a wimp or anything, but my inner goddess, if that was the best term, was badass.

Still, it was something of a letdown to watch the whole thing unfold; I'd assumed it would be my flesh and blood self, and not some strangely-coiffed representation of me who would be doing the actual shooting. Sure, I'd made the decision to come here and weave Joshua's fate, but now I felt a bit like the proverbial messenger, following orders rather than making them myself. Was I wielding the Bow of Destiny, or was it wielding me?

Or was I really fractured into two disparate halves?

Too bad there was no one I could ask. Thanks for not sending directions, Dad.

Before I could curse my father out loud, she let the arrow fly.

Insubstantial as a dream, it zinged through the throng of pedestrians to pierce Joshua's heart, where it immediately disappeared into a rose-gold ball of light, along with the glowing arrow.

For a split second, I could see it like an x-ray; one

brief moment of silence as his heart skipped a beat and then began thumping again to a slightly different rhythm than it had before.

The look on his face wasn't pain, and it wasn't exactly shock, either. *Dumbfounded moron* would have been a more accurate term, or maybe *lovesick fool.*

Ever since I'd gained the ability to watch the fates of a match play out before my eyes, I'd had to maintain physical contact with both potential lovers. Then again, I usually spend more time pairing them up. This time, the images funneled through the bow in a rush, showing bits and pieces of Joshua and Justine's past, present, and future.

But it wasn't the lovebirds who commanded my attention, it was the bearer of the bow. While she watched the series of images, I watched her to see what she would do next.

For all the good it did me, I might as well have been watching a snail race. One thing I could say, she had the best stone face I'd ever seen. Next to my grandmother's, of course. Not so much as the twitch of an eyelash betrayed her reaction when it felt like we were both sucked into a dream.

You know the kind I mean. The ones where you're playing the part of more than one person, and it's just plain weird.

I felt three versions of goosebumps—theirs, mine, and hers—tingle across my skin as desire flooded my senses. I experienced hope and wonder that this person, this one perfect soul mate could stand before me and be mine. During those moments, I was Justine, and I was Joshua. Our breath caught, and my knees trembled when our lips touched for the first time.

The world clicked into place, and my heart swelled with theirs during what I knew beyond all doubt was True Love's Kiss.

The vision faded like a chalk image being washed off the pavement and I came back to the present to see that I'd jumped the gun. In fairytales, when princess meets her prince, it's love at first sight. Justine and Joshua were candidates for true love's kiss, and so far, all they'd managed to share was a lingering look.

Still, bow song swelled as if the union was a done deal and my pink-haired half faded. If she melded back into me, I never felt a thing.

When the joyous notes faded, I noticed a shining symbol hovering over Joshua's head. He walked away before I could get a good look, but I'd seen something like this before. A new wrinkle in the process, but I assumed the seed had been planted.

Not that I worried, I'd just…sort of…been part of something wonderful. Something *forever*.

Yeah, I had a goofy look on my face for an hour—and for more than one reason—but I didn't care.

Chapter 5

Coming home to chaos is the measure of a normal day around my house. Faerie tempers run hot, and every time the godmothers get riled up, my life turns into a powder keg with a two-inch fuse in a room full of matches. The day I shot Joshua, the fuse burned merrily as I strolled up the walkway to find three out of the four godmothers on the porch pressing their faces up against the front windows.

"Can you see anything?" Evian changed positions and shoved in next to Soleil, which started a tussling match. Fire and water described more than their relationship, for those were the elements this particular pair of faeries commanded. Under the human glamour they habitually wore, my witch eyes saw the gloriousness of their real faces.

Evian's hair tumbled in luxurious sea-green waves and moved as though under water even when she was on land. One hand lifted while she contemplated using nails like mirrors to scratch out her sister's eyes. Soleil, by contrast, carried all the colors of a fiery sunset in the short cap of hair that flickered around a face so full of pale beauty it would make a grown man cry.

"Shut up, the both of you." Godmother number three warned with a dire tone and narrowed eyes the color of pink marble. Terra shook back her mane of mahogany hair and pointed a finger at her sisters. Her affinity for the earth element meant she could crumble the ground at her sisters' feet and allow it to swallow them whole if she so desired.

Anyone with half a lick of common sense could see the fight brewing under the tension, and after the past few weeks of relative calm, they were due for a knock-down, drag-out battle.

"What's going on?" I nudged my way to one of the windows to peek inside but saw nothing out of the ordinary. "Is it Clara?" With my grandmother back, and her sister Mag staying for an indeterminate amount of time, the house had surpassed its estrogen limit. An unintended side effect I should have foreseen, but didn't.

"Vaeta's lost her mind," Soleil muttered darkly. "Airheaded bimbo."

Uh oh. They were already at phase 2. Name calling.

"What happened?" Asking might contribute to the problem, but if I didn't know what was going on, how was I supposed to diffuse the situation?

Terra harrumphed and turned back toward the window while Evian explained. "Vaeta's dumber than a bag of dragon hair, that's what."

Not at all informative, and faintly dismissive of dragons.

Wait, what part of the dragon had hair? Maybe I didn't want to know.

"What did she do now?"

"She's in there with Rhys." Soleil flopped down on a rocking chair coated in faded green paint. "Rhys."

I knew she expected me to have a clue who she meant, but I totally blanked it. "Rhys?"

"We had to go drag her out of the underworld, and now he's back to fill her head with nonsense and trap her again."

The demon who seduced Vaeta into following him to the underworld for a hundred years. Rhys.

"You let a demon in my house? A demon? Are you kidding me?" I took two steps toward the door.

Evian held up both hands in surrender. "It wasn't us. Vaeta did it."

"Is my grandmother in there? Or Mag?" Granted, I hadn't known Clara very long, but I suspected her stance on demons in the house would be similar to mine. No. Just no.

"Left right after you did." Terra peered inside again, and then jumped away from the window. "Here they come."

The three sisters scattered like roaches when a light goes on. Watching Terra vault the porch railing and land behind a shrub with the finesse of an Olympic athlete shocked me enough to leave me standing there with my mouth hanging open.

I don't know what I was expecting to see when Rhys stepped out onto the porch. Horns. Red eyes. A curling mustache and a goatee. Maybe a cape. All my perceptions of hellbeasts come from Hollywood.

Vaeta's demon filled out a pair of faded jeans that went well with a belt buckle with an elaborately carved symbol, and the cowboy hat he wore tipped down low on his brow. No wonder she followed him to hell. Strong jaw, sexy glint in his eye, and when he spoke, a voice worthy of sending shivers down a woman's spine.

He turned once and gave her such a heated look it made me blush—and I'm no prude. Vaeta's porcelain-white skin remained tint-free, her face carefully neutral while their gazes stayed locked as if an entire conversation went unsaid between them.

An ear-splitting cacophony fired off in my head when the bow weighed in with its opinion. Unnecessary, since I'd already figured out this wasn't a good match, thank you very much. And now I had a headache to go along with the pain in my behind.

When he finally turned away, Vaeta shoved a strand of mist-colored hair behind one ear, and said to no one in particular, "What's for dinner?"

Thirty seconds of shocked silence followed the question—which is long enough to think about how long half a minute feels during these types of situations, but not long enough to frame a suitable response. Fury-born magic bled into the close space of the porch, and I knew what was coming next unless I could nip it in the bud. Faerie-tastrophe.

"Let's go inside." *Where the neighbors won't see you do anything weird.* Saying that last part out loud was the equivalent of throwing gas on a barbecue grill, but there are only so many ways to explain away flying pigs and Mrs. Chatterly had nothing better to do than spend a lot of time watching our house. Can't imagine why.

Three flouncing faeries led the way toward the kitchen, their favorite indoor fighting spot because what with the knives, cleavers, corkscrews, and the meat tenderizer there were more weapons in that room than any other. An absolute redundancy since the faeries themselves were the biggest weapons.

"What's everybody so upset about?" Vaeta had one of her clueless moments.

"You let a demon into my house." For once, I understood the impulse to throw a magical hammer at someone's head. Where was Thor when I needed him?

"Rhys? He was a perfect gentleman. You don't have to worry about him, it's fine."

A demon gentleman? Gullible much?

"It's not fine…" Before I could finish the sentence,

faerie magic shot past my head so close I felt the breeze stir my hair. Vaeta deflected the curse, which fell on Soleil instead. Vines slithered up her legs like snakes to bind her limbs tightly against her body.

"Sorry," Terra muttered from behind me while Soleil squinched up her face, engulfed herself in flame, and burned the vines to ash.

And then it was on.

Their magic fed off aggression like it was a succulent morsel or finest nectar, and grew so fast that it prickled across my skin in a breathless wave. I looked around and realized I was standing right in the middle between where Vaeta squared off against the others. Ground zero. Don't tell anyone, but I hauled my butt out of there while it was still attached to my body and took refuge in the hallway beyond.

"Something wrong?" Kin's voice in my ear triggered a fight or flight reflex that ended with the two of us plastered against the front door.

"Don't sneak up on me like that." An explosion rocked the kitchen. "Faerie fight," I explained.

"Shouldn't you go in there and put a stop to it?"

"Probably." I shrugged and caught a flying frog in my left hand. "Or you could try." I handed him the frog, bat-like wings and all. "Vaeta brought this mess on herself." I had no sympathy for her after what she'd done.

Kin held the frog up for better inspection. "If this is

the worst they do, I can't see how these fights are as bad as you make them out to be. This little fellow is kind of cute." Whereupon, the little amphibian belched fire and singed a swath of hair off Kin's arm.

"Dragolian frog. The snot's essential for certain spells, but they breed like rabbits."

"Regular rabbits or Dragolian ones?" He thought he was funny. Let a rabbit the size of an elephant with a brain as small as a pea loose in *his* backyard, and I bet he wouldn't be laughing quite so hard.

"You're not going to do anything?" Kin seemed surprised at my apathy, but not as surprised as he was by the tendrils of ivy creeping across the walls and ceiling. A particularly saucy stalk twined up his leg and goosed him hard enough that he yelped. "Ow. Stop that." He slapped at the questing plant, which took offense and tried to choke him.

"Terra!" I shouted. "Call off your minions." The vine retreated with a reluctant rustle of leaves. Kin rubbed his neck and swallowed hard.

"I had no idea things got this dangerous around here. It must have been an interesting place to grow up."

Interesting wasn't the half of it. All things considered, this was shaping up to a fairly tame fight thus far. I'd seen worse. Way worse. There was the time when I was six, and all the dust bunnies in the house came to life.

Talk about creepy. Hairy tumbleweeds with teeth.

No wonder kids have nightmares about the boogeyman. Actually, he's not all that bad when you get to know him. Excellent sense of humor and you get used to the smell after a while.

When the kitchen went suddenly silent, I began to worry. Silence during faerie wars is always a bad sign. Mist, dense and damp, built at the end of the hall, its advance toward us slow and ominous. Evian's work. The scent of fresh brimstone confirmed Soleil's fingerprints on the sound-dampening cloud as well.

Sighing, I dragged Kin toward the kerfuffle. Better the chaos you know than the chaos you imagine. Okay, that's not true, but it sounded like common sense at the time.

"Stay behind me where it's safer."

"I'm not a child."

"Then don't act like one," I snapped back and quelled the mutiny before it had time to ramp up. "Don't for one minute imagine that just because they like you, they won't let something weird happen to you. When they're in Armageddon mode, it's every man for himself. But, hey, if you want to take a chance you won't get turned into a toad, or something worse, knock yourself out."

"You're cranky," Kin helpfully pointed out, but my searing look failed to have any effect on him and set the bow to chiming out its temple-throbbing warning tone. Like I needed input from some sentient weapon on a perpetual ride-along in my head.

Huffing out a breath, I informed him, "Vaeta crossed a line, okay? I'm not sure I trust myself to step into the fray this time. I might be tempted to start tossing around my own magic." Hot blood coursed through my veins, sending my nerves twanging.

The faeries knew they were welcome to invite their eclectic blend of friends into the house with utter abandon. My home was their home, and I'd always wanted them to feel comfortable in it. For all I knew, many demons had made their way through the front door—it's not like I asked visitors to provide a pedigree and three references before they were invited in.

So why was I ready to chew nails and spit out bullets every time I pictured Rhys's admittedly-fine backside strolling down my front walk? I'm normally an even-tempered witch. Craziness sneaking up on me? After the past few months, who could blame me?

Well, I guess Kin could, given the look on his face. The hint of shock, the soupcon of disapproval, and the dash of fear said more than words could convey, and I didn't like the version of me that could write those things there.

"I'm sorry. The stress is getting to me, but Vaeta invited a demon into the house, and I'm not particularly pleased with her at the moment." Or with the babbling Bow of Destiny perched on top of the stress pile like the cherry on a sundae. "Come on, I'll go see if I can get them to take it down a notch.”

We made it halfway down the hall before I knew it was already way too late for that. The house wheezed and sucked in a breath like a bellows pulls in air, the force putting pressure on my eardrums. Before you could say boo, the kitchen belched a smell so foul you’d consider Eau de Rotten Egg the finest of perfumes in comparison.

Gagging, Kin spun and shot for the front door, and if I’d had a choice, I’d have been right behind him. But this *was* my circus, and those *were* my monkeys, so I pinched my nose shut and headed toward the big top instead of away.

I skidded to a stop at the edge of a pit full of bubbling goop that now occupied the space where the table and chairs used to be. I wiped my sleeve across my eyes to clear the stream of tears brought on by the noxious fumes. A mini snow storm raged in the newly doorless refrigerator, but other than those two things, the room looked the same as always.

Skirting the pool of goo, I made my way to the sliding doors leading out to the patio that separated the house from the back yard. Kin slipped through the side gate just as I stepped off the flagstones. Smart. He’d gone around from the outside to avoid the foul stench in the kitchen.

But dumb, because he was still here.

“You should have gone home while you had the

chance." I snapped unapologetically. It would be easier if I didn't have to worry about him carelessly wandering into something dangerous like a patch of faerie snapdragons. Not to be confused with the floral variety, these resembled flying turtles, traveled in packs and considered a good, juicy ankle the finest of delicacies.

"And leave you here to have all the fun?" Other than the swamp stench, he'd seen the most benign faerie fracas in history. Figures. Just when I finally wanted to give him a taste of life with Lexi, they go and…

I never finished that thought.

The world—well, technically just the backyard—shook like a dog after a bath.

"It's an earthquake." Kin shouted in my ear and then threw his body over mine like a shield. Cute, but unnecessary and besides, he knocked the breath out of me.

"Get off," I gave him a shove as soon as the shaking stopped. "It's not an earthquake, it's Terra. Come on!" Moving as fast as I dared, I led Kin in the direction that felt like the epicenter.

One of the perks of living with four elemental Fae is the spatial distortion that turns my urban sized backyard into acres of castle-worthy gardens straight out of the Faelands. On the downside, faerie fights tend to expand to occupy the entire space in which they occur. Faerie physics. It's a thing.

If I were lucky, I'd find them before we had a

scorched-earth situation on our hands.

"Don't touch that." I caught Kin just in time.

"What? This harmless little flower? You're a bit keyed up today." Fragrant petals the color of a bluebird's feathers begged for the touch of an innocent finger to test if they really were as soft as they looked.

"How could you have forgotten about that frog so quickly? I can still smell scorched arm hair, and that *harmless little flower* will wipe every thought out of your head for a full twenty-four hours. So unless you want to spend the rest of the day doing anything more useful than drooling, you'd better leave it alone." If he kept making comments about my attitude, I might offer him a bouquet.

Kin pulled his hand back quickly, wiped it on his pants before wrapping it around my own, and we continued on toward the booming sounds, sparkles rising above the trees, and loud voices.

"Almost there." Kin surged on ahead, his long legs eating the ground slightly faster than mine. He dropped my hand as we broke into the clearing and sprinted right into no man's land—the space between Vaeta and the others.

"Stop it, now. All of you." His commanding tone sent a little thrill up my spine. There's something sexy about a man willing to wade into danger and take control. Yum.

Still, if you're going to do that type of thing, I have

one piece of advice: know your audience. Make that two pieces: don't try it with faeries unless you're stronger than they are.

Okay, three pieces of advice: you're not stronger than faeries, so kids, don't try this at home.

Taking the hit from four different directions at once, Kin never stood a chance. Faster than you can say *don't do it*, he went down in a barrage of elemental fury. Evian's blast of water mixed with Soleil's gout of flame and intercepted Terra's ball of dirt. Vaeta jetted a shot of air toward the steaming mud ball, intending to lob it back at her sisters, but her aim was off. The gust tangled with the glob of mud and whipped it into a whirlwind of gunk that engulfed Kin like the world's most aggressive spa treatment.

Fury swept from the tips of my toes to the split ends of my hair (Flix needed to get back from his mad-at-me vacation and work his magic on my neglected tresses), and a ball of black witchfire began to grow in the palm of my hand.

"Enough." I spun around when Clara clapped her hands together four times in rapid succession. The fourth clap sounded like thunder, killed my ball of witchfire with a sizzle, and when the echo died, silence shrouded the clearing. A silence born from shock and surprise.

I wish I'd been watching the results of Clara's interference rather than the act itself because I would have loved to see her turn their own magic against them.

Four bedraggled faeries stood in a circle around Kin, who no longer looked like he'd been dipped in a swamp and hung out to dry. He was so clean he almost sparkled. My godmothers, however, had each found their elements returned to them. Forcefully, from the looks of it.

Evian was drenched and dripping while Vaeta looked like she'd taken a spin on the hairy edge of her own tornado, her face scoured pink with windburn. Terra, caked in dirt and grime, blinked her eyes at Clara and they were the only part of her that was clean. In that respect, she and Soleil could have been twins if not for the color difference between soil and soot. Where Terra sported all the browns of the earth, Soleil looked like she'd been rolling around in the blackest ash to ever grace a fireplace.

"I trust you will find a way to discuss your differences in a more civilized manner." Clara spun on her heel and departed for the house, leaving the godmothers in her wake and looking like chastised children.

"We're sorry Lexi, Kin." Terra braved the infuriated look on my face, and the others nodded in agreement but remained silent.

Knowing I couldn't respond with any sort of civility, I grabbed Kin's hand and stalked away.

Chapter 6

Clara

"Spoiled brats. Honestly, you'd think after an eternity's worth of years, those faeries would learn to act their age."

Mag looked up from her knitting, and the Balefire flared with red hot flames when I stormed back into the house. The hint of a smirk on her face sent my temper right back up to the redline.

"Don't get me started on your attitude. It's your fault Lexi grew up refereeing this nonsense. Was there some reason you, as her nearest living relative, couldn't be bothered to take care of my granddaughter? How do you think it makes me feel, knowing you all but abandoned her too?"

The question tore my soul on its way out, but it had

been simmering beneath my marble surface for over two decades and was determined to be set free.

My sister never had a family of her own, and if that bothered her, she hid the pain so deeply behind her sense of adventure that even she couldn't find it. Yet, I never thought she would turn her back on me and mine during a crisis.

Slowly and with great deliberation, Mag stabbed her needles into the ball of yarn, stuffed it into her bag, and went upstairs.

I followed and watched her yank open the top drawer of an antique oak dresser, scoop up the meager contents, and stuff everything into her knitting bag.

"I'll go. I should have known better than to think staying here was a good idea." Grim-faced, she tried to get past me, but I blocked the door.

"I didn't ask you to leave; I asked you why you weren't there for Lexi when she needed you."

"What answer will satisfy you, Clara? That I stopped coming around because my presence always made things worse between you and Sylvana? That I was furious with you for letting that brat walk all over you the way she did? Or that I didn't find out what happened to the pair of you for several months, and by then it was too late?"

The last was news to me, but I wasn't in the mood to forgive. "Flimsy excuses."

"Well, here's the one that caps them all, then. Kids

scare the bejesus out of me. It was probably a good thing I never had any of my own. I'd have made a hash of things."

Finally, a new truth. An embarrassing one if the dull red of her face was any indication. One I knew I could forgive.

"I know I screwed up, okay? I'd been tracking…Well, that's not important, but I was gone longer than I planned and I had no idea what happened. I stopped in at Athena's when I passed through the Fringe on my way home, and she told me some cockeyed story about you killing Sylvana, so I came straight here."

Hot acid still churned in my stomach, but I tried to picture it while Mag described finding Lexi happily ensconced with three faeries attending to her every whim.

"I hid in the bushes and watched the way they doted on her. She was happy, Clara. Smiling and laughing and I didn't have the heart to tear her away when they were taking better care of her than I ever could. So, I waited for Beltane that year and came in with the rest of the flame bearers for a closer look." Mag hung her head so I couldn't see her eyes.

Witches come in all different flavors of magical ability. Mine, like my mother's before me and Lexi's, showed itself in an innate affinity with the Balefire—all my other skills I learned through diligence. The Balefire certainly enhanced any strengths I developed on my own—save for divination, which I doubted I'd ever master. With my focus on home and family, I was the natural choice to become Keeper.

My polar opposite, Mag had exited our mother's womb with a burning desire to know what existed beyond the boundaries of our property. Where I struggled to See anything, the crystal ball showed her many things. I suspect some things it chose to reveal were painful for her, and those she kept to herself.

Instead, she regaled me with stories of scenes from far-away places, and when Mother finally gave permission, Mag wasted no time before setting off to find her way in the wide world. She stopped telling me the gory details of her exploits around the time she returned looking like she'd aged 70 human years in the course of a week. I knew Mag had done a lot of good for a lot of people, which makes it doubly distressing she didn't choose to raise Lexi when she had the chance.

Unless there was another reason. Of course, there was another reason, and it had nothing to do with being scared of babies, which was the dumbest thing I'd ever heard. Mag fears little in this world.

"You saw something." I knew I'd hit the nail on the head when she flinched. "You did. You tell me right now if there's something horrible looming in Lexi's future."

"Clarie, it's complicated." Mag using her pet name for me increased my suspicions.

"Then simplify it for me. I may have been turned to stone, but I don't have granite between my ears."

Mag tossed her packed bag down on the bed, eased her body back into the chair, and gestured for me to sit on the bed. If I needed to sit, her news had to be bad. "I knew."

"Knew what?" I prompted when she fell silent.

"All of it. That without intervention, Lexi's magic would never come. Did you really think I bought the story of you murdering your own daughter? I saw it in the crystal. You, Sylvana, the fight, the aftermath; and I knew if there was a way to keep Lexi safe, you would want me to take it."

The confession staggered me, and I was glad she'd made me sit.

"You thought you could keep Lexi from becoming a Fate Weaver if you let her be raised by faeries instead of witches."

"Lexi was born a Fate Weaver, as you well know, but that was Sylvana's choice and none of mine, dear sister. I walked away from her to keep her safe. A witch without power is no threat to anyone, nor is a Fate Weaver."

I stared at her as the implications set in.

"Choosing to do nothing wasn't easy for me, Clarie. It broke my heart to wait and watch her grow sadder as each birthday passed and she hadn't achieved her Awakening. Then Sylvana escaped, and I chose to follow her instead of watching over Lexi. I should have known that wily minx of yours would get past me and do damage. I'm not as fast as I used to be."

Mag tossed me a wry smile, but her eyes only stayed on mine for a bare second.

"She beat me back to Port Harbor by a matter of hours and gave Lexi the Stone of Blood. I missed my chance to put a stop to it."

"It didn't occur to you to break the spell on me so I could handle Lexi?"

"It occurred. Not in the cards. It had to be Lexi or no one." Finally, Mag lifted her head so I could see the tears she had been holding back. "Even knowing what I did, I traded your freedom for Lexi's safety, and I don't blame you if you hate me forever."

So many things clicked into place. "Is that why you never visited me? You must have known I could hear you, or at least considered the possibility."

The only sound in the room was the creak of her chair until she allowed, "Shame presents itself in many forms, sister dear. Haven't you ever feared to speak a truth out loud?"

Resisting an urge to indulge in a moment of extreme sentiment, I settled for patting Mag on the arm and mumbling something about it all working out the way it was supposed to in the end and that we needed to figure out our next move. Not that I had a clue in spell what that should look like.

I reached for her knitting bag. "Unpack your things and stay."

"In this madhouse?" Mag scoffed and yanked the bag out of my reach.

"Better than being bored, and I think you'll admit I've become something of an expert on defining boredom. Shall we pay a condolence call on Letitia? On the way, maybe take a look at what happened to poor Tansy?"

If there was anything Mag found irresistible, it was a mystery she could solve.

"You just want to get the word out that you're back and ready to take on Calypso Snodgrass."

I grinned back at my sister. "That might be part of my motive, but it's not all." The smile fell off my face. "You're feeling it too, right?"

"What? That Tansy's death is an omen? I don't need my crystal ball to see the handwriting on that wall. Speaking of which, I'm in the market for a few new supplies. Fancy a trip to Athena's?" Mag's lips twisted with wry humor. "I could stand to do some shopping." She gestured toward her pitiful bag of possessions and I knew our little tiff was over.

Standing in one place for so long had given me time to think, and I wanted to reconnect with my sister. Still, I wasn't above a little teasing.

"Well, I didn't like to mention it, but you could use a change of clothes. Something not quite so ..." The muumuu-style dress carried a sheen that marked it as some sort of polyester blend, zipped up the front, and was covered with tropical flowers larger than my head. The terms hideous, grandmotherly, and shapeless all sprang to mind and were dismissed. I wanted her to change her clothes, not get mad at me. "Casual." Seemed the safest bet.

"Excuse me for not wearing the latest styles, and what about you? You look like a throwback to the eighties."

"That *would* be the last time I bought anything new." Dust dry, the words fell off my tongue.

It was always this way with us—probably the same with most sisters who bicker over nothing and would still die for each other. Putting a stop to the pettiness before we ended up fighting like a passel of faeries, I dragged Mag to my room to rummage through my clothes for anything devoid of shoulder pads and geometric, color-blocked patterns.

We were not going out in public with her in the next best thing to a nightgown.

"No jeans. I can't abide the things," Mag specified. "And those high-waisted ones are way out of style."

"Actually, they're back in. Haven't you noticed what the kids are wearing these days." I tossed her a pair of black leggings and a long white tee with flowers on the front. "Here. This is the best I can do."

After struggling into the clothes, Mag faced the

mirror and grumbled, "I look like Barbie's grandmother," and I had to hide a snort behind a fake cough that didn't fool her in the least, but should have earned me a few points for trying. I opted for the pair of the jeans she'd scorned and covered up the dated front by leaving my blouse untucked.

"We'll hit Zayres on the way back," I pulled my purse from the hidden recesses of my closet and checked to see if the wad of cash I'd stuffed in there the day before my unfortunate incarceration remained.

"How much you got there?" Mag smirked at me.

"Couple hundred. That ought to do it."

Now it was her turn to snort, and she didn't even make an attempt to hide the sound. "Zayres went out of business years ago, and you don't have enough there to do any damage unless we're going to a secondhand store. Welcome to the new world, Sis. Is there any more where that came from?"

Funny how the world moves on when you're standing still.

"I can't believe we had to drive this thing," Mag grumbled from the passenger's seat of Terra's van. "Tell me again why we couldn't just skim from here to there."

"There's nothing like the feeling of a powerful piece of machinery in your hands." Not that Mag would know anything about that, having never learned to drive. There are faster ways for those of us with enough power and skill, but I wanted to look out the windows and let the breeze blow through my hair.

"Park it somewhere inconspicuous at least. Might as well wave a flag and have a parade. Draw less attention. Stupid thing looks like a clown's wardrobe."

Sighing, I did as she asked even though it had been years since Mag retired from actively pursuing rogue magic. She might still have an enemy or two floating around, though I doubted that was the case, and her worries were nothing more than old habits and an overinflated sense of propriety.

"The crime scene has already been examined and the park cleared for reopening. We're not doing anything wrong."

Mag raised an eyebrow, "We don't need to be doing anything wrong to stick out like a sore thumb."

Every step of the last twenty feet between the car and the square of earth where Tansy Blankenship's body had been found evoked the same skin-crawling sensation I remembered feeling when I was four years old and convinced something evil lived in my closet. Not even the sun's warmth banished the growing coolness that pebbled my flesh and sent a shiver through my limbs.

"You feel it, too?" Mag slowed to a standstill and inhaled as though scenting the air.

"I'd have to be a complete null to miss it." Hate prickled across my skin. The kind of hate that tiptoed through the world and aimed itself toward me and all of my kind.

"It's not possible, they're all dead, and I should know because this," Mag circled a hand in front of it to indicate the wrinkles and signs of advanced age on her face, "was how I paid for enough magic to make witchkind safe from the last of the Raythe."

Maybe not. "Unless there has been another one born since you retired."

For the first time, Mag's demeanor matched her frail appearance and it worried me how fast she turned pale and shaken. Any witch willing to give up her long-lived youth was a witch of great power and even greater heart. Witches can live for hundreds of years without aging at an equivalent pace, which is why I'm over 200 and still look like Lexi's slightly older sister. It's a fringe benefit meant to allay the burden of keeping the Unseelie court of Faerie from crossing into and wreaking havoc on our realm. Long story short, gifts can be taken away as easily as they were given.

In another minute, she'd pulled herself together again. "There have been no reports. I'm sure I'd have heard."

"Have I ever told you how much I admire you?"

"What? Am I dying?" Mag swiveled her head to get a better look at herself, and I was happy to see some of the color return to her face.

"Shut up. I'm not kidding, and you're not dying. Not ever." I dusted off my hands even though they weren't dirty. "Now, let's get to work and figure out what we're facing. If it is a Raythe, we're all in danger."

"It can't be. This is something else and my money's on it being a demon." Mag lifted the voluminous shirt to reveal a tool belt of sorts that she'd wrapped around her waist. No wonder she looked so chunky around the middle and walked as if she carried the weight of the world; she had a complete arsenal tucked into that thing.

Potion bottles peeked out over the leather loops that secured them to the outer surface, which looked like it could have been made from tanned dragon hide. Crystals hung in cages made from knotted string alongside pouches I could only assume carried whatever herbs and powders she deemed necessary for working magic on the fly. An athame and a boline rode special-made holsters, and a pair of wands tucked into their own carriers on the opposite side.

"Nice piece of kit. Where'd you get it?" While Mag had crazy skills in the craft, outside of knitting she hadn't ever been what you'd call crafty.

"Custom made by an old…acquaintance." My immutable sister blushed.

"An old boyfriend, you mean?" Evil still stained the air, but this piece of info was too much to let pass without prying a little. Mag liked to keep the juicy parts of her personal life hidden, even from me.

"I prefer men to boys, now get your head out of your hormones and help me collect some evidence." I suppressed a smirk, pulled out my wand, and tapped it lightly against the glass potion bottle she handed me. The bottle made sucking sounds as I waved it around to collect as much essence of evil as it would hold.

We spent a little time examining the area, and while Mag continued collecting samples, I ranged out to see if I could pick up any sign of a trail leading away from the scene of the crime. After crashing through the underbrush and getting tangled up in some thorny bushes, I concluded the twenty-foot radius we'd observed on our way in held up in a perfect circle with no break anywhere that I could find, even after a second rotation around its edge.

Heart heavy, I returned to where Mag was stowing away the last of her bottles with precise, but vicious motions that betrayed strong emotions.

"Find anything?"

"Dead end and not a single sign of a casting circle." I picked a twig out of my hair and tucked tousled strands behind my ear.

Grave-faced, Mag headed for the van. That she didn't even try for the driver's seat was a sign. "Let's go then. I need to get to the workshop."

Halfway there, she stopped and tilted her head to the side.

"That poor girl. Can't you feel the terror she left behind?" Mag's abilities in the divination department came along with a heightened sensitivity to psychic energies. A ghost could sit on my right shoulder, and I'd never have a clue, but I didn't need a ghost to tell me Tansy's sadness had settled over the clearing like a pall. I shivered, took my sister's arm and led her back to the van. "I can't stop thinking what if it had been..."

"Lexi. I know." I pushed back against the mental image that rose unbidden. First rule of witchery—and it goes without saying that this applies to everyone—is that what you concentrate on most is what will manifest in your life. Positive or negative. Life comes with this rule built in, and you can call it magic or positive thinking or whatever you want, but it pays to respect the process. "It wasn't, and we need to put that out of our heads."

"We're going to have to decide what to do about her at some point." Shifting back to our earlier conversation, Mag kept her tone neutral.

"It's a bit late, don't you think? Still, I think we should keep this little fishing expedition under wraps. She has enough trouble following her as it is."

"She needs to know what she's up against."

"Maybe, but not today."

The shopping trip and all thought of offering condolences forgotten, I drove slowly toward home.

Chapter 7

Lexi

Gran and Aunt Mag blew through the door like a hurricane, bringing with them a gust of crisp, early autumn air that tossed a pile of month-old mail off the entryway table. Several forgotten credit card bills fluttered to the ground, and I silently thanked Flix for setting up automatic payments on all my accounts.

"We've got work to do, follow us." Mag flicked her eyes and a withered finger toward the parlor.

"What kind of work?" I asked, trotting behind like a curious toddler or an obedient Jack Russel Terrier.

Mag fixed me with a stare hot enough to wilt lettuce, and Gran jabbed an elbow into her waist, "Don't pay any attention to your ornery old aunt. We might have a lead on what happened to Tansy Blankenship."

The thought of the witch's unfortunate death wiped

the smile off my face as I reached for the flame-concealed lever that would let us all into the space behind the fireplace. Something in the vicinity of Mag's waist clinked heavily as she passed behind the stone facade.

I soon found out the source of the sounds when she pulled a collection of palm-sized potion bottles from a belt strapped beneath the gaudy t-shirt she sported with more panache than you might expect.

"What on earth is in those?" I scrunched up my nose at the sight of what looked like brown sludge if brown sludge were a gaseous substance. Anything that can look like smoke and mud at the same time is extremely suspect in my book.

"Not exactly sure, but the fact that it's already begun to solidify should tell you plenty."

I stared at Aunt Mag blankly and received a look of utter disgust in return. "I keep forgetting you know nothing."

"That's what I tried to tell you," Salem chimed in, having slipped in through the fireplace in cat form without us noticing and then flickering into his human body—fully dressed, I noted with a mix of irritation and relief.

On further inspection, I decided Salem's outfit looked quite spiffy, and when Pyewacket trotted through the fireplace behind him, I realized why. One look at her sleek fur, and he seemed to gain an inch of height along with a few more around his chest. She curled up on a cushion near the fire, and even though he continued talking, his eyes flicked her way every few seconds.

"Only one kind of vapor turns viscous like that—essence of demon." He lectured with even more zeal than usual. Salem loves an audience, but I could have kicked him for pointing out my ineptitude in front of the one assembled before us now.

"You mean it was a demon that killed Tansy?" I squeaked.

"Possibly," Gran's voice was cautious, "All we really know is that there was a demonic presence in the location where she was found. Death attracts all sorts of creatures so I wouldn't be surprised if we found traces of multiple species."

"We must be thorough. Everything leaves a signature. This is magical forensics, and far more accurate than anything you'll see on *CSI*."

"I love that show!" Gran exclaimed. "Though I never imagined Sam Malone as a silver fox."

"Clarie, you're dating yourself," Mag rolled her eyes, "Poor Lexi doesn't even know what you're talking about."

"We have cable. I've seen reruns of *Cheers*. Can we focus here? There's a dead witch and possibly some kind of demon skulking about, and you two are discussing canceled shows and prime time television." I admonished.

Gran sighed, "You're right, Lexi. We're sorry." If I detected a note of sarcasm, I'd never mention it out loud. Salem had the good sense to stay out of the conversation altogether. I knew he despised cop shows almost as much as he abhorred dilly-dallying when it came to working magic.

Something short of properly chagrined, Mag went to work, and Gran explained what she was doing in a way that made me feel as though she were teaching a class of third graders. Assuming my education was well in hand, Salem catted out and curled up in a ball as close to Pyewacket as he could without actually touching her. Even though it looked like he was dozing, I could tell his whiskers were tuned in to her very movement.

"Your aunt is a master of alchemy, which is classified under the branch of—"

I cut her off in an attempt to prove I wasn't a complete dolt.

"The branch of elemental magic, involving the manipulation of naturally-occurring substances," I recited. "Salem says it's easier to understand than the mental branch and easier to explain than arcane magic."

"He's correct, though that's something of an oversimplification. Mental magic comes from within the witch or wizard; it's innate. You can't learn telekinesis, for example; you're either born with the ability to move objects using only the power of your mind, or you're not. Same with divination and capacity to create illusions. But, you can learn a spell or brew a potion with similar effects."

At least her recitation distracted me from what we were testing. Plus, it was good to learn from someone who'd actually been there and done that.

"Arcane magic—which encompasses such practices as summoning, binding, enchanting, and charms—involves harnessing as-yet unknown forces to accomplish a similar goal.

Mag has been trying to bridge the gap her entire life. She believes those forces can be analyzed using the principles of the alchemical—or scientific—method. If we can isolate all of the traces found at the scene of Tansy's death, for example, we can determine what branch of magic killed her. And that will tell us, first and foremost, whether she was murdered using magic or sorcery."

I already knew sorcery was abhorred in the witch community. A sorcerer is a person lacking innate magical talent—one who harnesses the power of another being and perverts the magic for his or her own gain.

My mind clicked into motion, and suddenly I understood what was so concerning. "You're trying to figure out whether this was an outside attack on witches, or if Tansy was killed by one of our own."

The two older witches exchanged a look I couldn't read.

"There is no good conclusion here, but we'd

certainly prefer if Tansy had tussled with a supernatural predator. I realize that sounds counterintuitive, but the alternatives are humans or witches, and neither bodes well for the future. It would mean we're either being split from the outside or splintered from within; either way, figuring out who's holding the ax is priority number one."

"Well, she's dead, so if it were one of us, wouldn't the killer have been," I flinched at having to say the word, "stoned."

"One would think," Mag said.

I thought back through all of Salem's lessons—even the ones I'd only half-listened to at the time. I remembered the tales of witch persecution even grade school history teachers couldn't ignore (I'd absorbed every detail of those, you can rest assured), and recalled the bedtime stories Terra, Evian, and Soleil had regaled me with as a child—especially the ones I'd assumed were complete fiction but could now recognize as flimsily-concealed truths.

"You're worried we have been or will be discovered," I stated simply.

Gran nodded, and Mag piped up, "Discovered, revealed, and eradicated. We can never let our guard down. There's more to being a witch than working magic. And you, my dear niece, have even more to fear, what with your particular brand of special gifts. Fate Weavers are considered a delicacy to a variety of creatures."

I swallowed the lump in my throat. Being referred to in the same manner as a slice of goose liver pate can be extremely motivating. "What can I do to help?"

"Just watch and learn. And don't touch anything." Mag barked. In all honesty, I preferred Salem's overbearing teaching methods to Mag's grumpy demeanor any day.

Gran began by lighting several white tea light candles while Aunt Mag rubbed each vial with a layer of herb-infused oil and placed each one in a suspended rack made of iron—for grounding, she explained—and laid out a pile of cardboard sticks in various colors.

"Each one of these testers has been steeped in a combination of revealing potion and the essence of various beings. We'll start with the basics—Fae, demon, witch, shifter, et cetera—and then narrow down the results as we go."

Mag lifted the stoppers off each bottle, inserted a different stick into each collection of goo. The red one gurgled, and the contents bubbled over the top of the vial, then crusted into shiny black crystalline shards. Yellow and blue produced no special effects, but the green one put on a miniature fireworks show before Mag deftly replaced the lid.

Another one of those looks passed between the sisters. The kind that smacks of adults conspiring to keep sensitive information from the ears of children.

"What?" Something failed the magical litmus test—perhaps failed wasn't the right word, but I wanted to know.

"Demon." Gran said.

"Coincidence? Unlikely." Mag referred to Rhys and his timely visit.

None of us noticed the Balefire dwindling to a bed of embers until the air had stilled to utter silence behind the clinking of glass and the shuffling of our feet against the stone floor.

"Um, you guys…" I pointed and rushed to the hearth.

When I reached for the handle nestled in behind the andirons, a feeble flicker of blue was all I could see above the glowing coals, and I felt none of the familiar tickle I was used to from the fire. The only other time I'd seen it close to this low was during the days before I'd gained my magic and this was worse. Way worse.

Thanking Hecate that part of my life was over for good, I gave the handle a yank and nearly landed on my butt when nothing happened.

"We have a problem." Another tug and the fireplace stood stubbornly still. The impossible room I'd made my own no longer felt like a cozy sanctuary. Every time I glanced away from them, it felt like the walls crept closer. We were trapped, and in another minute I might give in to the urge to voice the scream creeping up the back of my throat. Bracing my foot against the andiron, I grabbed the handle again. "This. Thing. Won't. Move." A grunt punctuated each word.

"Here, let me." Confident in her magic, Clara gently nudged me aside and, knowing I couldn't watch, I turned to survey the space for something that might help. Potions, powders, and books. Nothing useful unless…there was one book that might have something. The family Grimoire rested in its customary place on the pedestal in the center of the summoning circle.

The scents of old leather and parchment soothed the claustrophobia for about a second and a half—right up until I saw the room shrink another foot all the way around and realized it wasn't my imagination. Claustrophobia my left foot. You're only paranoid until they really are after you, and the room was getting smaller by the minute.

What would happen when the walls met? When the Sanctum dwindled to nothing with us locked inside? Would it spit us out the fireplace or would the walls eat us whole? I shuddered and renewed my efforts to find something to stop the inexorable slither of sneaking doom from closing in on us completely.

Meanwhile, Clara and Mag's voices rose with excitement, and not the good kind.

"Just crawl through."

"I can't. Remember we closed off the back of the fireplace when we installed the sliding door system?"

"Excuse my memory, I'm old." A sullen Mag

kicked the raised hearth with one surprisingly dainty foot. "What are we going to do, then? Because I don't want to spend the night fighting for space on the sofa."

"That's not going to be our biggest problem in a few minutes." Abandoning the book, I rejoined them near the hearth. "Haven't you noticed the workshop is getting smaller? What happens to us if it disappears? And by the way, isn't the door mechanism a mechanical thing?"

Clara ignored my first two questions and zeroed in on the last. "Runs on magic. I got that handle at a junk shop over in Palmer. The only way to get out of here is to feed the Balefire." She glanced toward the empty wood box, then at me.

"What? It's a magical fire, we haven't had to add wood to it since my Awakening." Fear sparked a touch of defensiveness, but at least I didn't whine. "Can't we use our magic?"

As it turned out, the answer to that question was a rousing no. Even with all three of us thrusting hands and power into the dying embers, we managed to raise nothing more than a brief flare of red before the coals darkened again. So much for the witch feeding the flame part of the Balefire lore.

"You didn't answer my question. What happens if the room disappears with us in it?"

"Best case, we get expelled through the fireplace. Worst case—we end up somewhere else, or dead.

There's no rule book or contingency plan for these things. We're witches, we work with what we have at hand. Let's worry about the Balefire for now, and figure out the rest later, shall we?"

"It needs fuel. Wood. It's the only way." Mag stated the obvious.

The walls inched closer. We needed something to burn, and I grabbed the only thing in sight besides books, which I could never bring myself to sacrifice to the flame: the three-legged stool tucked under the potions section of the table.

While I bashed the stool against a jagged border of stones lining the side of the fireplace, Clara and Mag rounded up an old newspaper and balled up a few pages to help coax the embers back to life. In their haste, they threw on more than we needed.

"Didn't there used to be a set of tools in here? I need a poker to stir this up before it suffocates the coals." Clara's voice sounded strained, and I hated to tell her the tools were in the garage.

Without thinking too hard about it in case of failure, I reached for the only long, pointy thing I had at my disposal and pulled an arrow from the invisible quiver on my back. *The* arrow, actually. The one I'd used to free Clara not so long ago. Of course, I didn't realize that until I poked it into the dying embers and gave the balled up papers a stir. When whatever remnant of the Balefire clinging to the arrowhead made contact, the paper caught and the pieces of stool went up like tinder.

Flames shot back to life with enough explosive force to push all three of us off the hearth and into a tangled heap. I happened to land in a position where I could watch the Sanctum walls scuttle back to their original dimensions so fast it looked like a time warp.

Gently extricating myself from the jumble of limbs, I yanked the handle hard, and the fireplace swung open. Crisis averted. For now, anyway.

You wouldn't think a thousand or so square feet could fit in the space between the back of the hearth and Soleil's room on the other side of the wall, but that's part of what makes being a witch so unbelievably cool. Just like the backyard, the sanctum occupied space in some kind of alternate universe, invisible to the naked eye but as real as anything else you can touch, see or feel.

I'd been happily unaware the workshop existed until I dreamed about thrusting my hand into the flame, feeling the soft tickle of fire on my skin, and pulling the handle to open the wall behind the chimney. Witches don't tend to doubt the wisdom of dreams the same way non-magical humans do; I trusted my instincts in real life and was pleased to find I couldn't be harmed by the Balefire.

Two minutes ago, I wasn't sure the coals could sear a gnat. But now, it roared to life in a hundred shades of the rainbow and fed off all the energy circulating through the house. Licking flames colored the bricks below the mantle a dingy shade of black that even faerie magic couldn't clean. Being confined indoors probably didn't please the Balefire; after all, it had once been a mighty beast of a bonfire that lived under an expanse of Celtic sky.

A couple thousand years ago the first Balefire witch, Esmerelda, created the Balefire to keep our realm—and witches—out of the civil war between the two Fae courts. From that time to this, witches have been distributing the same flame to one another, all across the globe. Back in Ireland, my great-great-great-and then some grandmother hosted a spectacular celebration each year on the day falling directly between the spring equinox and the summer solstice. Witches from all over the Celtic lands traveled the countryside for a bit of the Balefire flame. Beltane—a Gaelic term meaning *brilliant fire*—is now celebrated on the first day of May, which also happens to be my birthday.

Flame feeds witch, and witch feeds flame; that's the Balefire motto. Sure, our family Keeps the fire, but it belongs to all of witchkind. We brew our potions above it; we light our candles with it; we absorb and resupply its energy in a symbiotic relationship.

Globalization being what it is, distributing the flame has become a much bigger problem; and more important than ever. As long as the Balefire burns, our magic flourishes, and we're safe from the dark faction of Faeries—the Unseelie—who would love nothing more than to eradicate all witches and most humans from the planet. My godmothers, of course, hail from the Seelie, or light court, and have sworn to protect us from what the Seelie consider traitors to their race.

Around three centuries ago, my ancestors made the decision to move the flame to the New World, settling into the same plot of land on which I'm currently standing. With the population exploding during that time, what was once an honored celebration has turned into a logistical fiasco, and requires an entire committee to organize the distribution.

The witches who file through my parlor each year on Beltane bear little resemblance to the wild women who used to dance naked around the fire. They fit in with quote-unquote *civilized* society, passing for humans as the terms *eccentric* and *odd* are whispered behind their backs. We've all—and by *we* I mean supernatural beings of any and all persuasions—been relegated to the shadows in one way or another, effectively increasing the macabre stereotype by more than a few degrees. But, that's life, right?

Chapter 8

Clara

Cuddled into a patio chair on the front porch, I watched dawn paint pink light across a narrow ribbon of sky and sipped peppermint tea with enjoyment. After twenty-five years of standing still, I had plenty of catching up to do, but for this one minute, I didn't mind sitting down.

This early in the morning, the air often turns still and quiet like it's waiting for the sun's touch before coming back to life. That's the only reason I heard the soft exclamation drifting from the site where I'd been imprisoned for so long.

"Hecate's petticoats! She's gone."

I highly doubt Hecate ever wore petticoats, but I knew by the epithet exactly which witch had come to have a little chat with old stoneface. Now, I know I've been called evil a time or two, but I'm not. Or not more than most, anyway.

Scaring Millie Minkens out of her shoes only counted as mischief, not wickedness. Unless the degree of wicked can be measured by the amount of pleasure taken during a mischievous act—then it was totally wicked.

I crept across the front lawn and got as close as I could without drawing attention to myself. "Come to regale me with more tales of your superior nature, have you?" I let the words roll off my tongue, relishing the feeling of being able to speak my mind again.

"Clara?" Slightly stronger now, the sun gave just enough light for me to see Millie's hand rise to clutch her throat. Millie's biggest sin evidenced itself in a penchant for stirring up trouble by telling the kind of half-truths that made others seem stupid while she came off looking like an authority. That her habit was well-known and not only tolerated, but laughed about in the community was a piece of news she would ignore should anyone tell her. Anything that didn't fit with Millie's internal image of her own importance couldn't possibly be true.

"It can't be…Clara. Is that really you? But I thought…"

"…I was a stone cold killer?" I said bitterly. "Even after Sylvana turned up alive? Exactly who did you think I'd killed once that bit of truth came to light?"

The question put a stop to Millie fidgeting with the front of her dress, and she landed on the bench installed so witches could sit and contemplate my crimes before deciding whether or not to commit one of their own. Being pointed out to young witches as a bad example rankled more than I'd realized. It's not polite to carry a grudge, but it feels so good.

To her credit, Millie answered truthfully, "I don't think any of us really thought too hard about that side of things. You'd obviously been stoned, so we naturally assumed you did something to deserve the punishment."

"Naturally."

The support and warmth I'd hoped for from an old friend was not on the books, apparently. "Can you blame us for that? How were we supposed to know you were innocent?"

"A little faith might have been nice—especially coming from my own coven."

Millie had the decency to hang her head. "Calypso took over the coven after you…left…and she isn't your biggest fan." An understatement she delivered dryly. Calypso Snodgrass despised me almost as much as her daughter hated Lexi. And for as little reason. Her influence on my witch sisters couldn't have been good, and she was the only coven member who had never used me as a confessional.

"What really happened that day?" With guilt deflected onto Calypso, Millie was free to try and satisfy her avid curiosity, which left me with a small dilemma since she had trouble keeping even the simplest of stories straight. Anything said to Millie went in one ear and out her mouth. After taking a ride on the Tilt-A-Whirl in her head. No good could come from telling her anything important.

Unless there was a way to turn her insatiable need to know things to my advantage. I eyed Millie speculatively and tried to buy a little time to decide. "Tell me more about coven activities during my absence."

Eager to part with a load of gossip, Millie launched into a rambling tale that spanned the years I'd been out of contact. That her story hardly matched most of the one-sided conversations I'd witnessed during my years of standing still came as no surprise.

Picking the truth out of her self-aggrandizing narrative, I became increasingly dismayed at the direction Calypso had taken the coven. Maybe that's why I spit in karma's face and, using my amulet as a focus, whispered an incantation to wipe her memory clear of this conversation. I left her with the suggestion of a rumor that I was no longer among the dead and tiptoed away while it took effect.

Lexi

"Shh," Gran whispered as Terra glided into the kitchen for breakfast the next morning.

"You realize I could hear you from the end of the street if I wanted to, right?" My faerie godmother batted her thick lashes at us while absently flicking a finger and sending a cast iron frying pan zinging across the room. Salem and Pye ducked when the thing nearly beaned them on its way by. Mag let out a quiet chuckle.

The gas clicked to life as Soleil tottered in, still yawning, a few seconds later, Evian at her heels. In a flash, a fresh pot of coffee perfumed the air, and I inhaled deeply while pretending not to have any clue what Terra was talking about.

"Where's Vaeta?" Mag asked pointedly, ignoring her sister's request for silence.

"Still in bed. Morty Gunderson's retirement party raged on till almost dawn. Vaeta lost a bet against Terra and had to clean the bathrooms without magic, so she'll probably ignore us until the bleach smell fades." Evian piped up.

Soleil snorted, "Or until she forgets—which I'm betting will be around lunch time today, if not before."

"No more betting," I admonished, "Not today."

"Fine, fine." Terra brushed my statement aside. "We'll be good. Now tell us what the whispers were all about."

Earth and Air represent opposite ends of the elemental spectrum for a good reason; if Vaeta's mind was a sieve, Terra's was a steel trap. Nothing got past her, as attested by my countless failed attempts at sneaking out after curfew during my teen years. She might have let me get all the way to the end of our road a couple of times, but only for her own amusement.

"It's probably nothing, but we found some evidence that might point toward Vaeta's demon friend, Rhys. Inconclusive evidence," I returned Mag's elbow prod with one of my own, and heard her suck in a breath as I jabbed her ribs, "so it could have been an entirely different demon altogether."

Soleil let a hiss escape from between her lips as Evian's eyebrows lifted almost off her forehead, and Terra closed her eyes for a moment.

"You think it's no coincidence that Rhys shows up at the home of the Balefire Keeper right around the time a witch from her own coven was murdered." Terra directed the statement toward Gran and Aunt Mag.

"Essentially, yes. We're not suggesting your sister is involved—but she has a connection you can't deny would be hard for someone like Rhys to ignore." Clara's tone was diplomatic, but it didn't matter one bit to Vaeta, who had come around the corner, sleepily rubbing her eyes, at the most inopportune moment.

Now she was wide awake and more than a little ticked off. "Of course you witches think all demons are scum. I'm not surprised by your attitudes, except for you, Lexi. I thought you were more evolved than that."

I expected World War Three to break out, for hell to freeze over, or at the very least for a tirade of insults to start flinging around the room—but all of the faeries remained conspicuously silent. Apparently, Gran's presence was enough to keep them on their best behavior, and though I was grateful, it irritated me to no end that they could rein it in for her when they'd never made an attempt to shield me from nine levels of crazy.

"So you deny he had any involvement? How could you possibly know that?" Terra countered.

"Lexi just said the evidence was inconclusive. You think a demon was involved, but you don't know which demon, correct?" She continued without waiting for an answer, "So we're at an impasse, are we not?"

"I guess so…" I looked from Mag to Clara, who averted their gazes and let me take the hit for all of us.

"All right then. So when you have something a little more solid, we'll talk." Vaeta whirled around and stalked back out of the room.

Chapter 9

Flix still hadn't returned to the office, but he'd left a long, rambling message on the answering machine letting me know he'd taken Carl to his beach house up the coast and they'd be gone for at least ten more days. Thank goddess he took salon calls on a dedicated line, or I'd be knee deep in complaints from addicted clients who couldn't handle two weeks without one of his legendary blowouts. There had been a softness to his tone I took to mean he'd forgiven me, but for the time being, I was on my own when it came to FootSwept.

There were surprisingly few other messages, considering my lack of attention to business matters over the past several days. Strange, we hadn't seen a downturn in clientele like this…well, ever.

It had gone from boom to doom ever since the lonely hearts party cleared out my backlog of matches and then some.

Vacations are nice when you want to take them, less fun when you're not sure if you've been fired. I'd be thankful the bow hadn't made a peep if I wasn't worried I'd done something wrong. With it quiet around possible matches and my inner goddess a daily no-show, I wasn't sure if I was supposed to be fooling with people's fates or just waiting for a golden apple to drop on my head as a sign.

Whoever set up this Fate Weaving deal hadn't invested in direct deposit or a 401k plan, so I had to pay the bills somehow. Who was I kidding; FootSwept had always been a bit of a passion project. A way to parlay what little innate magical talent I'd displayed before my Awakening into something important.

Of course, I couldn't see the forest for the trees back then. With no idea my father was the actual Cupid of ancient lore, I hadn't recognized my power for what it was.

Was it possible I'd outgrown FootSwept altogether? Was I fooling around in an office when I should be strolling around town, watching for glowing signs and waiting for the bow to sing out that it's time to let my arrows fly?

The thought broke my heart a little bit, so I pushed it way down deep inside and hoped for clarity.

Or I tried, but it kept popping back up. I mean, think about this for a minute. Once I hit my groove with my weapon of mass love construction, how much business would I have?

Not that I was complaining because watching, even from a distance, that moment when hearts collide gave me a thrill. But, this bow and arrow thing seemed so cut and dried, so clinical compared to my previous work. If this was all there was to weaving fates, I'd be going from management to working on an assembly line.

I needed more.

I might not be able to maintain the business indefinitely, but for now, I wasn't ready to let it go, either. Even if it did mean having more time to spend with Kin, who was so busy we'd become used to seeing one another only in passing. His day job as radio DJ was a means to an end; his evenings were spent playing guitar with his band around Port Harbor, making connections for the day when he could finally open his own recording studio.

That man was almost too good to be true. Sexy as sin in a rock star-meets-nerd kind of way, he had a magical voice and hands to match. Thinking about Kin always put a smile on my face, so I let myself get lost in memories. How we'd met on the street in front of my house; the fear in my heart when I had told him about being a witch; and the way his lips felt when we'd shared True Love's Kiss.

And I still felt like we'd missed out on something wonderful. Our relationship started on fast forward—we went from strangers to being a fated match with almost nothing in between. We missed a lot of those moments I'd been giving my clients over the years. That breathless feeling when you notice him, or he notices you for the first time. Will he or won't he ask me out? What will I say? Will I be able to get the words out while my heart is thundering in my chest?

Kin made my heart pound from the first time I met him; that's not the point. We went from zero to sixty without going through any of the numbers in between. Sixty is nice. I love sixty. But twenty is a good number, too.

What was wrong with me? I'm Lexi Balefire, queen of setting the stage for love to build. If I could engineer romantic scenarios for my clients, why not for myself? All we needed was to replace some of the domesticity with adventure. The kind that is only dangerous to your heart, not your body. We'd had plenty of that already. If anyone could put a romance in motion, it was me.

Suddenly much more optimistic, I was just about to pick up the phone and get some appointments on the books when I heard a tentative knock at the door. A little girl, maybe twelve years old, with a determined look on her heart-shaped face stood on the other side. As I waved her inside, she pushed a pair of baby-pink glasses onto her nose and looked around curiously.

"I'm Hannah Aarons. It's very nice to meet you, Lexi." She spoke in a clear, precocious voice after I introduced myself and offered her a seat at one of the Chippendale chairs opposite my desk. I have to admit, I was a bit thrown. It wasn't every day—or *ever*, for that matter—a child comes looking to employ my services, and I had a feeling I knew just what she was after.

"What can I do for you, Hannah?" My friendly grin seemed to calm her, and she straightened in the chair and began her story.

"I want you to help get my mother and father back together." Just ducky, exactly what I feared.

"They still love each other. I know they do. My dad is lonely, and he still keeps a picture of my mom in his wallet. Mom's gone on a couple of dates, but she always comes back from her nights out looking disappointed. I can pay you; I have lots of bat mitzvah money left." Hope and fear vied for top billing as her eyes widened and then steeled against the onslaught of tears. I felt a rush of respect. Hannah Aarons was one tough cookie.

Formulating a response proved problematic, because the bow began to sing a sad tune, and my instincts screamed that I was supposed to help this little girl one way or another. It also appeared unlikely Hannah would take no for an answer.

"Sweetheart, I will not take your money. But I will do what I can to help you. I can't promise anything, though. Relationships are complicated, and just because two people love each other doesn't mean they're meant to be together." I couldn't *not* say it, though I hoped for

Hannah's sake I was wrong on this count.

Her hands fisted in her lap. "That's what everyone says, but I just *know* it's not supposed to be like this."

I had to admire her spunk and her determination. And let's face it, she tugged pretty hard on my heart strings, and if there was anything I could do to help her, I would.

"I'll need some information from you, and then I'll try my best."

It turned out Hannah's parents had been high school sweethearts—typical tale, and you'd be surprised how many soul mates are right under each other's noses. Proximity plays a big hand, and so does the heart. Except it's not the heart; it's the essence of one's very being that calls out to another, kindred soul. I've never been offered a 101 course on fate weaving, but that's what I've gathered. And good thing, too, because otherwise, I'd be trekking all over hell's half-acre to make matches.

According to their daughter, her parent's relationship failure sounded textbook: they married young, started a family quickly, and then allowed the fire to fizzle. Hannah described lots of seemingly pointless arguments and misunderstandings, but I could only take her observations with a grain of salt. After all, she was a kid, and though her point of view was valid, it definitely wasn't the whole story.

"They used to have fun together. We had fun

together. Look." She yanked a cell phone out of her pocket and keyed up the photo gallery to show me a blurry photo of a man smiling down at a woman with her back to the camera.

"This was last summer at Coachman's Bluff. We camp out in the caves for my birthday every year. Last year was the best. I got this phone for a present and took about a hundred pictures. But this year…well, we're not going of course. Because of the *separation*."

Hannah's despair touched my heart and reminded me why I was in this business, to begin with. This was exactly what I needed to get back into the swing of things at FootSwept.

Still, the closest I'd ever come to repairing a relationship was when my half-brother had used magic to screw it up in the first place, and this was different. My heart ached for Hannah, and I could only pray to the minor deities I wouldn't have to witness her disappointment if her parents weren't actually fated.

I reached across the desk to touch her hand and offer what little comfort I could, and as my fingers grazed hers, Hannah's need overtook my senses. This was becoming a regular habit.

In the vision, I was the tiny baby looking up into the glowing faces of two parents obviously in love with each other and their little bundle of joy. I felt safe and protected along with little Hannah. You don't have to experience loving parents to recognize them when you see them.

Over the years I lived through Hannah, Emily and Matthew's expressions altered, grew tense, and while the sensation of feeling loved never abated, we felt less secure as time wore on. Fights erupted on a consistent basis, and from the snippets, I could hear it sounded as though the stress had finally worn down their resolve to weather any storm.

My role of matchmaker typically means I'm helping to ignite a spark, not bring one back from the dead. I'd have to step up my game if I was going to have any shot at repairing this breach.

The *This is Your Life* episode served a second purpose. My LPS had taken the opportunity to home in on Hannah's parents in a big way.

I pried a few details out of her, then bid her goodbye, made copious notes on a little slip of paper in lieu of tappety-tapping them into my phone, and tucked it away inside Saturday's page of my day planner. Take some advice from me: if you don't want to work weekends, don't become a matchmaker.

"I want to talk to you about something." My brain heard the words, but I had trouble processing them while Kin's hands played over my feet. He could have had a career as a foot masseuse, he was that good. We'd finally been able to carve out some time for one another, and I couldn't think of a better way to spend it.

"Mmmm. Okay." The joyful kneading of my arch stopped.

"I'm serious, we need to talk." A phrase that has come to mean *uh-oh*.

"Sounds ominous." Was he about to break up with me? Dread shot my heartbeat up to a rapid flutter and robbed me of my breath. Just when I was about to launch my plan for pumping up the romance, it might be the end.

"I hope not. I want to talk about moving forward. You know, taking the next step." He twisted around, so we were facing each other.

Panicked, I tried to buy some time to think. "Isn't it usually the woman who initiates the *where is this relationship going* talk?"

Kin took a deep breath and blurted, "I think you should move in with me."

Once the initial shock subsided, I said, "You know I can't. I'm the Balefire's Keeper. I can stay away a day or two at a time, maybe longer if the flame is strong. But I can't move out."

Could I? If I went back every day? Kin said something I didn't hear while my mind raced through the possibilities. Could I treat the Balefire like a second job? Would that be enough to sustain it?

Keeper of the flame isn't something I *do*, it's something I *am*, just as much as being a Fate Weaver. Obviously, my father, the ultimate Fate Weaver, didn't wield the Bow of Destiny from his home—I pictured him living in a Greek palace with fluted columns in sparkling white.

Was I expected to travel around the world in my capacity as celestial matchmaker? How would that even work? FootSwept would certainly not be part of that equation. And could I fly commercial or would the bow show up on the scanners? Clearly, there were things I needed to learn about my new destiny.

"…she can take control of the Balefire."

"I'm sorry, what did you say?"

After a short, assessing pause, Kin repeated himself. "Now that Clara's back, she can take control of the Balefire, leaving you a bit more freedom." From his clipped tones, I assumed he'd condensed a longer observation to the bare minimum of information.

I opened my mouth to shoot down his proposal, then closed it again when I realized the idea did bear at least a modicum of thought. What if Clara could take over the Balefire? Would that really be so bad? Port Harbor is home, and I've never been bitten by the travel bug. This town has everything I want: nice people, good shopping, tall ships to admire, great restaurants, and I love it here. Watching over the Balefire and helping the lovelorn has always been enough for me, even before I saw my greater potential for doing both.

Going out into the world armed with an invisible bow and thwacking an arrow into anyone who needs it might sound like heaven to some, but not to me. Cupid, I assumed, could move from one place to another in the blink of an eye. Hell, even Santa Claus had more game than me in the magic travel department.

Truth be told, all I ever wanted was to get my full portion of witch magic. This extra stuff hadn't been part of the plan, and if I'd been given a choice, my answer would have been an emphatic *no* to almost all of it. How ironic is it that the thing I grew up wanting to do better—tending the Balefire—was the one thing I could now relinquish to someone else? Just at the moment I reached my full potential, too. Sometimes life sucks.

While all of that ran through my head, Kin interpreted my silence as disinterest.

"Never mind. Maybe I shouldn't have brought it up. I know you've been through a lot these past few months, and the last thing I want to do is pile more on your plate. I thought we wanted the same things, but I understand if you're not ready."

"Shut up."

"Shut up? Really?" Kin looked pained.

"I didn't mean it like that," I softened my tone, "Look, I know we haven't seen a lot of each other lately, and with the upheaval at home, we haven't exactly had much alone time. But do you really want to live with me? I can't cook, I don't do windows, and you'll find out exactly how big a mess I really am."

Kin grimaced, "That's a cop out, and you know it. I

already know you come with crumbs in the bed. And Skittles. And a closet that looks like it is organized when it's really chaos in disguise. But I'm still asking. If you don't want to, it's all right. I thought we were soul mates, but maybe you're not as sure about that as I thought you were."

"That's not it at all." I shook my head emphatically, "There are two separate issues here—our relationship and my living arrangements. That I might need a minute to think about one does not negate the other. I love you. I love spending time with you. The more, the better. All things being normal, I'd be home packing right now." I slid over to sit in his lap, and for once, his arms didn't go immediately around me.

"I understand that you can't make a snap decision and that this would be a big step for you. But will you promise me you'll just think about it? Clara's back, let her take the Balefire off your to-do list. You have enough other things to handle. Let her deal with four fighting faeries throwing magic around like water balloons." I could tell Kin was still bitter about the godmothers' transgression, but I couldn't help jumping to their defense.

"They're perfectly safe, I've lived with them my entire life, and I'm still in one piece." Relatively speaking, anyway, considering I split my personality with Demigod Lexi, shooter of hapless love targets. "And I don't even know if Clara would *want* the

Balefire back—or if it can be *given* back, for that matter. But I'll think about it. That's the best I can do right now."

"That's all I'm asking. Take all of your options into consideration."

How could I blame him for wanting more when that's what I also wanted—if in a slightly different format.

Right?

Or was I just feeling like this relationship was too good to be true because it had moved so quickly? Maybe what I saw as a boatload of too much convenience was only a front for the lack of trust that the universe would allow me this much happiness.

Clearly, I had some issues to work out.

Chapter 10

Faeries mystify me. Even after all these years of living with my godmothers, some of their motivations are as clear to me as mud. Like the way the four of them fawned all over Clara after she shut them down during the whole Vaeta-and-the-demon fracas. Then again, the one time I lost my cool and tossed a hissy fit, they responded with respect. If anyone ever offered a class in Fae ethics, I'd sign up in a heartbeat.

"Blueberry pancakes?" Soleil carrying the plate around the table was a subtle dig at Vaeta, who usually used her magic to jet serving dishes around the room. Not that the others weren't capable of doing the same, it had simply become Vaeta's task ever since she came to live with us. All Clara had to do was point the finger at Rhys, and her sisters were willing to throw out the baby with the bath water.

Vaeta's response was a complete freeze-out, and

none of us had seen much more of her lately than her back side as she tripped happily out the door to do whatever it is you do when you're cavorting with a demon. It amazes me sometimes that I grew up with any sort of moral compass given the pettiness practiced by my role models.

She'd had fallen off my list of favorite people, too, but I was starting to feel a little bad about it. After all, who hasn't had a thing for a bad boy at least once in their lives? I might have made a stab at brokering peace if the doorbell hadn't interrupted breakfast. The insistent peal of the chime triggered a burst of head-throbbing harmony from the bow that reminded me of the way two barking dogs feed off the sound of each other.

An ancient weapon with all the impulse control of a Schnauzer and it lives in my head. My life gets weirder every day. Another chime sounded, this one more frantic than the last, and I realized no one else planned to answer the door.

"Nobody move, I'll get it." I rolled my aching eyeballs in their sockets and went to see who was keeping me from blueberry fluffiness. Honestly, Soleil's pancakes are like heavenly clouds of yum.

"Don't look at me, I don't actually live here," Kin mumbled through a mouth full of pancake, his eyes half-closed as he chewed unapologetically. He can say what he wants, but he'd miss hanging out here in the mornings if I moved into his place. My idea of making breakfast involves a toaster oven and a pack of frozen waffles.

A steamroller waited on the other side of the door.

"Oh Lexi, is it true? I've just heard the news, and I wanted to come see for myself." At least I think that was what she said, it wasn't easy to hear with my head pounding and my face pressed up against the bodice of a hot pink sundress that lacked the wherewithal to adequately cover a pair of absolutely ginormous ta-tas.

Violet Bloodgood. The name swam up through layers of memory. One of the witches who came to every Balefire celebration, but wasn't a carrier of the flame.

"Oh, dear. Let me fix that for you."

Before I could ask what, Violet laid soft palms on either side of my head and pulled the headache out of me so fast I hardly had time to process what was happening. An empathic witch and a healer.

"Uh, thanks."

Violet tucked a lock of no-way-that's-her-natural-color blond hair behind one ear and presented me with a cheerful smile. "Better? I thought so. Now, about Clara—is it true? Millie told me she heard it from Bellona, who was shopping at Athena's when she thought she saw your grandmother walking by with that sister of hers. The one that used to live in the house of sticks until someone huffed and puffed all over it."

How she could talk so fast and not have her tongue dry out was beyond me.

"Gran! There's someone here to see you." I got at least that much out of the barrage of words.

Violet bounced and jiggled her way down the hall. She had to turn sideways to thread her way past bins and boxes labeled *Enchanting Events*. Making a mental note to finally have that conversation with Terra about the mess, I gave my grandmother a saucy wink when we burst into the equally crowded kitchen and noted the sliding doors leading to the patio were open slightly.

Aunt Mag must have moved fast to make it out in time. My grandmother's eyes cut to mine, then rolled up to the ceiling. The last thing she wanted was to be co-opted into a gab session with the biggest gossip in of all witchdom, but I hadn't given her a choice.

I'll admit it gave me a great deal of pleasure to watch my grandmother's face slam into the same spot mine had occupied only a few minutes before. Violet went all out with her hugs, and it didn't seem fair I was the only one covered in a thick fog of Chantilly Lace cologne. I coughed, partly to expel the cloying scent, and partly to cover a giggle I doubt Clara would have appreciated.

"Don't leave, Lexi. There were several reasons I came here today, and one is to see if there's a problem with the Balefire again. I assume it's all right to discuss this in mixed company?" Lips coated in candy-colored lipstick pursed and kohl-lined eyes slid in Kin's direction while Violet searched for a way to be diplomatic.

"Yes, of course," I responded dryly, lifting a subtle hand toward the godmothers to indicate they should mind their own business. Faeries are easily offended, and quick to react. I somehow doubted their involvement would improve the situation.

Violet cleared her throat and continued, "Ever since last Beltane, we've all enjoyed having that little bit of extra oomph that comes when the Balefire burns strong. The past few days, though, things have been…" Another pause. "Well, it hasn't been good. Look, we all felt bad when it took so long for you to Awaken, but keeping our powers balanced during those lean years required a lot of extra muscle, and it's been nice being able to perform complex spells with ease again."

Unapologetic, Violet leaned sideways to get a glimpse of the fireplace and the Balefire which had chosen that moment to shoot bright pink sparks across the rug. Lucky for me, the carpet was protected by Soleil's best anti-scorch charm.

Clara and I exchanged another glance, and this one contained no amusement at all. This trouble with the Balefire seemed to be having far-reaching repercussions, and I'm not sure either one of us had given the matter a proper amount of thought.

"Nothing more than a minor glitch, Vi. Easily set to

rights." Easing her way out of Violet's clutches, Clara put the kitchen island between herself and the overly affectionate witch before continuing. "Was there anything more? We have some pressing matters to…"

Moving through the kitchen like she owned it, Violet chose a plate from the glass-doored cabinet where they were stored, filled it with a stack of pancakes, and plunked down next to Soleil with a mile-wide grin on her face.

"Pass the syrup."

I curled my lips under to hold back a smile at the look on my grandmother's face.

"The blueberries were especially succulent this year. Real shame about Tansy Blankenship, don't you think?" Violet tucked into her breakfast with gusto, and before anyone could answer or ask if she knew anything about the case, she'd moved on to her next topic. "How perfectly awful these past few years must have been for you, Clara. It's a mercy you slept through the whole experience."

"Whatever gave you that idea?"

Violet paled. "You couldn't have been. Clara, are you telling me you were awake the whole time you were…during your unfortunate…ahem…incarceration?"

"Unfortunately." Dry as dust, Clara's answer triggered a wave of pink to wash over Violet's face.

"So you heard the things certain people might have said to you?"

What was I missing? The conversation reeked of unclear subtext.

"Every tiny detail." The sound of a fork tinkling against china signaled the end of Violet's appetite. "As you know, I pride myself on being the soul of discretion. After all, a good high priestess is one who helps her sister witches solve their…" A pregnant pause, "…most delicate problems."

Two inches of cleavage heaved when Violet sighed, "Too bad you couldn't have reined in your more…ahem…violent tendencies. The coven just hasn't been the same without that Balefire touch." Leaving her dirty plate on the table and ignoring more than one sidelong faerie glance, Violet wended her way toward the parlor as if she'd been invited to stay and visit awhile.

I know I wasn't the only one who noticed the way her gaze kept straying toward the fireplace, but what was I supposed to do? Ask her to leave?

"Come sit by me, Clara. I'll bring you up to date on everything you missed."

Call me a coward, but I used work as an excuse and hauled Kin out of there before Violet could draft me into the recent history lesson.

Chapter 11

"Where do you think you're going?" Gran's voice followed me as I edged toward the door.

"Uh, I've got a work thing. Big deal, lots of love to spread." Buh-bye.

Kin *and* a dirty look followed me out the door.

"You're going to the office? I thought we were…"

"Shhh. We're going to the market, I have a thing there, it won't take long. It's Saturday, the sun is shining, and I've got a hankering for roasted beet salad for dinner tonight, with goat cheese."

"You know how to make roasted beet salad?" He teased.

"No, but I'm sure we can figure it out." I twined my fingers with his. "And I know where to get the best goat cheese."

Comprehension dawned. "By *we*, you really mean *me*."

"You're the one with mad grilling skills, and you can teach me. I can brew a potion, that's like cooking, right?"

Thank goodness Kin is one of those boyfriends who knows it's smart to indulge his girlfriend when it comes to things like farmer's markets and yard sales. I have a sneaking suspicion he actually likes chick flicks, too, but instead of pointing it out, I've chosen to return the favor and be a good girlfriend. Why rock the boat when it means I get to watch Ryan Reynolds do his thing anytime I want?

Besides, there was no way I was leaving him alone at my house today. I always worry about his safety, especially since he seems to be developing a talent for making himself a target for my enemies. It's one thing to worry about outsiders but protecting him from my own family borders on the ridiculous.

Unfortunately, with the Balefire acting wonky and the godmothers on permanent edge, the possibility that he could get caught in the crossfire was just not something I was willing to risk. Removing the concern would fall nicely into the pro column of the whole *moving in with him* list of factors to consider. At least Clara and Mag were around to balance out the wrath until I made my final decision.

My life had begun to feel like a high-wire balancing act to stay in the middle ground between witch and demigod, and learn how to tame the Balefire flame with another, more powerful Keeper living under my roof. Or, I supposed, it was really her roof. Things were complicated.

How to stay sane in the face of so many variables was a complete mystery to me, but I was trying my best. The permanent imprint of teeth on the tip of my tongue proved how many times I'd clamped down on my own irritation and frustration, and yet complaining made me feel like a big crybaby.

Sure, my life had changed in unexpected ways, but I'd gained more family out of the deal, so it balanced. Of course, I felt a bit stressed out about work stuff, but now I had the Bow of Destiny on my side and could make a bigger difference than ever before. Once I figured out the rules for using it.

Baby steps might keep me from plummeting off the wire.

"…I hate playing phone tag, don't you?" Guess I'd better give back my A+ girlfriend medal. Kin had been talking while I was preoccupied.

"Yes, it's the worst."

Or close to the worst. I'd trade a rousing game of it now for a moment of silence. After an extended period of relative quiet, the bow had decided it was speaking to me again. Gentle persuasion toned down the volume, but not the distraction.

It seemed to have something to sing about for nearly every person I passed; sometimes a gentle hum of satisfaction, or a lament for those who were, I assumed, as yet unmatched but not quite ready to meet their mate. Once in a while, it would forget and crank up the tunes again. Loud enough to rattle my teeth until I muttered the command under my breath and my not-so-silent companion mercifully lowered the volume by a few decibels.

It worked for a few minutes.

All my effort went into listening as attentively to Kin as I could while trying to assess the sounds. The music, I knew, was one key to unlocking my Fate Weaving potential.

Port Harbor's historic district was more crowded than usual, vendor tents full to overflowing with locally grown fruits, vegetables, flowers, and potted plants from this year's harvest. Saturdays, when the square transformed into a farmer's market, were my favorite days to wander the cobbled streets.

As if in answer to a prayer, Kin said, "Hey, there's Darius. Mind if I go have a word with him about the schedule for next week? I promise I'll only talk shop…"

"…Just long enough for me to hit my favorite vendors. Go on, I'll be around when you're done." I gave him a kiss that promised it would be worth his while to find me later and turned left while he went right.

With Kin occupied, it was time for a little test. Orienting myself using the most plaintive tune, I locked in on a man in his forties: attractive face, not much fashion sense, and definitely lonely. He needed the goddess and her pointy friend more than most.

Hello? Dead-eye bow shooter, are you in there? Calling to her didn't work, so I squinched my eyes, tensed my whole body, and tried to force her out into the open. The chuckle I heard came from my imagination. Probably.

Nothing worked, so I finally pulled out one of my enchanted business cards and moved close enough to drop it in the bag of apples dangling from his left hand. If you can't shoot them, match them the old fashioned way. Maybe FootSwept was in less dire straits than I thought.

At the first stall, I snagged a bunch of fragrant lavender and tucked it into the canvas tote hanging from my shoulder, tossing a couple extra dollars into the tip jar on my way past. Of course, we have herbs growing in the back yard, almost every kind you can name, but it feels good to support local growers.

"Hiya, Lexi, the usual?" A plump, red-faced man with a stubble-covered chin waved a hand and winked in my direction.

"Extra tomatoes today, and make it two, please." We chatted about the end of growing season while Frank piled organic greens onto homemade flour tortillas, loaded the wraps with veggies and his secret recipe vinaigrette, and expertly rolled them up into sheets of brown paper for Kin and me to enjoy come lunch time.

Finally, I located my quarry. Hannah Aarons' mother, Emily, displayed artisanal cheeses in a booth toward the back of the market, and the opportunity to combine business with pleasure didn't hurt my feelings one iota.

As I approached, Emily Aarons, in what seemed like a practiced spiel, explained the process of cultivating goat's milk to a young woman who listened avidly.

Perched on a stool next to her mother, Hannah, the sour expression on her face proclaiming she'd rather be anywhere else than hocking what amounted to rotten milk at the crack of dawn on the weekend, played with her cell phone. When she caught sight of me, she grinned and put down the phone. I squelched her greeting with a wink of my eye while scanning the contents of the table thoughtfully.

"What can I help you find today?" Emily asked with a genuine smile. Wide eyes the color of toasted hazelnuts framed with thick lashes showed a few deep-set lines as if the expression were her default—but a few thinner ones around her forehead spoke of a rising stress level in recent years. She looked like an older version of her daughter and was a prime example of how a healthy lifestyle can slow the ravages of time. If Emily Aarons had walked into my office, I'd have thought her an easy match based on appearance alone, for she radiated warmth and vitality.

"I'm not really sure, what would you suggest?" I feigned ignorance and elicited a flurry of a response.

"Well, that depends on your tastes. Here, take a cracker and try this cranberry coated chevre. It's fabulous with wine and a nice, crusty bread." I closed my eyes with pleasure and got distracted from my mission for a split second as sweet and tart berries blended with the creamy, tangy goat cheese.

"That is excellent. Do you make all of this yourself?" I snapped my focus back to my goal and fished for information.

Emily hesitated for a fraction of a second, her forehead wrinkling as though she were trying to push away an unpleasant thought. "Yes, and my daughter, Hannah here, helps me." She wrapped a protective arm around Hannah, but you don't work with people as much as I do and not develop the ability to sense when they're feeling fragile.

"I help milk the goats in the mornings, and after school." Hannah beamed but couldn't hold back an eye roll. "They're cute but smelly."

I chatted with Emily long enough for my LPS to kick in and discovered that unless it was off by a mile, her match was also at the market. Coincidence or fate?

Had to be fate.

Planning to follow my gut and scope out her match, I picked a few items from the table and handed over my cash. Just as Emily deposited the change into my left hand, Hannah passed me the bag of cheese, and as both mother and daughter's fingers contacted mine, I got caught up in another vision.

This was becoming a regular thing.

That might be an understatement. I didn't so much get caught up as sucked into it. I watched Hannah Aarons' life play out in a slow motion montage, musical accompaniment provided by the Bow of Destiny. You'd have thought when I absorbed the essence of the bow, it would have done a quick scan of its new host and tailored its playlist to my liking. As it was, twangy country tunes didn't really float my boat, and elevator music was nearly as far down on my list. But, that's neither here nor there.

What I saw proved Hannah's future happiness rested on a pivot point anchored in the decisions her parents would make over the coming weeks. For her sake, I hoped the man my gut said was right for Emily would turn out to be Hannah's father. If not, the girl was headed down a path that led nowhere good.

I know, it sounds a lot like the butterfly effect; one small change influencing all the future events of a person's life—but doesn't that make sense? We're never the same person from one moment to another. We know more, have felt more, have changed our minds and chosen an alternate destiny every second of our lives from the instant we're born until the second we die. Did that mean affecting positivity was pointless? No, it means it's necessary if we want to keep the world from going to hell in a handbasket. We still have to live in it, after all, and some of us for longer than others.

Though the vision played out in excruciating detail, it passed in the blink of an eye and no one seemed to notice I'd gone blank for half a second. "Thank you for your business." Emily dismissed me like any other customer, and Hannah's frown deepened. I gave her a wink to let her know I was on the job, and she winked back. Cute kid. No way was I letting her have a dismal future.

The tug of my LPS pulled me across the square and down the path toward the parking lot. Another two minutes and I'd have missed my chance to lay eyes on Hannah's father as he slid behind the wheel of a beat-up truck. As it was, I only caught enough of a fleeting glimpse to recognize him from the photo she'd shown me.

Well, that should make things easier, I thought. Or maybe not.

My watch said I'd been gone longer than planned, but when I passed back by her booth, a glowing symbol popped out of thin air over Emily's head. It was the same symbol I'd seen above Joshua Owens. It had to be a sign.

Duh, it's a symbol, by its very nature, that makes it

a sign.

Quit worrying about semantics, Lexi, and get on with things.

Don't tell me you don't argue with yourself sometimes, too. I can't be the only one.

With Joshua, I couldn't be certain whether the symbol appeared before or after I'd winged my arrow at him. To be honest, I hadn't been paying close enough attention. But, there was a symbol, and shooting him had turned out so well, it must mean I should do the same for Emily.

If anyone needed magical intervention, it was this family, and they were going to get it.

No more of this wishy-washy wondering who was in charge of my Fate Weaving destiny. I am the carrier of the bow. It will respect my wishes.

It did, too. I let the power flow through me to the secret place in the depths where the bow lingered and called it to life. Like turning on a faucet, it was that easy. And natural—it felt like the most natural thing in the world. Demigod Lexi stepped out from my body like a badass twin sister, her almond-shaped eyes glowing with pink fire. I don't think I'll ever get used to seeing things other people can't—knowing things other people don't. An invisible rope of energy flowed between my astral self and me as if I could tug her back inside if I so desired. That was new.

This time, the choice was mine. My goddess peered at me over her shoulder, the question in her eyes. Confident in the memory of what happened when my arrow struck Joshua Owens, I wanted to feel that shift in the cosmos again; needed it with a hunger I hadn't anticipated.

Demigod Lexi shrugged before fitting arrow to string with the very tips of her fingers. She pulled back with as much ease as if she were handling the five-pound draw weight of a child's practice bow. Emily's back straightened, and her eyes turned stormy as soon as the arrow made contact with flesh, but she shook her head as if to clear an uncomfortable thought and carried on with business.

Her heart didn't skip a beat. The stars didn't align. And I sure as heck didn't feel like I'd done the world a favor.

Not what I expected, and it didn't seem as though the Bow of Destiny was pleased either, judging by the slow rendition of "Can't Hurry Love" pounding loudly in my ears. If it had been a car stereo, I'd have yanked it from the dash and chucked it out the window.

Emily was already married to her soul mate, so her reaction probably would be a little understated compared to Joshua's. All I'd tried to do was reinforce that connection. It can't hurt to freshen things up from time to time, right?

Demigod Lexi shook her head at me before fading into the ether.

Great, now I was mad at myself. Sort of.

My life gets more complicated every day.

Chapter 12

When I padded downstairs for breakfast the next morning, my eyes were full of sleepy seeds, and I hoped a good, strong cup of coffee would wash the images of a nightmare from behind my lids.

In the dream, I'd been running; endlessly running from a dark, hooded figure on a giant black steed. In one hand he carried a scythe, and in the other a long chain, on the end of which hung a glowing lantern full of souls. I got the distinct impression he wanted to add mine to his collection and woke up in a pool of sweat.

Mercifully, the kitchen was quiet for a change. Grateful for a reprieve from the insanity that was the Balefire household, I did a little dance across the floor. The godmothers—sans Vaeta, as far as I could tell—were out organizing another spectacular event, Salem had taken Pyewacket fishing, and I couldn't have guessed where Mag was if I tried. Gran, however, I found hunched over a tray table in the parlor, staring intently at the television while devouring a plate of eggs in a nest.

I stopped to watch her dip a toast round into the runny yolk and pop it into her mouth with a look of sheer pleasure on her face, but I wasn't sneaky enough to have gone without notice.

"Thank the goddess so many people are raising free range chickens again; this tastes just like the way your great-grandmother used to make it. Whatever was in that carton in the fridge tasted like dirt, but Mrs. Chatterly has a couple of hens in her backyard, and she owed me a favor." She took a sip of milk to wash it all down, "if only she had a milk cow out there as well. What have they done to it? I can taste the plastic from the carton and not much else. Yuck."

"There's a guy at the farmer's market who sells milk in glass bottles. I wish I'd have known to pick some up when I was there yesterday. Come with me next time." I'd never gone on an outing with her before, and shopping with another woman always opens a window onto their temperament and personality.

She waved another piece of toast. "Just say when."

I fixed myself a cup of coffee and, curious to see what held her rapt attention on the screen, joined Gran on the couch.

Apparently, Clara liked her soaps, since the DVR was full of Days of Our Lives and The Young and the

Restless. Shaking her head in disgust, she checked the clock and switched to the morning news, "I'd really like to know what happened to Reva Shayne, but it seems they've canceled Guiding Light while I was…gone."

"Well, it did run for several decades, so I suppose it was time." I murmured quietly. "I can look it up online if you want."

"What is it, dear?" Gran's witchy senses, or maybe just her womanly ones, zeroed in on my distracted state of mind, and I'd already learned once she caught a scent, she'd sniff out the details like a bloodhound.

"Nothing, really. Just a dream. I've been feeling a bit out of sorts ever since I repaired the Bow of Destiny; like maybe I need to be watching my back. I think it just came out in the form of a nightmare."

Gran shot me a scathing look, "Don't underestimate the importance of your subconscious. There's a goddess inside you, and she might be trying to tell you something. It's not easy being what you are, and there are those out there who would love nothing more than to stop you from matching one more soul—and they wouldn't raise an eyebrow at using physical force to do so. Weaving fates is a dangerous game."

How? I wondered. My job seemed menial at best. See an unattached soul, shoot an arrow. The bow or the fates or someone else chose the targets and I wasn't interacting with them in any other way. Frankly, being a Fate Weaver was boring compared to when I'd happily matched the lovelorn.

Before I had a chance to respond, the petite blond from channel five news flashed up on the screen, carrying a rehearsed expression of empathy, "In local news, the police have issued a statement in the death of a local woman named Tansy Blankenship. No cause of death could be determined. Police found no evidence of foul play, but have stated that autopsy results on the twenty-six-year-old woman have not yielded enough evidence to rule the death as natural or accidental. We'll keep you updated as we learn more about the case. I'm Alicia Simpson, reporting for channel five news."

Gran's eyes widened, and she pulled a weathered coin out of her pocket, pressing her index finger to the raised initials on the back that would let Aunt Mag know she was needed, and then turned slowly to face me, "Get dressed; it's time to rally the troops. We'll continue this discussion later."

Clara

It's a common misconception that it takes thirteen witches to make up a traditional coven. In truth, a coven is the size it needs to be. Thirteen or thirty members makes no difference unless you're the person in charge and the higher the number, the more frequent the headaches. Standing before mine, I searched every face for subtle clues to how many might have my back and which of the witches would only stand behind me if there were a good chance of pushing me off a cliff.

At a quick tally, I judged my approval rating to be somewhere around 60 percent—give or take a few undecideds. Only Winsome Warner, a complete mouse of a woman, was so flabbergasted at the sight of me she tripped over her own shoes on her way into the room and smacked Violet Bloodgood on the backside with a vividly-printed purse the size of a shopping bag. It seemed the news about my miraculous resurrection hadn't spread all the way to the smallest tendrils of the grapevine.

Whispers slid from the corners of mouths set into faces paled or reddened by the sight of me, but when I stepped in front of Calypso Snodgrass and waited for everyone to take a seat, silence fell so hard you could almost hear it thump on the floor.

Calypso's daughter, Serena, sat next to her mother, her nose wrinkled in distaste. I imagined she'd rather be anywhere but inside this house with this particular assemblage of women. In fact, she looked like she was about to throw up which, considering she was still in her first trimester, might be an accurate assessment.

My eyes narrowed at the loose peasant blouse Serena wore, and the absence of any of the coven members fawning all over her cemented my conviction that she hadn't announced her pregnancy yet. The girl wouldn't meet my gaze, even though she'd been my most frequent visitor over the years, and I probably knew more about Serena's life than Calypso did.

"I'm sure some of you are surprised to see me," I let my dry tone punctuate the sentiment as my gaze traveled around the room. Yes, I noted plenty of surprise displayed along with a host of other emotions as I counted how many happy, upturned faces balanced out the number of dismayed frowns.

"I'm surprised to be here, all things considered." I directed a warm smile at Lexi, who leaned against the doorway to the parlor and watched the proceedings with caution. Never having been an active part of the group, she wasn't sure of her place, and I didn't blame her for that.

My sister, always a solitary witch, also sat somewhat apart from the rest and let her crossed arms and fierce expression speak volumes. I'd asked her to observe only and estimated the chances of her remaining silent at somewhere around 50/50. Respecting my need for a coven was no promise she would respect the group.

"What did you…how did you? But, Clara, you were stoned. You killed," Winsome's voice dropped to a scandalized whisper, "your daughter."

"No, she didn't." Bless her little heart, Violet spoke right up. "Sylvana is alive and probably out wreaking havoc right now." Interesting blend of defense and condemnation. "Catch up, Winnie. That news is positively ancient.”

“Then who *did* you kill?” Winsome reached conclusions with great difficulty and very little speed. “You’re supposed to be dead.”

“Clearly, I'm not.” I gestured to myself for emphasis. “My daughter and I had a slight magical mishap in the midst of a heated discussion.” The details of which, I had no intention of sharing. “And I was the victim of my own bad intentions.”

“You were stoned. You killed.”

“Keep repeating it, Winnie, but that won’t make it fact. Let my experience be a beacon of truth for you all.” I raised my voice slightly. “The strongest of emotions can color your intentions black, and two angry witches in the throes of a heated discussion can create unpredictable results. I’ve spent the last twenty-five years in a granite prison. A lesson to remember and a cautionary tale you should all keep in mind. No one died that day.”

With a tilt of my head, I tossed a verbal bomb, “Unlike today, when one of our numbers really is dead, and not from natural causes.” Notably absent from the proceedings were Letitia Blankenship and her cousin, Hattie.

“Are you saying you killed poor Tansy?” Poor Winnie. Dimmer than a blown-out candle.

“How many times do I need to say it? I. Didn’t. Kill. Anyone. If I had, I’d still be made of stone. You *can* see me standing here in front of you, right? Do you need to touch me to make sure I'm warm and breathing?" My voice rose in frustration while several of the assembled witches shushed Winsome loudly.

Despite the suspicion aimed at me from certain factions, being among the coven soothed some of the raw places inside me. "While I understand the temptation to cause harm, I'm not a killer."

Having waited long enough to measure the response, the woman who had taken control in my absence nudged me aside. "Thank you for clearing the air, Clara. Now, if you would please take a seat." She indicated a ladder-backed chair to her left, pulled a gold-plated pen and a clipboard from the messenger bag slung over one shoulder.

"There are a few questions we'd like you to answer before we consider what, if any, position you will retain here in the coven."

"Thank you, Calypso, but *I* called this unofficial meeting to talk about the tragic death of Tansy Blankenship, not to stand trial for imagined transgressions." In my own home, no less. The nerve.

On a typical day, Calypso Snodgrass looked like someone had permanently mounted a pickle under her nose—or shoved one where the sun doesn't shine. Her sour face matched an equally sour disposition, and I wondered what kind of coup she had pulled off to rise to the position so quickly.

"Calling meetings falls within my duties as high priestess. You should have followed protocol and contacted me first."

"Official meetings. This is not one, and would you have convened the coven if I asked you to?"

"I see no reason for alarm. The girl's death hasn't been ruled murder."

"Thank you for making my point, and if you'll indulge me, I'll make another. The role of high priestess is largely ceremonial, mainly to do with providing moral support where needed, and we don't adhere to a set of bylaws. Therefore, any coven member can convene a meeting if he or she wishes to do so."

A shrug of her narrow shoulders dismissed my objection. "I'm sure we'd have come around to discussing the untimely death of Ms. Blankenship in time." She sniffed. "You've been a very naughty girl, Clara."

My eyebrows shot up to my hairline. I'm at least a hundred years older than Calypso, and her attempt to talk down to me would not be forgotten. Or forgiven.

"As I've said, I was the victim of a magical accident, and there's no need for more explanation. I don't answer to you." My glance included the collected group and lingered.

Like a Pitbull, Calypso refused to let it go.

"If you wouldn't mind, I think we'd all appreciate hearing the exact details. Unless your memory has gone hazy during the last twenty-five years of sleeping in a stone cocoon." Calypso leaned forward as if to brace herself for a particularly dirty piece of gossip.

"Sleeping? No, not exactly." Deliberately, I directed a series of brief but meaningful looks at a few of the women who had come to babble out their misdeeds in my stone ear during my statue-like days and confirmed their worst fears. "I heard and saw plenty."

The ploy worked and Calypso lost support like she was the sinking Titanic and the rest of the witches were rats.

"Now, Calypso, I don't think we need to go dredging up Clara's painful past. It's enough that no one was killed and I, for one, am thankful to have her back with us safe and sound." Lobelia Morningside, for all that hers had been the most salacious of confessions, lifted her chin and returned my gaze with a resigned shrug. "In fact, I'm hoping she will consider returning to her former position as high priestess."

The perfect way to make sure I stayed quiet about her sexual transgressions along with everything else I'd heard. High priestesses are the souls of discretion. Maybe not Calypso, but in general.

Gasps and more than a few snorts followed the bold statement, and I stole a look at the current leader out of the corner of my eye. If it had been physically possible for steam to come out someone's ears, Calypso Snodgrass would have given her best impression of a teakettle about to whistle.

"Thank you for the suggestion, Lobelia, but I think we'd all agree a period of observation is in order—just to make sure Clara hasn't suffered any ill effects from her experience before we consider making any changes to the leadership of the group." Calypso turned to me, "I have to wonder what kind of psychological problems your *ordeal*," she may as well have made air quotes, "might have brought on, and we've all felt the results of whatever is going on with the Balefire lately."

On cue, heads swiveled toward the fireplace where the Balefire flickered cheerfully.

Some women will smile sweetly while they drive the knife deep into your back, and Calypso was one of those women. "Should we assume you're taking steps to ensure these disturbances will not continue?"

She'd issued an open challenge to my past authority wrapped in an insult to my mental state, and I was in no position to make assurances at the moment, so I changed the subject.

"I came here to talk about the *murder* of Tansy Blankenship." A hush rippled over the room from left to right, and all eyes were on me.

"Murder?" Someone gasped. Mag gave me a pointed look and a deliberate, but barely noticeable head shake. She didn't want me to mention the demon for some reason.

"Yes, murder."

"Are you certain it wasn't a spell gone wrong?" This from Violet Bloodgood.

"No, it was murder. I'm certain."

"Well, it couldn't have been any of us since we're all walking and talking. Unless there's a way to avoid the inevitable." Eyes flickering my way, Violet issued the statement with a delicate, but exaggerated shudder. What was that about? I was beginning to think Violet was a human ping pong ball the way she went back and forth with her opinions.

"I'm not accusing anyone in this room of murder. What I *am* trying to make you all understand is that some*thing* or some*one* killed Tansy, and if the crime was committed by a supernatural predator the police are going to hit a dead end. They're simply not qualified to handle something like this. I shouldn't have to remind any of you what happens when humans catch wind of our existence."

Pansy Pinkerton cocked her head and challenged me. "What do you expect us to do about it, Clara?" Having been friends with the mousy brunette for upwards of a century, I'd hoped for a warm homecoming and been sorely disappointed. "Go poking around in a dead girl's business, and then wind up dead ourselves? No, thank you."

I let out a discouraged grunt. "If my sister and I are the only ones with enough guts to figure out what's going on here, then so be it. But I swear to Hecate, if any of you withhold information that could be helpful, I'll make sure you regret it."

It probably wasn't the greatest idea to threaten the women I was trying to convince of my sincerity, but sometimes I have no filter and tonight was one of those times. I could feel a muscle twitch in my shoulder and knew the tension I'd been carrying around would turn into a splitting headache if I didn't find some way to relieve it. Releasing my wrath on the rest of the coven would make me feel marginally better—for all of two seconds. So I clenched my teeth and ended the conversation.

Mag stood and spoke aloud for the first time, further delaying the coven's exit to the chagrin of Calypso, who suddenly looked like she had a giant slice of chocolate cake in the fridge, and couldn't wait to get home to it.

"Wait just one more minute. The state of the Balefire has been questioned by several of you tonight, and I think it's about time we all had a discussion about something—my grand-niece, Lexi, and your treatment of her over the past twenty-five years."

You could hear a pin drop when Mag paused and passed the gauntlet, leaving just enough time for Calypso to open her mouth before allowing me to cut her off again. I'd waited a long time to speak my mind, and relished the thought of unloading a quarter-century worth of irritation on the group.

And my resolve to keep the peace had all but evaporated, so what the hell?

"Lexi was your Keeper, was she not?" I stared into the eyes of each of the witches who had enough guts to hold my gaze and glared at the tops of the bent heads of the cowards in the room. "Lexi was, by right of birth, a member of this coven, was she not?"

They all knew the ways of witches as well as I did.

"Clearly, you all could see that she was struggling. Any one of you could have had the decency to lend your support; to guide her whether she had Awakened or not. But you didn't. All because you assumed if I harbored a secretly wicked heart, then Lexi must have one, too. Well, I'm not a wicked witch, and neither is Lexi. I'm ashamed of the lot of you. Some more than others."

I let my eyes flick to the top of Serena's bowed head and then to her mother. "Would any of you have treated your own daughter as poorly as you've treated Lexi? A coven is a family, and we don't forsake our own, no matter the transgression. I've spent twenty-five years paying for bad behavior. How long do you think you'll have to pay for yours?"

Lexi

Serena didn't offer one of her customary insults or even make eye contact with me as she shuffled past amid half a coven of shame-faced witches and a few who still refused to admit any responsibility and kept their noses firmly tilted toward the ceiling. I couldn't really tell which emotion Serena was feeling, but I guessed relief at finally having been dismissed as a major contender for top billing.

I knew Serena was still angry with me about her lover boy having been blasted into the Faelands, but according to Flix he'd escaped unscathed. Not that Jett had come scurrying back to her side, which was probably a big part of why she'd stopped harassing me about it. Jett had made his own bed since he'd tangled with me and mine, but I was guessing he'd be sleeping on the couch for quite a while if he ever bothered to try and get back into Serena's good graces.

All of this I noticed in passing. Watching Gran and Aunt Mag read the coven the riot act for having shunned me all those years brought up a wealth of emotions. Of course, I was grateful for the gesture itself, but what really had me choked up was how happy I was to call myself a Balefire. I'd always regarded my position as Keeper with the utmost respect, but familial pride had ended there. I was, after all, descended from the wickedest of witches.

Except I wasn't, and it felt good for all those old biddies to realize it. The young biddies, too.

Chapter 13

A waning moon cast writhing shadows against the back door of the mortuary. Between the chill darkness and the knowledge of what type of business we were breaking into, I wondered how long before my total revulsion of things most of my kind took for granted would require me to turn in my witch card.

I am witch, hear me cackle madly at creepy things. Nope. Not me, not so much. Not when we were about to step into a darkened house of the dead. And not the part where bodies are put on display in doily-lined boxes like macabre candies, but the hidden area where all the mysterious preparations take place.

The days of wrapping a witch in a clean white cloth, taking her into a clearing, building a pyre, and feeding her body to the hungry flame while her sister witches chanted and danced around her were long behind us. There's little of ritual to be found in a crematorium, but we abide by the rules, and Tansy's body lay somewhere inside, awaiting its turn in the burning box.

"You're going to get me arrested before this is over," I grumbled while my grandmother reached into her pocket. "Feels like the world's worst role reversal when the adult is the one dragging the next generation along on an illicit mission."

Arched windows trimmed with newly-painted molding lent a tasteful gingerbread-like air to the Victorian-era building that had housed Crandall Funeral Home since the late 1960's when Morticia Crandall decided to live up to her first name. Set into a shallow alcove, a plain back door matched the less showy side of the old home.

"Quit complaining, or I'll start to wonder if you've got any more guts than the rest of the coven," Mag ordered while I waited for Clara to cast a spell on a door lock that looked like it had been the best security money could buy. In 1976.

"Don't be such a killjoy."

Killjoy? A shoe-in for a Miss Marple lookalike contest winner was calling me a killjoy? "No one says that anymore."

"Hush up." Clara put an end to her sister's sharp tongue and my tendency to bicker when feeling nervous. "I'm not sure I remember how to do this." To my utter shock, she pulled out a credit card instead of a wand and proceeded to pop the back door with a flick of the plastic.

"Killer security system. I mean, spring for a deadbolt at least."

"Shh." The command slid out between Clara's gritted teeth as she slipped into the dark recesses beyond the open door. Mag gave me a shove when I didn't move fast enough to suit her, and I practically tumbled inside. How had I let them talk me into this? Oh, right, the alternative was being branded a coward—that's how.

Faint witchlight conjured into Mag's palm threw more shadows against a wall lined with steel-fronted drawers and my heart sped into a double-time drum roll that beat a tattoo against the back of my ears.

"I see dead people." No one got the joke because I forgot to play to my audience. Didn't matter anyway, since the two sisters ignored me. Clara prowled the line of cold storage drawers and cast her senses into the spaces behind clinical steel until she found what she'd been looking for.

"Here." Gently and with stealth, she twisted the handle and began to pull. Can you throw up and faint at the same time? I thought I might test the theory when a low screech of metal on metal announced the sudden appearance of Tansy Blankenship.

Pale and perfect she lay in death's slumber, and the twisting in my belly shouted it was a cardinal sin to disturb her peace. But, disturb it we must. Mag twitched the pristine sheet down Tansy's body inch-by-inch, and revealed the Y-shaped horror left by the medical examiner's scalpel.

"You think there's any paperwork with the body that tells the cause of death?"

"How would I know?" I answered Mag's question sharply then paused while an idea struck. "I'll look for the files." Anything to keep from looking too closely at Tansy's face.

The current generation of Crandalls now worked the family business while Morticia enjoyed her retirement in Florida. They kept the place tidy, I gave them credit for that. Tansy's folder was neatly stowed in the filing cabinet under B for Blankenship. I pulled it out and scanned through it quickly.

"Tox screen came back negative. The cause of death listed as unknown/natural. Looks like there wasn't anything definitive to find."

"They have their ways, we have ours." Clara chanted an invocation that built in rhythm until the room thrummed with her words.

"Ladies, light your flames," she ordered when the sound of her voice had finally echoed into silence.

Color by color, we ran a series of conjured witchlight over Tansy's body. Red, orange, yellow, green revealed nothing out of the ordinary. As the blue and then the indigo light rimmed their faces in shadow, I watched Clara and Mag's expressions turn grim and then grimmer until, in the violet flicker, a sigil surfaced on the death-blued skin covering Tansy's collarbone.

I heard Mag draw in a quick breath on a gasp. "Holy Hecate. Do you see that? We were right. It's a demon mark."

"I'm not blind, am I?" Clara hissed. "You recognize it?" Her face took on the blank look of someone rooting through the back rooms and recesses of memory.

"Not off the top of my head, but I swear I've seen it somewhere before. What about you, Lexi?"

"I'm the newbie, remember?"

Mag prowled around the room looking for I don't know what, then returned and, hovering a finger over the glowing mark, traced its contours several times .

"What are you doing?" I asked.

"Committing the shape to memory," she said absently. "Unless you've got a notebook on you somewhere." The quick look she swiped over me carried more than a hint of condemnation for wearing tightly fitted clothes with little room for stashing away tools of the witchly—or, more importantly, of the cat burglar—trade.

"No, but I have something better." I pulled my phone out from where I'd tucked it into my bra and clicked off a couple photos while ignoring Mag's raised eyebrow and smirk. "Are we done?" I'd had just about all the fooling around with dead bodies I could stand for one night, and if they even thought about asking me to help turn Tansy over, I was taking my heebie-jeebies and going home, thank you very much.

"A couple more things, and then we're done." Clara stared down at Tansy's face with a mix of compassion and regret. Not regret for her own actions, but for the loss of someone who had barely had time to get started in life.

Laying one palm against the dead woman's head and the other against her heart, Mag assessed the situation.

"The killer was after her soul, not her body." She paused and closed her eyes to divine information about Tansy's final moments. "Didn't get it all, though."

Despite feeling squicky, I was curious enough to take a long look at Tansy's body. "How can you tell?"

"By the design, of course. It's a soul binding, not a drawing." To Mag she might be stating the obvious, to me she might as well have said *hibbitygibbity*, so I waved a hand to get her to elaborate.

"A demon's mark can only be burned into the skin when soul essence is present. The brand usually marks a soul to be drawn and sent to the underworld after death. This one bound the soul to the body."

"Okay, but couldn't Tansy have been marked before she died? Or even while he was killing her?" My questions made Mag look at me with grudging respect.

"Smart, but no. A binding like that was meant to

hold the soul. See this pattern here? The way it curves inward." She pointed to the spiral that made up the outer ring of the mark. "That bit in the center, that's the demon's signature."

She no more than finished the sentence when Clara whipped a ceremonial athame out of some hidden pocket and slashed a pentagram shape in the air above the light-tattooed sigil. Her eyes glittered as the color of her witchlight turned red and she pressed it into the mark. There was a flare, then the ball of flame dimmed.

We all watched the mark writhe against pale skin like snakes in the grass before dissipating in a wisp of shivering smoke, a tiny tendril of which Mag inhaled and then swallowed. My eyes were still dazzled by the flare, so I couldn't swear I actually saw what I thought I saw, but it looked like her irises flashed to black for a split second, and a new wrinkle etched itself into the corner of her mouth.

Gran's forehead crinkled enough that she looked a few years closer to her actual age, and a round depression appeared in her cheek as she nervously chewed the inside of it. "Are you all right, Maggie?"

Aunt Mag declined to answer, fixing Gran with a quick, pointed look and a raised eyebrow. Then she nodded, but I suspected the nod was the answer to a different question. One Clara hadn't asked in front of me.

"Is it safe to mess with the mark when you don't

know more about why or who put it there?" Sometimes I'm as fascinated by magic as any straight mortal.

"We had to free Tansy to move on."

"But did you have to…you know." I mimicked her breathing in the essence of ick. The light wasn't so dim I couldn't see the way Mag's gaze shuttered or the tightness around her mouth. Or my grandmother's enigmatic expression. There were secrets between them, lines they might have crossed, a history I would never share, but that defined their relationship.

"I'm not a child," and, of course, the necessity of making such a statement only proved it false. When it became clear they weren't having this discussion—whether here and now, or *ever*, I couldn't have guessed—I reluctantly gave in. "Fine. Are we done here?"

"Just about." If I sensed a gentle mocking flavor to Grandmother's tone, I ignored it, and when she laid her lips on Tansy's forehead, I held back a shiver. Did I mention dead people creep me out? Sorry, maybe that makes me a substandard witch, but it's true. "Blessed be, little one."

"You didn't forget the charms, did you?"

"Why does everyone think my head is still full of rocks? Of course, I have them." Using a magician-like flourish Copperfield would envy, Gran called an old coin and a crudely wrought straw doll into her palm.

"What are those?" I asked.

"A coin and a poppet."

"I can see that much for myself. What do they do?"

"Coin's a relocation charm and the poppet," Mag plucked a single hair from Tansy's head and handed it to Gran who wrapped the hair tightly around the neck of the straw doll, "will provide misdirection."

Clearly, I was missing the point of all this, so I circled a hand to indicate I needed more information.

"Taking the body would alert the authorities, would it not? And performing the proper rites and rituals isn't something we do in public, so…"

Oh, I got it. The charms would send Tansy to the place of ritual while allowing the mortician to think the body had been properly cremated. Very sneaky. I guess I was wrong about us adhering to the letter of the law when it came to dead bodies. Wonderful.

Gently, and with great reverence, Gran tucked the poppet into Tansy's hair where it would be safe, but stay concealed until needed. Next, she placed the coin on Tansy's heart, and it sank into her breast where it would remain until activated.

"Blessed be and safe passage, little one." A tender kiss landed above Tansy's brow.

"Blessed be," Mag added her kiss, and her blessing then looked at me expectantly.

"Oh, no. Nope. Not happening."

There are looks, and then there are *looks*. Some of them weigh little more than a feather and caress the soul with their lightness; others carry the weight of displeasure and expectation. Very heavy. Enough that I crumbled under the pressure.

The way Tansy's skin felt so cold and lifeless made mine crawl. It would be one thing if this were a beloved family member who lay before me and needed my benediction before traveling on to the Summerlands, but Tansy was a stranger.

"Blessed be," I murmured half-heartedly, my mind on getting this over with before my lips tried to crawl back inside my mouth.

"Need." Tansy's voice whispered through my head, and her hunger yawned over me. The smoky quartz pendant I'd worn for protection frosted over, and I didn't care if Clara and Mag wanted to paint the word *coward* across my backside, I was out of there.

Out. Of. There.

A herd of rampaging centaurs couldn't have caught me between the mortuary and the van we'd parked a couple blocks away—not the best vehicle for a stealth mission given its size and a paint job that looked like Rainbow Brite had barfed all over it.

I drove while my aunt and grandmother carried on a cryptic conversation.

"Are you sure?"

"Yes, Clarie, I'm sure."

"But I thought you said they were all gone."

"Well, I guess I was wrong. Thanks for pointing out

my mistakes." Now Mag was annoyed, and she wasn't the only one.

Glancing at them in the rearview mirror, I asked, "What's all gone? Or not all gone? What aren't you telling me?"

"Pay attention to your driving," Gran advised and her tone was cooler than normal.

I couldn't get anything more out of them as they huddled over the photo on my phone and speculated what type of demon might have left such a mark.

"We're not looking at some low-level Fury, here. It takes a fair amount of power to do that type of a binding." Mag's voice dipped so low I could barely hear the next words she spoke. "This sigil reminds me of when family crests were popular. That means it's one of the old ones, and that's doubly bad for us."

If they were practically whispering, I knew I should listen harder and so I did.

Gran muttered, "Demons don't bind souls, or take them from the living. They have the common decency at least, to wait until after death to harvest. And they don't associate with Raythes. It would be like owning a pizza place and buying from your competition."

"Clarie, you're dimmer than a box of blown light bulbs if you buy that steaming pile of horse manure. Do you also still believe Lee Harvey Oswald acted alone, or that they didn't find anything fishy on the dark side of the moon? Come on, if the American government can convince the people everything's hunky dory, imagine what a faction of ancient demons might be doing behind closed doors. Wake up and smell the conspiracy, Sis."

I didn't know what a Raythe might be, and I only understood about half of the words coming out of their mouths the rest of the ride home. But I'm no fool, and filing away as much as I could, I pretended I hadn't heard a thing.

If they thought I wasn't going to get answers to my questions—especially the ones I didn't have enough knowledge to formulate right now—they had another think coming. I was not content with my brand as "uninformed newbie," and I would not be kept in the dark any longer.

The fact that I believed I could get either of them to do what I wanted them to do if it wasn't what they wanted to do in the first place just goes to show how much of a newbie I really was.

Chapter 14

Back at the house, I went upstairs to change, stashed the chilled pendant in a box with a shiver, and headed back downstairs to join in the discussion of what to do next. More research, exactly what I'd feared. Here I'd thought being a witch would come with some cool perks like, I don't know, *practicing magic*. Instead, I wound up perched on a hard wooden chair surrounded by massive leather-bound volumes while my elders went about their business.

"Oh, look" Pyewacket stretched to pull another sizable tome from a shelf. "This is a compendium of demon glyphs." I'm not into women, but even I couldn't help admiring the lines of her when she reached up high. A dancer's lithe figure paired with naturally bronzed skin and silky hair made for a lethal combination.

"Dude, roll your tongue back up, no woman appreciates a drooler," I warned Salem in a whisper.

"Huh? What?" Poor thing, he had it bad. "I'm just going to help with the search," and with that, he wandered off toward the object of his current obsession. The next time I looked, they were curled up on the sofa in a ball of black and tawny fur.

"What exactly is this Raythe thing you two keep whispering about?" I finally asked during a lull in the tinkling noises coming from Mag's work station. "And stop trying to shield me from whatever you consider unpleasant. If I've got a right to be part of the coven, then you should be able to be candid with me."

Mag shrugged and tossed a glance at Gran, "I happen to agree with Lexi."

"Fine," Clara threw her hands up in the air, "you tell it since you're the authority."

My aunt abandoned her experiments, and we all settled into more comfortable accommodations in the form of a pair of Victorian-era settees positioned catty-corner to the Balefire hearth.

"You've heard the term *null*, I imagine. Witches and wizards born without power?"

"Um, yeah, I sort of was one." I reminded Mag.

"You obviously had power, you just hadn't unlocked it yet," Mag rolled her eyes, "but I'm talking about daughters and sons descended from powerful magical lines, yet somehow devoid of any magical abilities of their own. It's not common, and some of us believe the phenomenon stems from the efforts of certain branches of the first families who wanted to control the more powerful blood lines.”

Bile burned the back of my throat as I realized what she meant, “You mean incest, don’t you? So many icks.” I pushed the image of my disgusting half-brother back into a dark corner of my mind and wondered what I’d done to deserve being grossed out this many times in the course of one evening.

“Yes, exactly. You can probably imagine the dismay when the elitists learned their poo didn’t actually smell like roses.”

“Nice analogy, Mag,” Clara grinned despite the gentle chiding tone.

“I call it like I see it. Anyway, for all the efforts to fortify the bloodlines, there are still witches who, come Awakening day, learn they don’t have enough power in them to levitate a frog.”

“So what do nulls have to do with this—if they have no power, they’re no threat, right?”

Turning in her chair to look at me, Aunt Mag wagged a finger at me. “Right, except for one tiny problem. When a witch and a null love each other very much they…”

“Oh, for Goddess sake, Aunt Mag, I’m familiar with the concept. What happens when a witch gets knocked up by a null? A magic-less male witch.”

“Nice mouth.” She shrugged it off and continued, “They have a null baby.”

"Okay, I'm not seeing the ominous here, it's not an interspecies relationship or anything."

"You're talking physical genetics, this is magical. The active magic that would have been born to the child—" Mag searched for the right words. "Has nothing to latch onto, and goes rogue, if you will. Born wild, unaligned with the host witch, the wild magic takes physical form and turns on witchkind. We call the creature a Raythe."

All the hazy pieces of last night's conversation went crystal clear. "There's one loose in Port Harbor, and it killed Tansy by eating her soul." I swallowed hard. It seemed the more I learned about the supernatural world, the more I wondered why I had been so keen to join it in the first place.

"How many others are out there?" It was the exact wrong question to ask given Mag's response. She turned the air blue with a streak of language not fit to repeat.

"Until now, I thought there were none left alive." She sighed. "What I'm about to tell you can't leave this room. Swear on it." I did. With blood.

"Witches aren't exactly the most prolific breeders in the world, to begin with, and it's rare enough for a witch to have a male child, rarer still when a male null is born. There haven't been all that many in my lifetime."

"Enough," Gran bit the word out. "Mag thinks she's the Raythe slayer."

Cue the mental image of fluffy-haired old Aunt

Mag wearing one of her flowered muumuus, crouched in a fighter's stance, clutching a stake in each hand while the words: *in every generation a slayer is born* played in the background. I held back the smirk, but I'm sure my eyes twinkled. For half a second, anyway. This was serious business.

"How do you kill them?"

For the first time since I'd met her, Aunt Mag blushed. "Taste of their own medicine, but that isn't important right now. With a demon involved, we're up against a whole other level of predator."

Standing, I arched my back against the ache from sitting for so long. Plus, the look on Gran's face and the tone in Aunt Mag's voice had me thinking this was information I shouldn't take sitting down.

"So why all the secrecy? You think I can't handle the thought I might be considered prey? It's not pleasant, but it's not exactly novel, either. Everything is prey to something else."

Gran cut her sister off before she could answer. "This isn't a typical predator/prey situation. Killing Raythes and releasing the souls they've eaten comes at a cost. I'd like to keep my sister from spending more than she already has."

"What can I do to help? I can't look at another book, give me something else to do." I leaned over Gran's shoulder to take in the contents of the table. There were no potion coated litmus sticks this time, no series of apothecary bottles full of evidence. Only a crystal grid laid out in a spiral pattern with the clearest quartz crystal I'd ever seen anchoring the outside end and a tiger's eye the size of my fist in the middle.

"Another pair of eyes won't go amiss. Keep watch now." At her sister's nod, Gran tapped her wand three times against the center stone and whispered an incantation in a language I'd never heard before. I heard chimes, and not from the bow this time. I saw mist, sparkling motes of light, and when it cleared, the crystal had grown to form walls and an enclosed top. The whole thing reminded me of a display from seventh-grade science class of a shell sliced in half so you could see the way each chamber created a new part of the spiral path leading to the middle—only this was made from crystal as clear as glass.

Mag leaned in close and blew the gentlest of breaths into the open end. A wisp of the essence she'd taken from the mark on Tansy's body flowed through the circling pattern until it got to the center and the Balefire chose that moment to have the worst fit so far.

A wall of flames shot toward the ceiling and the magical pressure built so fast it made my ears pop. Enough raw energy pulsed in and around me, I thought I might blow apart if it didn't stop soon. With a crash and a tinkle, the crystal test enclosure imploded, bursting inward with such force nothing was left except a tiny pile of fine powder. Maybe it was a coincidence that the powder took the shape of a witch's hat, but I was too shell-shocked to think about it now.

I reeled from the sensation of feeling like I'd been turned inside out, and I wasn't the only one. If Mag learned anything in the split second before the Balefire's burst, I never heard about it. We all stumbled out of the fireplace as fast as we could.

"Yuck, I need a shower, but all I want is food. Maybe I can get Terra to cast one of her no-dirt spells on me instead." I muttered as we ducked back through the sanctum door and became tangled in the sticky strands of a recently-woven spider web. Since the return of the elder witches, Terra had removed her cleaning charms from the area. This was not an improvement in my book.

Aunt Mag grunted, which I was beginning to realize constituted a language in and of itself, and Gran scoffed, "No granddaughter of mine should be forced to run to her faerie godmothers for every little spell. There's no earthly reason why you can't perform this one on your own. If you don't want to smell like musty dust, then do something about it."

"What about the rule of threes? No magic for personal gain. Doesn't that count?"

"Pish, posh!" countered Mag. Seriously, she used those exact words, and the phrase didn't come off quite as charming as it did for Mary Poppins.

"Are you harming anyone else by making your life easier? Do the faeries get slammed with karmic mojo when they make the pots and pans fly around the kitchen or grow us a tree for freshly-squeezed orange juice? Of course not. We're talking about a little locomotion here."

The curious look Gran pierced me with implied she'd like to add something along the lines of *How did you get to be so uptight?*

My gut response was something whiny about not having had a suitable teacher in the house, but I kept my thoughts to myself. Maybe she was right, and I'd been, as usual, over-thinking things.

"I don't know how." I raised my hands in defeat. Or maybe shame. And a healthy dose of humility.

Clara grinned, and for a moment it was as if I had caught my own reflection in a mirror. We both get the same glint in our eye when we're excited, and the lines around our eyes when we smile are nearly identical. If my mother were in the same room, we'd be mistaken for triplets. I think two of us is quite enough, but something told me we'd all be together again at some point, whether the thought scared the pants off me or not.

"Just clear your mind, focus your power into your pointer finger—we've got to get you a proper wand—and let your will alter the world around you. Make up a chant or a rhyme if you feel it helps. It's all the same, just a method of focusing your intent. Once you get a feel for it, you won't need to speak the spell anymore."

"Very useful in magical combat." Mag nodded.

Was that a thing?

"Shhh, Maggie. Let her concentrate. Meet us in the kitchen when you're clean, Lexi." Gran smiled encouragingly and forcibly pulled Aunt Mag from the room.

For a solid five minutes, I stood in the doorway, trying to come up with a rhyme at the drop of a hat. The best I could manage was:

Rub-a-dub
Need a scrub
Wash me clean
And nix the tub

Try saying that five times fast.

Turns out, a slow chant works much better. I let my inner power gather in the space beneath my breast, and directed it down my right arm and out through my forefinger. My magic felt heavy at first, as though it were resisting my desires—and then I realized the only thing resisting was *me*. I had it in my head I shouldn't do this, even though there was no evidence to support my theory.

As soon as I let go of the notion, power shot out of my fingertip, and a gentle gust of wind began to blow. It caressed my face, tangled in my hair, and raised the peach fuzz on the backs of my arms. Just as suddenly, the wind dissipated, and I felt like a newborn baby, freshly scrubbed. I doubt I had even a speck of dirt hidden beneath my pinkie nail when it was all over.

In the kitchen I found Gran and Mag seated at the island, embroiled in a heated discussion about whether or not it was socially acceptable to wear shoulder pads anymore. I got the sense Mag was tired of this particular argument when she thudded her fists on the counter top and roared, "For the love of the Goddess, Clarie, spring for a new wardrobe! You haven't spent a cent for twenty-five years."

"We'll drink to that!" Terra's voice floated into the room, and I heard the familiar slosh and clink of a bottle of Twinkleberry wine.

Half a glass of Terra's home-brewed concoction was enough to send me to a happy place with fluffy, pink clouds crowding all the stressful thoughts out of my head, but not so much I'd end up dancing skyclad on the front lawn. My neighbor, Mrs. Chatterly, got an eyeful of my naked backside on the night of my twenty-first birthday and the two of us haven't made eye contact since. I'd feel bad about it if she hadn't elevated hiding behind the curtains and watching my house to an art form.

Does it make me a bad person if I admit I didn't even make an attempt to warn Gran and Aunt Mag about the potency? Hey, I'm allowed to have a little bit of fun every once in a while, and seeing the two of them with lowered inhibitions was too tempting to pass up.

Terra flicked a finger, and the dining table dressed itself in buttery, cream-colored linens and a display of hand-blown glass stemware I knew had to be worth a fortune. I suppose when you've got access to a warehouse full of place settings and the ability to conjure whatever the heck you want, it's easy to score a grand slam in the home decor department.

I noticed Vaeta's absence, which had already caused some palpable tension lately but continued to ignore it as I was expected to do. Gran and Aunt Mag followed suit, for which I was grateful. Twinkleberry wine fights are the worst, and I'd prefer not to have another five-alarm blowout if I could possibly help it.

"Cheers!" We all clinked our glasses and took a sip. Aunt Mag let the brew wash over her, and every muscle relaxed. She let out a loud belch, and raised her glass again, "To family. The Goddess has blessed this home, and I'm proud to be surrounded by women like all of you."

"Hear, hear!" We toasted once more, and I caught Salem rolling his eyes and gesturing to Pye that perhaps it was time for the two of them to make themselves scarce. One of these days, I'll get him to drink some Twinkleberry wine, and see what sort of information I can glean from a drunken familiar, but today was not that day.

"We'll be up in your room watching a movie if you

need us," Salem snagged a few items from the fridge.

By the time Salem and Pye hit the bottom stair, the rest of us were three-quarters of the way through our first glasses, the table had redressed itself for a game of poker, and Mag was shuffling a deck of cards while reciting the Balefire house rules for Deosil Draw.

It didn't sound much different from Texas Hold'em to me, except for the duels. No buying back, and if you got knocked out of the game, you had to beat the winner of the hand in a magical battle—fail, and you'd spend the rest of the game as an Azurian Muckwalker, which looks a bit like Jabba the Hutt covered in blue slime.

If Deosil Draw was anything like faerie game night, it could last for days. Not a fun prospect for the losers, but it didn't seem to hamper anyone else's spirits, so I settled myself in the chair and began organizing my chips into neat stacks.

"Remember the time Roselia Clatterwall cheated, and Mum caught her?" Aunt Mag raised an eyebrow at Clara, who loosed a laugh that shook the entire house.

"How could I forget? By the end of the night, Rosie had turned herself into a Dragolian frog to escape the Muckwalker curse and made it a point to scorch every one of those ugly dining room curtains Mum loved so much. I don't think she ever forgave Rosie for that."

"That woman was such a mouse; I didn't think she had it in her."

"You'd be surprised. It's usually the ones you least

expect who have the dirtiest secrets." Gran slurred and chugged back another swallow of wine.

Soleil, who up until now had only exchanged a few abbreviated pleasantries with either of the new(ish) members of our household, clunked her glass down on the table with a bit more force than necessary and leaned in close. "Tell us, Clara, tell us some of the secrets you heard while you were standing in that clearing. We won't breathe a word, cross our hearts and hope to die."

Evian and Terra nodded in agreement, and Gran switched into storytelling mode, the card game forgotten, at least for the moment. That's right, godmothers, ply her with wine and then get her to spill. Faeries are much more manipulative than people give them credit for, but my grandmother and my aunt had no clue about that particular nuance of their personalities. Or maybe they were just too many sheets to the wind to care.

I chose to stay silent, because, well, I'm nosy.

"Take your pick, ladies. I've got a million tales of botched spells and misdirected curses. I could tell you who's a hoarder, and who's a thief. I could tell you just how many witches like to pat themselves on the back for every random act of kindness—and the ones who congratulate themselves when they avoid a karmic kickback, no matter how temporarily. But I'm guessing your curiosities lie with the truly scandalous deeds tossed at my granite feet."

You'd have thought we were in the front row of a Tony award-winning Broadway play, all hunched shoulders leaning expectantly toward Clara, practically drooling on our shoes.

While she took center stage and held court like a trained actress, all I could think was that if you could bottle charisma, it would have a photo of my grandmother on the label. She may not look a day over forty-five (and a well-preserved forty-five at that), but a couple of centuries was plenty of time to cultivate the air of *je ne sais quoi* most women only understand about five minutes after they've gone far enough over the hill it doesn't matter anymore. And if you told her any of this, she'd laugh herself silly.

By the time she wound down, I knew I'd never look at Lobelia Morningside the same way again. The woman had more notches on her bedpost than a comb had teeth.

The last thing I remember was dancing around a roaring fire in the backyard—something I'd promised myself I'd never allow to happen again, but at least I was wearing clothes this time. Wedged between Soleil and Aunt Mag, I caught Gran's eye across the flames as she, Terra, and Evian swayed to the beat of a Stevie Nicks song.

I don't think I can say it was a dream come true because when I was younger, any dream of my grandmother coming back from the dead would have qualified as a nightmare. Not once did I ever imagine I had a great aunt who kicked magical butt and I never considered sharing my godmothers with anyone.

Someone wise once said the best things in life are the things you never imagined. Ain't that the truth.

Chapter 15

A heavy weight lay on my chest as I fought my way toward consciousness and tried to take a full breath. Disoriented and confused, I reached for magic and pushed until the dull pressure was gone and my lungs filled with air.

"What the hell, Lexi?"

Kin's annoyed exclamation punched through the last vestiges of sleep with a vengeance, and I popped my eyes open to find him balled up in the corner with Salem, a pink polka-dotted bean bag chair, and a tangle of sheets and blankets.

"What happened? Did I do that? Are you all right?"

I'm not a morning person on my best day, and not even waking up in the middle of an adrenaline rush was enough to poke my brain into full gear as I blinked and tried to make sense of what had happened. Kin's presence in my bed was still a novelty for me, as he was my first real boyfriend and the only person to sleep over. Ever.

My Twinkleberry-induced inebriation had caused a total blackout, and I didn't even remember him showing up the previous evening, but I chose to keep that confession to myself.

"I'm fine," came the disgusted reply.

"Speak for yourself." Salem forgot to add clothing when he morphed from cat form to human. "You landed on top of me, you big oaf." He grabbed the bean bag, tossed it back to its customary position at the foot of my bed, and started untangling Kin from the sheets.

"Clothes, Salem. Please."

"Sorry." He flashed back to cat form and then reappeared in a pair of pajama pants with Santa Claus all over them.

"Cute jammies." I tried to hold back a snort, but it sneaked out and twinned the one that came from Kin. I loved that we found the same things funny. Salem, however, was not amused.

"I was going for silk boxers."

Ignoring that for the time being, I focused my attention on Kin and repeated, "What happened?"

"It's a bit of a blur. We were spooning." Now it was Salem's turn to snort. "And I remember giving you a little squeeze. Next thing I know, I'm shooting out of bed like it was a slide at an amusement park. You used magic on me in your sleep," he accused.

"I'm sorry. I…that's never happened before. Is that normal, Salem?" He'd know better than I would since his magical experience was a whole lot more extensive than mine.

"No, it's not normal." His voice sounded funny, and I looked back at him to see why. Rapidly alternating between cat and human form, Salem rotated through a different outfit each time.

"What are you doing?" I asked, and he froze wearing nothing but a pair of black leather chaps and a look of consternation that told me he hadn't been going for the Magic Mike cast member look.

"Dude, seriously." Kin tossed Salem the sheet to cover up with and then said to me, "We're going to have to rethink our sleeping arrangements again." We'd already moved Salem out of the bedroom once, but with Clara and Mag here, he'd returned the bean bag to his favorite spot in my room.

"One catastrophe at a time, if you don't mind." It would take a gallon of brain bleach to wash that image out of my head. "Something feels off." I took stock of my mental and physical selves. The flow of magic I'd come to rely on having at my command now hovered at the edge of my grasp. Like when you're reaching for a jar on an upper shelf, and it scoots back just far enough that you can only touch it with the tips of your fingers. In the time it took to finish that thought, everything changed, and the power engulfed me hard enough to raise the hairs on the back of my neck.

The smell of smoke beat the shrill alarm of the detector to my room by half a second. Salem reacted fastest and disappeared out the door just ahead of Kin. I suppose their manly need to fix the problem outweighed any instinct to see the womenfolk to safety. Not that I needed any help, mind you, it was merely an observation on their behavior.

"Thanks for leaving me to burn," I muttered.

I hit the bottom of the stairs right behind Kin and peeled off toward the parlor to check on the Balefire. Flames danced merrily behind the andirons with no sign of a disturbance. Shouts drew me toward the kitchen where the rest of my family members were busy trying to direct the smoke cloud out the patio doors using towels, a plate, a flattened cereal box, and a large palm frond. Perched on a chair, Terra smothered the shrieking alarm with a flower-covered tea cozy, but the thing kept whistling merrily despite her efforts.

"Did a bomb go off in here?" I grabbed the first thing I could lay my hands on to help with clearing the room and wondered why the faeries hadn't used their magic to take care of the problem.

Stepping off the chair, Terra opened a lower cabinet drawer, pulled out a hammer, climbed back up, then bashed the smoke alarm to bits with a grin of satisfaction.

"Soleil burned breakfast," Vaeta supplied, having

apparently returned sometime during the wee hours of the morning. "Maybe she has a hangover from your little party last night." I detected a hint of hurt at the thought of us having a good time without her, but I still wasn't ready to discuss the subject.

"It wasn't my fault. Everything was going fine like always, and then something happened, and I lost control of my magic. Next thing I know, the pancakes are flash charred, and the pan of bacon goes up like a mushroom cloud. There's smoke everywhere, and my eyes are watering. Vaeta tried to blow the smoke outside, but her air only fed the flames and just when Evian tried to douse the kitchen with water, the magic dipped to almost nothing and…"

Soaking wet, Evian pressed her lips into a straight line and turned eyes gone the deep blue of a storming sea up toward the ceiling in an exaggerated roll.

"…that didn't work, and then the alarm went off, and you saw the rest."

"The Balefire's acting up again," Mag followed Clara in through the open patio doors, and I wondered if they'd passed out in the yard the night before. Twigs twined through Clara's hair, a coating of dust turning the deep chestnut to a dull gray that nearly matched the pallor of her face.

By contrast, Mag's flushed features appeared unnaturally red. Yet, neither of them looked the least bit hung over. Not fair, considering my head was pounding to the rhythm of a djembe drum.

"I know, but why is it affecting Fae? I thought only witches draw on the power of the flame."

Shamefaced, Terra stepped down from the chair and sat on it with a thump. "That's how it's supposed to work, but when you didn't Awaken, we had to align our magic with yours to help keep the Balefire alive, and now we're tied to it."

"Permanently?" That would partly explain the meltdown when my mother had returned, and the faeries thought they were going to be evicted.

"Not entirely." Between her tone and her shuttered expression, I could tell Terra didn't want to explain, so I let the subject drop. We had bigger problems at the moment.

"This," Clara waved a hand to indicate the kitchen and confirmed my suspicions, "is nothing." She snatched the remote off the table and turned on the television with a frustrated gesture. "I've been recording the news ever since Tansy went missing." She pulled up the early morning edition and fast forwarded through the national news to get to the local report.

A clip of the wicked witch flying through the skies of Oz played behind the announcer, a perky blond with even teeth who described a similar sighting over Port Harbor in the affected rhythm adopted by news personnel to sound more convincing.

"It looks like Halloween has come a bit early this

year, folks, as we investigate a citizens report of a witch—yes, that's right, a witch—flying over the city. We received this clip anonymously, and can only speculate that someone in Port Harbor has an interesting sense of humor. "

Amateur footage replaced the movie clip, and my mouth dropped open as the unmistakable silhouette of a woman riding a broomstick passed against the peachy pink light of the rising sun. Clara hit the pause button and activated a zoom feature I didn't even know the TV had as an option. "Recognize her?" Taken with a cell phone while its user was on a dead run, the short video lacked clarity, but even fuzzy and in low light, I knew Violet Bloodgood when I saw the shape of her. Those boobs were one of a kind. Or two.

Despite the alarm of seeing one of us blazed across the news, I had to give Violet props. "I didn't know she had it in her."

"This is no laughing matter, Lexi. It's a disaster on several levels." Clara started ticking them off using her fingers. "First, that was just plain stupid. It takes immense power to ride if levitation isn't one of your natural talents, and I happen to know it was never one of Violet's strong suits. She's drawing on the extra energy from two keepers feeding the Balefire."

The remote hit the table with jarring force. "Stupid witch. Riding temporary power like that. What did she think she was going to do when it failed? Flap her arms and glide. Honestly.”

“You can’t be responsible for everyone’s choices.” The gentle reminder earned me a narrow-eyed look.

“She was seen. You understand what that means? They'll be coming for us with pitchforks and nooses if we’re not careful. You’ve heard of a little thing called the Inquisition or don’t they teach history in school these days?”

Rather than get into a discussion about changes in the educational system or venture my opinion about how society is more accepting of witchcraft these days, I waited for my grandmother to continue.

“Mark my words, nothing good will come of this. We’ll be in the middle of another witch hunt if this keeps up and none of us will be safe from persecution.”

While I felt Clara might be overstating the situation, she had good reasons. My great-grandmother, Tempest, left a detailed memoir in the Sanctum of her experiences during the time of the Salem witch trials and it hadn’t been pretty. I like to think we’re more enlightened these days, that we understand more about how it’s our choices that make us who we are, not the circumstances of our birth. Ten minutes viewing the vast array of dirty laundry aired out on the Internet was enough to prove me wrong many times over.

Before I had a chance to venture an opinion, the doorbell chimed three or four times and the door, left unlocked all night, banged open to admit a gaggle of harried-looking witches, several of whom flashed me tense smiles or nods.

"Clara Balefire, you have a lot to answer for." Calypso Snodgrass led the way.

"It's my fault Violet Bloodgood doesn't have sense enough to fly under the radar? Sure, and when I get bored, I arrange for solar eclipses and tsunamis. You're the high priestess, Calypso, so why aren't you banging down *her* door and asking for an explanation? Go lead, and leave me alone." Maybe Gran had a little hangover after all.

Calypso straightened to her full height of at least five foot eleven inches, towering over the rest of us with a look of contempt on her narrow face. I wondered briefly whether she, like her daughter Serena, had been pretty at one time, and what had turned them both into the biggest sourpusses I'd ever met.

"Don't try and pawn this off on me. Twenty-five years of peace under my guidance and it all goes out the window in less than a week. What's the common denominator here? You. The great Clara Balefire and her half-powered spawn. Do you think I can't recognize a campaign to wrest control of the coven when I see it?"

Harm none. Harm none, I reminded myself like a mantra to keep from breaking the Rede I live by. Calypso Snodgrass wasn't worth losing my self-respect over.

"It might surprise you to know that I have no

interest in taking over the coven. Standing in one place gives one plenty of time to think about one's life and choices. It's time I saw a bit more of the world than what lies between the county lines. Once I've reacquainted myself with my granddaughter, I'll be taking an extended vacation." My grandmother's response elicited gasps of surprise from the rest of Calypso's entourage.

A sneer and a disbelieving sniff were Calypso's reactions to the news. "Don't bother climbing up on your high and mighty broomstick with me. If it's your presence in the house making the Balefire erratic, why don't you have the decency to leave so the rest of us don't have to deal with the fallout?"

"Because I've told her she's needed here right now." In Clara's defense, Mag got right up in Calypso's face. "All signs and portents point to these being dangerous times." If she'd been peering into the crystal, it was news to me.

It looked like Calypso couldn't decide whether she dared to lean in closer, so she moved back and ignored Mag's smirk.

"Maybe the times are dangerous *because* she's back. What does your crystal ball say to that?" I didn't see who threw out the challenge, but several of those who had smiled tentatively at me earlier now refused to make eye contact.

"Banning witches from the coven is always a

difficult choice, but if we all agree it's necessary—"

Mag, already bristling, closed the gap again, and deposited a loud slap across Calypso's cheek. "Don't you *ever* insult my niece or my sister like that again, Swampscum or I'll make sure you're sorry for the rest of your pathetic life."

Even the crickets stopped chirping while Calypso's face flicked through shock, anger, and indignation. I had to admire her self-control because I can tell you right now; I'd have gone wild if someone had the guts to slap me like that.

Chapter 16

"You've never jumped in a pile of leaves?" Kin tilted his head and appraised me with a pitying look. "I knew your childhood was different, but you really missed out." He leaned his rake up against the fence and grabbed one of the tall paper bags he'd just filled with a red and yellow confetti of crunchy leaves. "It's time to rectify that particular oversight," and all his hard work spilled back out to add to the heap at his feet.

I'd always loved autumn, but that year, it seemed to have set in early--or maybe I'd just been so preoccupied I hadn't counted the days and weeks passing me by in a blur. At least I was paying attention now. The colors, the scents, the crispness in the air.

Can't say I've ever thought about rolling around on a cushion of nature, but if Kin felt I'd missed out on an experience, I'd happily give it a try. A second bag of leaves joined the waist-high pile.

Kin, a goofy smile on his face, took a running start and managed an impressive flip into the mountain that closed over his head with a rustling sound. Seconds later, he popped back up with an even goofier smile that made my heart flip over and set things in my belly to fluttering.

"Your turn."

"Do I have to do the flip?" I preferred to avoid looking like an idiot whenever I had a chance to choose. What if I missed? Despite all evidence to the contrary, we were still in that stage of the relationship where I sneaked out of bed in the morning to brush my teeth. Landing on my butt in front of Kin ranked low on my list of girlfriend activities.

"Just jump. It's fun. You'll love it." People say things like that all the time, but that doesn't make them true.

Except for this time, it was. I plunged into the heap of dried leaves and relished the almost musty fragrance as they closed around me. If Terra had known how much fun could be had with something so simple, she would have created piles the size of a house and set up a diving board to leap into them. As it was, she had always relied on faerie magic to keep the yard clean of such debris.

"Lexi Balefire, come home now!" As though the mere thought of one of my godmothers had been enough to conjure them up, Evian's preferred method of communication issued from my pocket. I dragged a small shell from the denim depths and spoke into it.

"Can't you handle one day without me playing referee?"

"Oh, get over yourself. There's a situation, and your grandmother needs you." She barely got the words out before I was up and sprinting toward the sliders overlooking Kin's back yard from his living room. I heard the pounding of his feet right behind me. Good man.

A part of my brain recorded that the front door hung ajar, but I was already past it before the fact registered with the rest. Excited voices drew me toward the parlor where the Balefire flickered in a manic dance that sent more puffs of smoke to color the ceiling with soot stains I feared would become a permanent reminder of the past month.

"…not since last night according to Serena." Violet Bloodgood's tone sounded unnaturally strident to my ear. "You don't think she's in danger, do you?"

"How should I know? I have other things to do besides keeping tabs on the habits and whereabouts of Calypso Snodgrass," Clara's annoyance came across loud and clear. "Shouldn't you be gathering the coven together to decide how best to proceed? I can't imagine why you'd come here. Calypso made it quite clear my services were no longer required." She didn't outright tell Violet to piss off, but the woman would have to be really stupid not to pick up on the dismissive tone.

"Clara Balefire, I'm surprised at your lack of concern. Where else would we go? With Calypso gone, you have to take over the coven," Millie perched on the edge of the sofa, her hands nervously fluttered against the purse resting on her knees.

"You must. We need someone with your experience. Calypso should have stepped down as soon as you were cleared of any wrongdoing." Millie might as well have been surgically implanted on Violet's backside these days because wherever one went, so went the other.

"This is the worst thing that could possibly happen. A second unexplained death is going to draw more media attention, and you know very well we can't afford another round of bad publicity." Eyes glittering with a host of emotions I couldn't fathom, Violet shook her head slowly and deliberately.

Maybe my radar was off, but it seemed like she was enjoying the idea of scandal and media coverage more than she should. "You really should have considered the good of the coven, Clara. This situation puts us all at risk."

Did she just subtly suggest my grandmother had something to do with Calypso going missing? Heat followed the rise in my blood pressure and painted my neck and face with damp pink. I'd better be wrong, or Violet was going to get a taste of Balefire wrath from a source she never expected.

"Are you saying…" I started and subsided when Clara raised an eyebrow slightly and shook her head at me. Behind her, the Balefire's flames evened out and began to burn a red so deep it looked almost black.

Witch feeds the flame, and the flame feeds the witch. Too bloody right. I siphoned off my rage and fed it into the primal fire before the emotion turned into something wicked and uncontrollable. At least a minute had passed before I tuned back in to the conversation.

"There'll be burnings before this is over, you mark my words." Millie was so keyed up she reminded me of Don Knotts in The Ghost and Mr. Chicken, one of my all-time favorite movies. "Burnings." Her voice dropped to a scandalized whisper. Her bugged-out eyes only enhanced the resemblance.

Satisfied no one in the immediate family had been hurt or worse, Kin had taken himself off to the kitchen where he could hear everything without seeming to eavesdrop. Given a choice, I would have joined him. During the ten years between when I should have come into my powers and when I actually did, I'd been left out of coven politics so completely I still felt like an outsider.

"You know there were never any…"

Violet cut me off. "The less the outside world knows about us, the better." Her eyes cut toward the doorway Kin had walked through moments earlier. "We don't tell our secrets to every Tom, Dick, and Harry who winks in our direction."

"Channel. Five. News." I forced the words out between clenched teeth. Wild unicorns couldn't pull me from the room now. "*I* wasn't the one caught on video." Probably because I didn't know how to fly a broomstick, but that's a conversation for another day.

Clara gave a delicate snort while a flush crept toward Violet's hairline.

"Well, I never," Violet puffed up at the offense.

"Indeed, you did." A flower might have wilted under Clara's gaze, but Violet only raised her chin another notch and let the accusation fall into a heavy silence broken seconds later by Millie letting out a noise that sounded like someone stepped on a mouse.

"I can't stand all this fighting," she wailed. I thought we'd been quite civil, all things considered. Five seconds of a faerie tiff would send Millie cowering under one of the beds curled into the fetal position. Probably not the worst place to be during one of their battles, but not the kind of witch you'd hold up as a shining example of the breed. "We need to do something. A memory spell, perhaps."

"Yes, that's a wonderful idea! Make the entire city forget all about the strange goings on lately." Of course Violet agreed with her lackey.

Aghast, Clara opened her mouth to speak, but before she got a word out the doorbell rang again. A second group of somber witches filed into the house amid the sounds of rattling pans coming from the kitchen.

Leaving my grandmother to handle the witch invasion, I dodged into the kitchen and caught Evian's eye. "Party?" I waved a hand to indicate the food appearing on table and counters.

"Nope." A nod indicated the growing group.

"Thanks." I let my smile include all four of the busy faeries and, pretending their motives were entirely altruistic and they weren't just being nosey, returned to Clara's side.

No amount of finger food was going to make this a merry meet.

Aunt Mag managed to sneak out while the room filled with the buzz of concerned voices. Crowds weren't her thing, and she refused to indulge in coven politics after the last blowout. It was tempting to follow her upstairs since I'd have bet my favorite sweater her crystal ball was already getting a workout. Talking a situation to death wasn't Margaret Balefire's style.

Apparently Millie and Violet were the only coven members concerned about the involvement of four faeries, considering the speed at which they snarfed the crab puffs and mini quiches circling the room. I could see the lines of Gran's face twitch in an attempt to suppress an eye roll, but she stood in front of the group with authority and chose to be the bigger witch.

"First of all, we haven't received definitive proof

that Calypso is dead, so let's not assume we've lost our priestess," she even managed to keep all traces of contempt from coloring the word, "just yet. We need more information. Who here is close friends with Calypso?"

I followed Gran's gaze around the silent room and saw nothing but sideways glances and guilty expressions.

"Clara, who are you kidding? Calypso doesn't have *friends*. She has loyal subjects, and it certainly isn't because of her benevolent nature," Lobelia chided.

Gran sighed and tried another tack, "All right, then has anyone tried scrying for her? I would assume Serena has, but since she's not here maybe we should give it a go. Pyewacket, gather the supplies, and bring the clearest quartz pendulum you can find."

Her voice kept a low tone even though Pye was two rooms away.

"Winnie, you're the strongest at scrying, so you'll do the honors. We just need something of Calypso's as a focus." Winsome Warner had hidden talents. Who knew?

Violet's face lit up as she plunged an arm elbow-deep into her duffel bag sized purse, "I've got something. In here. Somewhere." She grunted and fished; finally producing the thin gold pen I'd seen poised over Calypso's clipboard the night Gran called the meeting to announce her triumphant return.

"I wanted her blueberry scone recipe—say what you want, but Calypso's scones are always so perfectly moist—and then I must have tucked the pen away in my purse by accident." Violet babbled as she handed it to Gran.

"Well, it's a good thing you did. Pye, everything set?" The familiar nodded silently and ducked back into the kitchen, presumably, to report back to the rest of the eavesdroppers.

Winnie knelt down before the makeshift altar in the middle of the parlor, the pen clutched in one hand and the crystal pendulum in the other. She blew lightly on a white candle, and the wick gently flamed to life. We all waited with bated breath while she held the pendulum's chain above a Port Harbor city map and willed the crystal to touch down on a location.

"Nothing. We'll have to widen the search." Gran replaced the thin sheet of paper with a state map, and finally one of the entire northern hemisphere. Still, the quartz pendulum refused to indicate a location, only hesitating over our tiny town in Maine, then a blank expanse of country outside St. Louis, and finally the mountains of Oregon.

Each time the pendulum wavered, the Balefire shot pink and blue sparks up the chimney until finally Winnie threw her hands in the air and admitted defeat. "Either she *is* dead, or she's skipping all over the place, or she's performed an advanced cloaking spell. I'd be surprised if she had it in her, to be honest with you."

Didn't surprise me one bit. I'd seen Serena dodge my pendulum, and she had to have learned the skill from someone.

"We're at a dead end, excuse the expression, and we've got a funeral to attend. Everyone keep your eyes and ears open. Watch your back. Don't go out alone. Regardless of what's happened to Calypso Snodgrass, there's a witch killer on the loose, and we all need to look out for one another and ourselves. Let's all give our support to Letitia, and we'll reconvene once we've said our goodbyes to Tansy. Agreed?" Gran looked around the room.

As if anyone had a choice.

Chapter 17

Clara

"I can't believe you made me wear this thing." Lexi shrugged the heavy blue velvet back into place to keep the clasp from digging into her neck. "It weighs a hundred pounds and smells like old lady." She slammed the van door with extra force. It really was time to think about buying a car that wasn't covered with garish advertising images.

"Watch who you're calling old, that's my second best robe, and I can't believe you don't own a single ceremonial garment of your own. What is wrong with those faeries?"

"Leave them alone, they did the best they could. It wasn't like the coven offered up any witchy parenting advice."

If she was going to become a proper coven member, I thought Lexi needed to start learning the ways of her people. And I needed to take her shopping for her own things. My old robe started shedding fine blue hairs over every inch of the simple black dress she wore underneath.

"Wearing black to a funeral." I tsked. "Who ever heard of such a thing?"

"Everybody has." Lexi cast a disbelieving look over my choice of a tunic dress in a lovely eggplant color over a pair of burnt orange stockings. At least they didn't have stripes on them. I'm not a total cliché.

"Shut up." Mag's tolerance for bickering—unless she was one of the bickerers—was smaller than the head of a pin. "Have some respect for the dead and them that were left behind." When she's upset, Mag's grammar goes out the window.

Poor Tansy.

"Sorry." Lexi and I spoke together and followed my sister down a grassy embankment.

"I told you those shoes were a bad choice," I whispered to Lexi, knowing Mag's sharp hearing would still pick up every word. "We're taking that trail through the trees." I pointed to a grove of pines up ahead.

Lexi's nose raised a fraction of an inch but, with admirable stubbornness, she refused to respond. *She's nothing like her mother*, I thought for perhaps the hundredth time. Or if I was counting the stoned years, the thousandth. Sylvana would have to forgive me for wishing she was more like her daughter, though I wasn't sure I'd ever forgive myself. Not for the comparison, and surely not for the act that made me miss out on my granddaughter's formative years.

But I still suppressed a grin when her three-inch heels sunk into the pine needle-covered earth. Moist, early autumn air had turned their soft golden hue to a deep, russet brown that contrasted with lush green mosses and ferns lining the path.

We'd driven several miles north to a rocky, uninhabited stretch of coastline. No highway noise or mindless chatter pierced the serene quiet of these woods. Only the soft crashing of waves against the nearby shore sounded between the chirping of birds and the rustle of a few curious chipmunks. It was the perfect place to say goodbye to Tansy.

The entire coven had assembled save for Calypso, who, as high priestess, should have led the Summerland ritual according to ancient custom. I hoped Letitia could get through the ceremony without breaking down. We witches understand that death is an inevitable part of living, and we also believe our souls will return to this plane of existence in the form of another life. But that doesn't mean we don't feel the loss of a loved one just as painfully as anyone else.

Losing a daughter was something I could relate to. During all but the last few months spent in my stone prison, I'd mourned doubly knowing not only was my Sylvana dead but that I was to blame. I'd thought I deserved my punishment and believed my incarceration no different from that of other murdering witch. I wished I could alleviate some of Letitia's pain, but there is no act of kindness with that amount of power.

The woods opened into a clearing, and beyond that, visible through the border of trees, lay an undisturbed expanse of sandy beach. Two large, square stones formed the base for a wooden funeral pyre, on which lay Tansy's linen-shrouded form. I heard Lexi's sigh of relief when we approached the altar, and it became clear she wouldn't have to come face-to-face with Tansy again.

Each witch had added something to the border of blooming flowers surrounding the altar: items of sentiment; strange powders and potions designed to ease her soul's passage into the Summerlands; and protective charms.

When we had all assembled into a circle, Letitia raised her hands, head, and heart skyward to begin the ritual.

From the Goddess, we have hailed
And to her breast, we shall return

Once you walked upon the earth, grounded in her
stability

*Once you breathed the air and reveled in her
freedom*
*Once you played with the fire and lost yourself in
her passion*
*Once you bathed in the water and got lost in her
dreams*

Now you dance with the spirit

You have become that which encompasses us all
You have passed into the lands of Summer

We will meet again someday, sister witch
Blessed be

Letitia, tears running down her face, choked on the last few words, then raised a golden, wine-filled goblet and took a sip before passing it to the next in line. Every member of the coven followed suit, each swallow punctuated with an echoing "blessed be."

Lexi

I don't think these witches realize how creepy it is to actually burn a body nowadays. Yes, I get it: ancient ritual passed down for thousands of years. Blah, blah,

blah. This is 21st century America and, might I add, it's probably against the law.

I reluctantly participated in erecting a barrier to keep us from attracting the attention of prying eyes, noses, and ears—and by that, I can only assume, they meant those of the police or any rational human who might summon said police.

Then, we each took our place at the edge of Tansy's pyre, carried it to the shore, and prepared to push her out to sea.

I barely heard a word of Letitia's parting remarks, because this was the part of the day I'd been dreading. Don't get me wrong, I was sorry for Tansy's death and the somber nature of the occasion had not escaped me. But no one had told me my part of the ceremony until we were standing next to the covered body.

"Here, Lexi." Aunt Mag produced a candle from beneath her robes, its wick flickering behind the bubble of a charm designed to make transporting the flame less of a fire hazard. "Are you ready?"

As I'll ever be. I *so* didn't want to be the one to do what needed to be done next.

"Blessed be," My voice sounded full and confident, even though my fingers were shaking as I touched the tip of Mag's Balefire candle to the edge of Tansy's shroud.

The flame traveled slowly as the pyre drifted out on the receding tide, finally engulfing it and Tansy's body as the last rim of the sun disappeared over the horizon.

Clara

With that, the more formal part of the ritual was over. Wine flowed, and cakes were passed around as a symbol of flesh and blood. Sounds creepy, but what do you want from me? We are witches, after all.

Stories of Tansy drew a picture of a young woman with great promise. I learned she loved to dance, and she'd been a scholar, particularly adept at translating ancient languages. With wine loosening tongues, I decided this was the right place and time for a bit of judicious prying into poor Tansy's life for clues to how she might have ended up dead. I'd taken the white, powdery image of a witch's hat as a portent. What could a demon and a Raythe have against her? And where, if at all, did a witch fit into the equation?

Only Tansy knew, and she was beyond the ability to tell.

The next best thing would be to find out more about her, so I listened intently to every story in case there might be a clue.

"Tansy was the sweetest person. When I came down with witchpox last year, she brought me an anti-itch potion that worked like a charm, and she didn't even care that I was contagious."

"She was the best at finding things. I lost my second-best wand in Tidewater Park," one young witch revealed. "And I panicked, but Tansy found it. In the pocket of the boy I wasn't supposed to be dating." She blushed prettily.

As each tale unfolded, I regretted not having the chance to get to know the young witch. Genuinely caring, willing to help anyone in need, it was a pity her life had ended so soon.

"It's too bad she was the soul of discretion," Hattie Blankenship, three sheets and a set of towels to the wind, Tansy's aunt slurred her words. "I bet she learned plenty in that new job of hers." My ears perked up. Literally, and the sensation startled.

"What new job, Hattie? Do tell." It seemed Gran wasn't averse to a bit of prying, either.

"Calypso hired her to transcribe some of the old coven records. Births, deaths, and the lists of grievances for the last half a century. Bet there were some secrets in those old records. Scandals, too."

It was the most interesting piece of news I'd heard all day. Not only had Tansy been able to access sensitive information, but she'd also been involved with Calypso, who was now missing. A connection where none had been before.

Chapter 18

Magic tiptoed across my skin leaving a trail of pebbled flesh in its wake. Now what? Was there some reason I couldn't have one single day without some new catastrophe rearing its ugly head. There were times I missed the simpler days when I longed for magic without truly knowing what a giant pain in the patootie it would turn out to be.

Not that this magic had anything to do with witches, it was all Fae and reeked of fury. The godmothers were at it again.

"Stupid no-fighting compact…should have known it wouldn't last…worse than herding kittens…thousands of years old and it still feels like a daycare center full of cranky toddlers hopped up on Pixie Stix." I grumbled as I followed the trail of magic down the stairs. After the funeral, I'd begged off spending the night with Kin. I still had some thinking to do, and I'd been too tired to deal.

Every one of my goosebumps had sprouted goosebumps by the time I stepped into the parlor where my godmothers were in a three-against-two face-off with Vaeta and her demon on the lower side of the equation.

Not this again.

I fixed the pair with an icy stare and felt power rise up inside of me like water filling an empty vessel.

"Did I not make myself clear that he," I pointed at Rhys, "is not welcome here?"

Vaeta bristled like Salem when he's in cat form and someone steps on his tail.

"It's not what you think. Rhys would never do anything to hurt you or anyone else I love." Her eyes stayed on mine while his kept straying toward the Balefire as though searching through the flame for something. "You have to listen, Lexi. Rhys isn't who you think he is."

At that point, her sisters chimed in with accusations and recriminations stemming back to Vaeta's departure to the Underworld while she defended herself hotly and Rhys stepped closer to the fireplace.

Despite fury elevating their power, the faeries restrained themselves to using words as weapons, probably to keep from running afoul of my grandmother's wrath. I had to give her props for applying witch rules of magic to my godmothers since the karmic payback hadn't been an issue for them until she showed up.

A stroke of genius and one I'd love to have come up with on my own, but I was new enough to possessing power that it never occurred to me. Not sure I'd have had the stones to implement it if it had.

Whether her spell had been temporary or permanent, the magnificent Fae were clearly loathe to tempt fate again and find out. Their own medicine must have left a bitter flavor on the tongue.

When they switched to their native language, I watched Rhys to see if he understood the conversation any better than I did. Soleil tried to teach me once, but human vocal chords can't reproduce certain sounds. The alien words of the language might be different, but the tone and the passion on their faces told the story.

We were at the name calling phase, which usually preceded the flinging of magics, followed by all-out war. My role had always been that of mediator, but when it came to Rhys, I lost my sense of balance and landed firmly on the side of no. No demons in my house.

Dark power begged for me to dip into its well and sample the heady sensation of losing control as it washed through me like thunder.

"Don't do it, Lexi!" Salem said urgently in my ear. His hand dropped heavily on my shoulder, and I shrugged it off. Where had he come from, anyway? The pursuit of Pyewacket had kept him busy and out of my hair for days.

The heat of battle, the determination to defend my home, and Vaeta's betrayal of my faith wrapped themselves into a hard ball that lodged in my belly and demanded to be freed. Freed by magic. Black witchfire magic like my mother used to wield. A dark spark arced and snapped in my left palm. All I had to do was lift my right hand to make the connection and let the magic seethe and build.

The half a goddess who lived in my skin had no problem with what my inner witch wanted to do. Odd, given her affinity for love. Even odder that I felt detached enough to observe the two parts of me when I thought I'd finally fused them into one. Had absorbing the bow divided me into bits again?

I don't want a life lived in pieces. I don't think anyone does. Getting through the day without flying apart at the seams is an all too human problem when the little stresses start building up into a wall of obstacles. Having the power to manifest my reactions to those stresses in a tangible way came with certain caveats that I fully intended to honor.

I wasn't sure the goddess side of me enjoyed the same level of conscience. That would be the best explanation for why I experienced ambivalent feelings at weird times. Times like this one, for instance.

The godmothers might scoff if they knew I envied the depth of their connection to the elements since, as a witch, my affinities are similar even if I'm not as grounded in my magic as they are in theirs. In contrast, my inner goddess seemed more interested in the intangibles. Life, death, love, morality. Those sorts of things.

Nothing odd there, really. We all battle the same elements and everything is made from duality. Dark and light, earth and sky, heart and soul. It's just that my halves have the potential to create havoc unless I stay vigilant.

Chasing that line of speculation distracted me long enough for the destructive urge to ebb, and when I came back to the present, it was to find myself the silent observer of yet another Fae standoff. You know that breathless moment when the roller coaster crests the hill and is about to drop? Welcome to my world, because that's where the faeries find ways to torment each other at every possible opportunity.

"We're not doing this. Do you hear me?" I shouted into air so heavy my words thudded to the ground like stones. Vaeta's wary expression transformed into a triumphant smile, and she let the air pressure drop back to normal.

"Please, Lexi. You have to listen, Rhys is just trying to…"

Terra pulled the rug out from under her. Okay, it wasn't just the rug, it was the rug, the floorboards, and about twenty feet of earth that swallowed Vaeta whole while Rhys reached for her and missed.

"Bring her back." His voice, deep and commanding, danced across my nerves in a way that could have edged into either pleasure or pain. Flipping through my mental catalog for information about demons produced a whole lot of scenes from television shows and the preconceived notion that demon equals evil. Preconceived and unshakable, it seemed, because I couldn't quell my edgy and tense response to him even though he hadn't done anything to me or mine. I think those three words were the first I'd heard him utter, come to that.

"That's rich. You telling me what to do after you basically kidnapped my sister and held her in the Underworld for a century." Evian and Soleil punctuated Terra's response with noises signaling their agreement.

Rhys couldn't have looked more surprised if she'd told him his pants were on fire. "Lies. All lies."

Accusing the Fae of telling an outright lie is not only baseless, but it's also a high insult. Bound to tell the truth, or at least as little of it as they can get away with, my godmothers believed Vaeta's incarceration to be fact or Terra could never have made the statement.

Holding out both arms to keep them apart, I stepped between Rhys and the three women ready to pound him into a greasy stain. Vaeta was in no immediate danger from Terra having briefly entombed her, and we needed to get to the bottom of this before it escalated into all-out war.

"Vaeta said…" I got no further before the faerie in question erupted from a crack in the floorboards, her body turned to little more than light and air in order to squeeze through the narrow space.

"I said nothing if you recall. You were free to draw your own conclusions, and I can't be blamed if you drew them incorrectly. Rhys is not here to hurt you," Vaeta's pointed finger indicated each of us in turn, "but I can see your minds are already closed. You will never see me as anything more than Vaeta the airhead who is too stupid to know when she's being seduced by evil. Whisper sweet nothings in her ear, and she'll follow you anywhere, even to Hell." That last was directed at her sisters.

"No one ever said you were stupid," Evian defended hotly while Soleil stared at the floor.

"And what is the difference between calling me stupid and calling me gullible? It means the same to me. Come, Rhys. I think my time here is done." Pulling him along behind, Vaeta stuck her nose in the air, flounced down the hall, and out the door without a backward glance. Rhys cast one enigmatic look toward the Balefire but allowed himself to be pulled away.

The house seemed inordinately emptier without her there.

"What just happened?" Soleil slumped down on the sofa. "Do you think she's gone for good?"

Following her example, the rest of us took seats and tried to parse the past ten minutes for subtext. Had Rhys indicated Vaeta hadn't actually been confined to the Underworld? Then why had she gone to such lengths to make it seem like she was in need of rescue?

Vaeta's ruse had spurred her sisters into teaming up with Adriel, a former guardian angel who had her own reasons for storming the nexus where Vaeta was supposedly being held. When the dust cleared on that day, we had freed Adriel's friend along with my mother, even if I hadn't known that at the time. Coincidence? Maybe, but now I wasn't so sure.

"With any luck, for another hundred years." Terra's tone held an undercurrent that belied the words. Sadness and fear all wrapped up in anger and defensiveness. I knew she only half meant it because I had witnessed the dichotomy between earth and air on more than one occasion. There's a reason polar opposites attract, and in the hands of the Fae, the two elements complement and elevate one another the same way a rhythm and a melody can create a beautiful song.

Without Vaeta, Terra was yin without her yang; a single tricycle wheel trying to balance the dual forces of fire and water.

An hour later, Evian hiccuped daintily and shook the last drop of wine from the bottle. That it missed her glass by two inches went unnoticed.

"That's your third bottle," I pointed out, then

squirmed under the gaze she leveled at me.

"To Vaeta." A mirror tipped hand waved the delicate crystal glass around in an attempt at a toast. "Long may she stay wherever the hell she is."

"Hear, hear," an equally inebriated Soleil echoed. I'd never seen them get tipsy so quickly. Terra must have added extra dragonfly wings to the batch. I made a note to cut myself off at half a glass.

"You know what Vaeta needs?" Terra slurred her words and the three of them giggled as if they'd heard an unspoken answer to the question. The giggles had an edge to them that would cut glass. Mean and diamond hard.

Water sloshed out of the hole Terra had gouged, with the wave of one hand, out of rock and soil to form the circular space Evian had filled with crystal clear spring water. No one wanted to admit the whole magic hot tub experience felt slightly lacking without Vaeta there to supply the bubbles. Still, Soleil's heat and light show made up for a lot. Scented steam drifted skyward while night birds serenaded us with tender melodies and the occasional honk (some of the residents in my back yard are from the Faelands).

Time alone with the godmothers had been about as rare as a dodo bird lately. What with them being tied up at Enchanting Events and me dealing with my newly expanded family, work, and the fallout from the Balefire having a fit of the wonkies, we'd barely seen each other for days.

Changing the subject for the moment, I said, "You've been busy lately, big wedding?"

"Twinniversary." Terra sounded sober all of a sudden.

"A what now?"

"Two sets of twins got married in a double ceremony thirty years ago, and now they're having a blowout anniversary party. Two of everything. Identical cakes, table settings, double the flowers, the whole shebang."

"It's uncanny," Evian said. "Almost creepy in a way."

"I assume Fae don't run to multiple births," I swear I wasn't prying and it didn't matter anyway since the leading statement went ignored.

"Well, I think it's sweet. Such perfect carbon copies, but their personalities are different." Leave it to Soleil to look past the superficial. It was one of her more endearing qualities. "Vaeta was supposed to…"

"Stop." Terra speared a finger toward the end of Soleil's nose and nearly made contact. "She's a traitor *and* an idiot, and as far as I'm concerned, she doesn't exist."

I checked my watch to see if we'd gone back in time. Three faerie godmothers were an embarrassment of riches and, growing up, it never occurred to me that earth, water, and fire were missing wind. When Terra cuts someone out of her life, that person stays out.

Except that Vaeta had come back a few months before and I'd have bet the farm she would again. Terra might grumble, but she'd welcome her sister back. After a suitable period of time spent in paying penance, of course.

"Did anyone ever ask she-whose-name-we-must-not-speak why she came back when she did? I'm genuinely curious. Was it a tiff with that demon of hers or something else?"

Terra snapped her mouth into a straight line, launched out of the tub and stomped away. But not before turning the tub into a big vat of mud. Warm mud—people pay good money to wallow in the stuff—and it actually felt good, so no one complained.

"I guess I should have kept my big mouth shut."

"It's not your fault, Lexi. For all her bluster, Terra has the softest heart, and that means she's the one most easily hurt." Evian added more water to the mud and wiggled down deeper into it.

"She'll forgive and forget eventually."

I'm not sure if you can snort internally, but I tried. Forgive, yes, but forget? Never.

Chapter 19

Walking into the popular nightclub named Driven had become even more like a family reunion since I'd started dating Kin, though I'd known the owner and several of the employees from my matchmaking activities. I'd always played an active role in mating souls, and sometimes that meant taking clients out to see what kind of people they find attractive.

Trying to talk a stone cold yuppie into dating a rocker chick covered in tattoos is about as difficult as you'd expect, regardless of whether or not they have a million things in common and are destined to be together. At least when I know what I'm up against, I can formulate a suitable counterattack.

On my way in, I was accosted by regulars who now knew me either by name or as *Kin Clark's Girlfriend*, which wasn't a moniker I minded in the least. In fact, it was kind of cool to be treated like a member of the band,

and I'd dressed to the nines tonight to look the part. A pair of opaque black tights hugged my legs below a pleated denim mini skirt, and the late summer air had cooled enough to allow for a pair of ankle boots with pointed toes that reminded me of witch shoes.

I enjoy my little private jokes. A white off-the-shoulder top showed off my bronzed décolletage one last time before my tan would begin to fade and turn my skin back to its normal peaches-and-cream hue.

Would this be what it would be like to join Kin on Rain of Thirteen's concert tour? None of the slated venues were anywhere near as small as Driven, so I doubted the atmosphere would be quite as homey. Still, it would be an experience to remember, and the thought of missing it all was beginning to bum me out. I hadn't felt comfortable discussing the subject with anyone else, and it ticked me off to no end that my best friend, Flix, was MIA right when I needed some sound relationship advice.

Given the state of affairs at home, I didn't see how I could leave. In fact, I hadn't even broached the subject with a single one of my housemates.

"Hey Lexi, how's it hanging?" Shouted someone from the group of drunk fraternity guys playing darts at the far end of the bar, his gaze traveling the length of me with a glint in his eye until I raised an eyebrow and sent a tiny flick of magic toward one leg of the bar stool he was lounging on. Instead of simply knocking him on his butt, it skidded across the floor on a slick of spilled beer, and he let out a whoop as his forehead collided with the edge of a nearby table. Oops. I should have known better, given the unstable state of magic lately. After making sure he was no worse for the wear, I vowed to be more careful.

Kin was busy tuning his guitar when I approached him from behind, letting out a low, exaggerated whistle of appreciation at the sight of his backside, "Hey, baby, how you doin'?" I attempted a Joey from Friends-esque pickup line.

"However you want me to be." Kin replied in kind and set aside his guitar to wrap his arms around me. His hands slid through my hair and down my back, pulling me toward his muscled chest with passionate intent as he kissed me breathless. Don't ever listen to women who try to say they're not attracted to musicians because it's a total lie. Watching a man's hands slide over the strings of a guitar is about as sensual as you can get, and being serenaded by a sultry, sexy voice turns bones to mush. Every. Single. Time. "I can't wait until we're out on the road."

"Mmmm," I murmured, pulling away reluctantly, "I'm going to go grab a drink and try to find a good seat. Good luck, Babe."

"They're saving your favorite spot at the end of the bar, and my tab is open. Love you!"

I added an exaggerated wiggle as I sauntered

toward the bar a little slower than necessary, throwing a mischievous grin over my shoulder knowing Kin watched me walk away.

I tossed a wink at Tiny Tim, who stood with his hands clasped in front of him at the stage entrance, a formidable expression on his robust face. A teddy bear of a man inside the body of a grizzly, he broke character with an enormous grin and gestured for me to come closer.

"Sandy's pregnant!" Tim shouted while I was still several steps away. Matching him with his wife had almost been an accident, back when I had no clue how to use my powers with any sort of intent. I've seen them go through some ups and downs since then, but their commitment to one another has never wavered. Now, Tim and Sandy were one of the yardsticks by which I measured my success.

"Congratulations! How far along is she?" I pelted Tim with questions and squeals of delight, taking care to avoid offering my babysitting services once the little one arrived. You never know when these things are going to come back around to bite you in the butt. Don't get me wrong, I love babies and would like to have children of my own one day, but hanging out with faeries and witches could scar a human child for life.

When I finally made it to my saved seat, Kin had already begun to strum the intro to his opening song. Carlos, who had recently been upgraded from a waiter-slash-barback-slash-gopher into a full-fledged bartender, slid me a vodka and soda with a twist of lime and waggled his eyebrows toward the stage.

"How's everyone doing tonight?" Kin's husky, sexy voice floated out over the crowd who cheered and woo-hoo'd with gusto as he launched into a sped-up cover of A-Ha's *Take On Me* that had become such a frequent request he'd finally decided to add it to the set list. Even those who chose to remain seated couldn't help swaying to the beat.

The fact that Kin's goal had never been to become a rock star was a testament to just how talented he really was. Driven started out as a side gig; inspiration for Kin's artistic motivation, but this offer for a tour could be the start of something else, and any sort of publicity is good publicity. He might think he wanted to hunker down in good old Port Harbor for the rest of his life, but things change. Bright lights have been known to turn even the most steadfast head.

I couldn't hold him back, especially if it meant a boon to his career. Not to mention, I'd never ask him to give up a dream just to stay near me and keep playing the same gig every week. I was lamenting the possible loss of the love of my life to the rock gods when a conversation down the bar caught my attention.

I tuned in to my witchy senses and spotted a man and woman whose resemblance marked them as brother and sister. I'm not ashamed to say I blatantly eavesdropped; it comes with the territory, and I admit it: I'm nosy. And good thing, too, because as it turned out, the man was Matthew Aarons, whom I'd almost forgotten I'd drawn here with a spell.

"What am I supposed to do, Michaela? I love her, but she won't even talk about our marriage anymore. This was supposed to be a trial separation, but I don't think she's ever going to forgive me."

"Why do you think she's so angry?" It sounded like Michaela had a background in psychology and was grilling her brother for information; her voice conveyed the practiced nonchalance of a professional therapist as she steered Matthew into revealing the root of the issue he needed to confront.

"She said we'd turned into a stuffy old couple like her parents, and she was right. I focused on work, and she focused on raising our daughter. Then it was all about the business, and even though we both loved what we were doing, it wasn't enough. We'd become one of those couples who watch Netflix and chill without the *chill* part." He tossed back half his drink and thumped the glass back down on the bar.

"Emily made it clear that she was only thirty-seven, and she didn't want to spend the rest of her nights watching television and ignoring each other. Everyone talks about that seven-year itch, and I've always thought it was a bunch of nonsense, but I've realized that's when things started to go downhill. We've been treading water ever since."

"The seven-year itch is definitely a thing—I mean, come on, they made a movie about it—but what most couples don't realize is that if you can get past it, what comes next is even better than those first few passion-filled years."

His empty glass hit the bar, but Matthew didn't motion for a refill. "How did you and Elliott make it through? You've always seemed like the happiest couple in the world. What's the secret?"

"No secret; just hard work and understanding. And plenty of compromising."

"Well, duh, Captain Obvious. Isn't that the textbook answer to all relationship issues? I thought you'd have more insight than that. I feel like I do compromise." Matthew's voice turned just a tiny bit whiny.

"Everyone does. That's the problem. You compromise every day on little things you don't even realize, and then years go by, and it adds up to feeling unappreciated even though you were probably never asked to make the concessions you've made. And Matthew, I bet Emily feels the same way. The question is, what do you want to do? Is she worth working for, even if that means waiting until she makes up her mind? Even if it means still more concessions and a lot of additional effort on your part?"

Matthew was quiet for a long moment. "All I want

is to make her feel like the most beautiful, amazing woman in the world because that's what she is to me. And I want to feel loved the way I used to when she'd look at me across a room. We'd share that secret smile, and it let me know everything was going to be all right. But I'm not willing to live on a one-way street. She's not the only one who has felt forgotten and ignored. Our sex life was…"

His sister shoved a raised palm toward Matthew's face.

"Okay, okay, that's all I need to hear. I don't care what I do for a living, hearing about my little brother's sex life is creepy and way too much information. All I'm going to say is this: give her the space she's asking for. And take some for yourself while you've got the chance. Get a hobby, or pick back up an old one. Spend some time doing the things you like to do for *you*—like coming out to a dive bar and watching a great band. When she's ready, have a conversation. An adult conversation. It's got to start somewhere."

Their talk turned to more mundane matters, and I tuned back out and completely missed Kin's second set as I pondered what I'd just heard. Simple advice, easily accepted; that's what I'd witnessed—and my intuition was echoed by the bow playing a few bars of You Can't Hurry Love. Again. You can't force someone to feel the way you want them to feel if they aren't ready.

All the signs were pointing toward me leaving

Matthew and Emily to their own devices because this wasn't something I could fix. Not with one of my patented setups, or even with Cupid's bow and arrow. It wasn't a problem of the heart, it was one of the minds.

Except I'd already stuck my nose and my arrow into things, and since I had no idea how to reverse my actions, I'd have let the fates decide what to do with the Aarons. I hated the idea of breaking the news to Hannah, but you can only lead a horse to water. If it doesn't want to drink, it staying thirsty isn't your fault.

When I let myself into the house at nearly two o'clock in the morning, I hadn't expected my grandmother to still be up and about, but there she was sitting next to the Balefire with a pair of knitting needles in her hands. Uttering a few words from the faerie's naughty no-no list—*she* didn't wind up with a mouth full of soap bubbles as punishment, I noticed—Clara chucked them, yarn and all, into the Balefire.

The flame lurched and then let out a sound that could only be described as a belch, and flung one of the needles across the room where the tip embedded itself into the door frame about three inches to the right of my ear.

Clara followed its trajectory and took in my outfit with a raised eyebrow. "You look like a school girl in one of those dirty movies," she commented without the shadow of an apology.

"Thanks, Gran." I grinned in spite of the insult; for

one thing, she was kind of right, and for another, it was nice that she cared. The godmothers who, let's face it, had never been the pinnacle of modesty, only commented on my outfits if they wanted to borrow something. I'd worn a dress code-restricted tube top to the last week of high school, and they'd batted nary an eyelash when the principal threatened to withhold my diploma. "I was out watching Kin perform at a nightclub. It's the required uniform for that sort of thing."

"Hmm, yes, I suppose so."

I took a seat in the armchair on the other side of the fireplace to watch the Balefire twirl and bounced back and forth between us like it was playing a game of eenie-meenie-miney-moe.

"What's on your mind, dear?" Grandmother asked, having tiptoed through my emotions and zeroed in on the undercurrent of indecision in which I was currently mired.

Sighing because it was the first time I'd had a concerned family member with dating experience to dump my drama on, I said, "It's Kin. You know this is my only real relationship, like, *ever*, right?"

"He's a lovely man, dear. Gentle and patient, and he's taken much in stride given all that comes with loving a Balefire witch. You shared true love's kiss, so what's your worry?"

"True love's kiss isn't the answer to everything." I

wiggled in my seat a bit, "Do you think long distance relationships ever work out?"

"Well, I think it's silly to say something *never* works out. We know how much life can change—sometimes in a split second—don't we? Assuming you can't weather the storm is just setting yourself up for failure in my book. You can do whatever you set your mind to, and things are different nowadays. Technology has made "long distance" a relative term. Why do you ask? Is Kin going somewhere?"

Clara would never be one of those people who struggled with technology. She could do things with a computer that I'd never attempt, and she'd only been warm and breathing for a matter of weeks.

"He's been offered a spot on tour, and it might lead to something more—at the very least some work composing, which is what he really wants to do. And he's asked me to go with him, but of course, I can't. I have responsibilities here; my family, my business, and obviously the Balefire. With all these messes to clean up, it's just not feasible." I tried to keep the touch of sadness out of my voice, but there was no getting anything past Clara Balefire. "We might be soul mates, but there are no guarantees he'll return."

"I can't imagine what your mother told you about her father, but the truth is we weren't soul mates. I reckon you'd know more about that than I do, and someday I might have you work your magic on *my* love life. What I do know is that there was a time my daddy couldn't find work here and he took a job away from home. It nearly broke my mother in half. Of course, she worried about him, but it was more that she couldn't bear to lose one second with him considering he was human and their time was limited to begin with. But if it's more than that—if your heart wants to fly free, then this isn't strictly about Kin. It's about your own future, which I'm guessing feels a bit uncertain right about now."

I thought about Clara's statement for a long moment. "I love living here, and I love my duties as Keeper of the Flame. But I love Kin, too." I replied simply. These were the facts that were pulling my life apart. Seems like I couldn't catch a break.

The creak of my grandmother's rocking chair was the only sound apart from the crackling of the Balefire until she finally spoke.

"I know how difficult it's been for you, Alexis, with the pressure to keep this flame lit when you had no idea how to Awaken your magic. I prayed to every goddess I could think of while I was stuck inside that stone; asked for guidance and received little in return. I should have been there for you. Should have taught you what you needed to know and trained you to handle whatever life threw at you. If going away with Kin is what you want to do, then you should go."

"I don't know what I want yet, but you're right. I need to figure it out, and soon."

"There's no rush dear; you take your time. I'll be here."

Chapter 20

All the stuff with Matthew and Emily kept bringing the issue of parenting to mind, and I knew I had a difficult task ahead of me. I needed to go talk to the last person in the world I wanted to see.

It's not as though I didn't know the witch community could be brutal to their own. After all, I'd spent my entire life branded a wicked Balefire witch, and the ones who believed strongly enough in that truth had been more than willing to continue throwing my family name under the bus even with definitive proof that Clara hadn't killed anyone.

I also couldn't deny Calypso Snodgrass had done her level best to further tarnish my family's legacy, but I'd come to realize, after my last run-in with her daughter, Serena, that she was just as lousy a mother as she was a high priestess. It didn't sit well for me to feel sorry for someone I'd long considered an arch-nemesis, but at a distant point in the past, Serena had been my best friend.

Now, she was carrying my half-brother's child, and about to become a single mother. I doubted Calypso had provided any support before her disappearance, and I couldn't imagine what it would feel like to be pregnant and completely alone. With guilt from how I'd treated Serena over the years keeping me company, I slowly walked the three blocks to her house. All the way there, an internal battle raged. Should I knock on the door or just keep going?

I spent some time examining the front hedge, which had clearly borne the brunt of whatever love Serena's mother did have locked inside her shriveled heart, and realized just in time that walking up to a witch's front door uninvited might not be the best idea I'd ever had.

Witch senses burning, I placed a hand out in front of me to feel for the protective enchantment's energy signature. Nothing; not even a tingle, as I slowly stepped forward and braced myself for a magical onslaught. Feeling watched, I reached for the doorbell.

Directing my intention to harm none out through my index finger, I squeezed my eyes shut and pressed the button. A sharp zap similar to what you'd feel after shuffling your feet over shag carpet and then touching something metal prompted me to take a step back, but then the door creaked slowly open, and I finally let go of the breath I hadn't realized I'd been holding.

"Come in, Lexi Balefire." I heard Serena's thin voice call out from somewhere beyond the threshold. Talk about walking into enemy territory. On the edge between fight or flight, I reminded myself that coming here had been my idea, and crept into the living room where Serena was curled up on an armchair.

I'd never seen her look so drawn. Dark circles ringed Serena's sunken eyes, and her pointed nose and thin lips were lost in a sea of paste-white skin. She pulled an ancient-looking checkered afghan up to her chin and glared at me from behind limp blond hair that had begun to show mousy roots. I wondered why she didn't just glamour it back to rights.

"Are you all right?" I asked, holding my hands up in a gesture meant to indicate I'd come in peace.

"Do I look all right to you?" She tried to snap, but her voice lacked the strength to make the words bite with poisonous intent. Serena really was in a low place if she couldn't keep up our ongoing verbal sparring match. "What do you want? You couldn't possibly have come here out of genuine concern."

I sighed and took a seat even though she hadn't offered me one. My choices were the tattered La-Z-Boy I knew to belong to Serena's father or the contrasting Victorian armchair that was probably Calypso's favorite spot.

"All you're doing is proving to me that you've never known me as well as you think you do. As counterintuitive as it may seem, I actually do care about you." I fired back, realizing that my words were truer than I'd even guessed. "We were friends once, after all."

"Yeah, until you stabbed me in the back."

"I'd call getting rid of my good-for-nothing brother a favor rather than a betrayal." This conversation was taking the turn I'd hoped it wouldn't. I'd come here to mend fences, and now I was going to have to tear through a brick wall. I supposed I couldn't blame her for seizing the opportunity to pelt me with lame insults. You don't hate someone with the fervor Serena has always reserved for me without putting plenty of mental strength behind the action.

Serena fixed me with a gaze I couldn't decipher, and we stared at each other for a moment before she finally spat, "That was you stabbing me in the front. I'm talking about when we were kids. You've always been rotten, ever since I got invited to Jennifer Johnson's birthday party and you didn't. I heard you tell her I didn't even like her, and that I thought her unicorn theme was stupid, and she made my life a living hell until we graduated."

Was she freaking kidding me? "That's not what happened at all. You wouldn't even talk to me after you Awakened. I wasn't witch enough to be your friend."

"No, that's not it at all." I think we regressed back to our thirteen-year-old selves for a moment as I contemplated replying with an *is too*.

I decided to be the bigger person for once in our sordid history. "Look, I'm sorry for whatever I said to hurt you back then. I really am. I remember always feeling like the odd girl out, and you were the only one I could be honest with. You think it was easy for me to make friends with four faerie godmothers living at my house? I could have had the best birthday party in the universe, but no one would come. And then you abandoned me too."

Wow, it felt good to get that off my chest. My ire toward Serena had always been born from the pain of betrayal, and now that I'd said what I needed to say it deflated like a balloon. I thought I detected a measure of softness in her eyes as she took in my apology, but she hadn't enough emotional strength to let it spread.

Head down, she picked at the afghan with shaking fingers. "It doesn't matter anymore. Nothing matters. I'm barely making it through the day."

I leaned forward, my eyes pleading, "You don't really believe the Balefires had anything to do with your mother's disappearance, do you?"

Serena was quiet for a long moment. "No, I don't. I wish I did, it would be so much easier than…this. Not knowing where she is or whether she's all right. I know she wasn't the greatest mother in the world, but…"

"She's still family, and you love her. I understand completely." And I really did. My mother was no prize, either, but I wouldn't want anything bad to happen to her.

"I can't even do anything about it." Serena moved the afghan aside and indicated her swollen belly, and I had to choke back a gasp of shock. On anyone else, the baby wouldn't have been showing quite yet, but Serena had always been stick thin, and stress had rendered her more gaunt than ever before.

"Serena, why don't you come stay with us? We've got a packed house, but we can make room." I blurted before I'd thought the invitation fully through. "Someone, in fact everyone there knows more about supernatural pregnancies than I do, and Terra makes a tonic I'm sure would perk you right up."

She actually thought about it for a split second before declining. "I can't. I've got to stay here and take care of my dad. Besides, if mother returns or they find out anything more about her, I should be here."

"Okay, I get it. But can I at least bring you anything? That's my niece or nephew in there, you know."

"No, I can fend for myself. But I'll keep it in mind."

That was more than I expected and was shocked to realize it felt good to put our stupid feud to rest. Serena's eyelids began to droop, so I whispered goodbye and headed back home. Terra would give me that tonic, and I'd talk Gran into taking it over. No one says no to Clara Balefire.

Chapter 21

Magic had nothing on Elvis when it left the building, or to be more accurate, the world. It was the worst time of my life. About a minute after getting used to having more than the latent spark of magic all witches carry until the day they Awaken to their full potential, it all drained away like liquid through a siphon.

The Balefire, an unearthly blue for the past week, half-heartedly issued a handful of sparks and turned generic orange. I didn't need to poke my hand into them to know the flames would sear my skin and even if I could, by some miracle, grab hold of the handle, there was no magic workshop on the other side of the hearth.

Knowing Salem might have been in there triggered the beginning of a freakout, but then he bolted into the room, stared at me with bugged-out eyes and his tail puffed up like a bottle brush, and I relaxed. I preferred him stuck in his cat form to squashed into the studs behind the fireplace when the workshop winked out.

If you really want to see what someone is made of, take a look at them when they are having their worst day. That's when you see whether their spines are made of bone or jelly. If it took more than two minutes before the jelly-spined among the coven started lighting up the phone lines, I'd eat one of my favorite pairs of Jimmy Choos, sautéed with butter.

It took two seconds.

Clara picked up on the first ring and held the receiver away from her ear. Her face went a dull red, and I could hear the screeching from across the room.

"What did you do? Whatever it is, you fix it right now! Right now! Do you hear me? FIX IT!" The caller, who declined to reveal herself, disconnected and the phone rang again in Clara's hand.

With Calypso missing and the coven now looking to my grandmother for de facto leadership, she was left shouldering the blame when things didn't go exactly right. Maybe Mag did have the right idea remaining a solitary witch with fewer ties to the group. Less hassle all the way around.

"You might want to turn off the ringer and get ready for the physical onslaught. I predict the doorbell will start chiming any minute now," I said ruefully. "Or we could run away. I know a place no one will ever find us. Well, if Evian's magic still works." Then again, an underwater grotto only accessible by magical means probably failed the safety test. "Maybe I'd better go check on the godmothers."

I left Mag and Clara, heads together and speculating over what, if anything, there was to do about the situation while I hurried toward the faerie's section of the house. Eerie silence met me at the threshold. Faerie silences, while not rare, usually signal they've hit battle stations—the last thing I needed right now.

"If you're fighting again, you need to stop, we've got a situation on our hands." My voice echoed through the space, so I pulled out my phone to check the calendar app where I tracked their events. Nothing on for today, so where had they gone? It wasn't like Terra to skedaddle without leaving a note.

Added on to the back of the original house to form a reversed L shape, the faerie wing boasted three bedrooms, two baths, and a sitting room. Vaeta, since her arrival some months prior, had been sleeping on the couch as penance for having followed a demon to hell.

Between them, they could have magicked up a palace for her, but that was none of my business. Connected to the main house by the shared kitchen, which Terra had doubled in size during the building phase, the many-windowed faerie wing presented a modern contrast to the original structure.

"Terra? Soleil? Are you here?" No answer, only the shushed hum of a fly against a window screen. "Evian! Where are you?" The fly buzzed its lonely sound again.

"Hmm. Must have had something they didn't put on the books." Frantic now, the fly pinged off the metal mesh.

A fly? Sometimes I'm just too dumb to live. Houseflies were not allowed in that section of the house. I refocused my attention on the long hallway with sliding glass doors at the end leading to a private patio. They were there—the three of them—tiny faces pressed against the screen, delicate wings beating the air.

Something seemed off. Way off.

In their winged form, the godmothers are every bit as perfect and beautiful as they are at full size. More actually. Imagine the petal softness splashed across a fragile butterfly's wing mixed with the iridescent quality that creates sparkle and glows when a dragonfly flits through a patch of sunlight. Even if you have the biggest imagination in the world, you'll still come up short.

Evian landed on my left shoulder and Soleil on my right—and yes, I did get a quick mental image of the angel and the devil in their place, but I wasn't dumb enough to tell them about it. Terra plastered herself to my waist, tiny hands firmly clutching my clothes to stay anchored there. When I gently placed her in my palm, I felt the tremble of fear—something I'd never known from any of them before, and it brought a tear to my eye.

Soleil spoke first; a spate of words in Fae language that I could barely hear and sounded like a cat walking across the strings of an out-of-tune banjo.

"I don't know what you're saying." Why is it when

we try to talk to someone speaking another language, our voices rise, and our speech pattern slows down? It seemed like she understood me and I felt like an idiot standing in the middle of the hallway draped in faeries and trying to communicate.

"You know you all weigh more than you should for your size."

Yep, they understood me all right. Dirty looks require no translation. I moved toward the seating area and transferred my passengers to the coffee table.

"Can you understand me?" Just making sure. Three heads nodded, so that was progress. "I assume the loss of magic forced you into this form." Three more nods. "It's the Balefire." The duh expression also required no translation.

"What am I supposed to do about it? I know all that business about the flame feeding the witch and the witch feeding the flame, but it's more complex than that. Maybe I should just leave. Gran was here first, and it's her right to take back control. I should have listened to Kin and moved out weeks ago. All of this is my fault. I swear I'm the worst jinx in the world. Everything I touch turns to poo and—" My tirade ended abruptly when Terra stamped her feet on the coffee table to get my attention and what followed was the most important game of Charades of my life. Every faerie game night had prepared me for this moment.

Terra pointed at me, shook her finger and fixed me

with a stern expression, then pointed to the door. Her head moved deliberately from side to side.

"You don't think I should leave."

She gave me a terse nod and spent the next half a minute in conversation with her sisters. When they were finished, Evian took over. Pointing toward Soleil's fiery head with one hand, she used the other to point toward the general area where the Balefire burned and followed that up by making a fluttering motion with her fingers.

"The Balefire," I guessed, and she nodded so hard her wings dropped a sprinkling of faerie dust. Next, she pointed to her sisters and then to her head, and I didn't have a clue what she meant.

"You hear the Balefire?"

A frustrated head shake met my guess, and she pointed to her temple again and lifted her eyes toward the ceiling. Ah, I got it. Think.

"You think?" A nod and a smile told me I was on the right track and she repeated the Balefire gesture.

"You think the Balefire…"

Evian exaggeratedly clutched at her throat, stuck out her tongue, and then tipped her head sideways and let her eyes drop closed.

"Sick. You think it's sick. I already knew that." Another frustrated shake of the head and she mimed drinking something and then the same throat clutch, tongue out, faked death scene.

"Poisoned? You think the Balefire has been

poisoned?" Terra held her palm out and tipped it back and forth in the gesture that means sort of, but not quite.

"Not poisoned." I let my brain follow the concept to another conclusion. "You think someone tampered with the Balefire. Did something to it that isn't exactly poison, but has the same effect."

Not only did they exchange high fives, but they also did the faerie version of the chest bump jump thing while I contemplated the theory. Tampered with. Why didn't I think of that?

Besides, what kind of poison would work on fire? I knew for a fact that the Balefire sneered at water. You don't live with the equivalent of a water nymph on steroids without a few mishaps.

Witch feeds the flame.

"You're sure it's not because there are two of us feeding the fire?"

Three emphatic head shakes.

"Will you be okay like this?" Raised eyebrows confirmed the stupidity of my question, and I shrugged. "Had to ask. I'll go poke around in the fireplace, but I'm not going to promise I'll find anything."

I left them there with a backward look and detoured into the garage where I hoped to find the set of fireplace tools we'd used before my Awakening. There hadn't seemed to be any reason to let them gather dust in the house when I could use my hands.

Ever since losing my beloved pink scooter to an

accident, the garage felt like the empty space left behind after having a tooth removed. You know you should leave it alone, but you can't help poking your tongue in there until it hurts.

Ten minutes later, I emerged victorious, if slightly disheveled. A smear of greasy dust decorated one cheek, my hair looked like a spider's house, and it occurred to me that Terra neglected the garage in her tidying efforts. I brushed myself off and headed for the parlor with a poker in one hand and a small shovel in the other. Lexi Balefire, superhero. Not.

My prediction about how soon to expect the onslaught of powerless witches must have been off by a bit since it was still quiet inside the house. Other than the sound of the phone ringing off the hook and Gran placating coven members, that is.

Bypassing that mess, I headed straight for the fireplace. The next few minutes I spent moving partially-burned logs around with the poker and pretending I had some idea what to look for. Nothing jumped out at me as being off. It looked like a normal fireplace with normal logs burning in a normal way. Except the very normalcy of it all *was* what was off. Any resemblance to the magical fire I'd tended all those years was gone.

Salem dashed into the room and, plaintively yowling, twined his body around my legs like he was trying to tell me something. I don't speak cat. Maybe

I'm supposed to, and had just ignored that part of my training as I'd ignored so many other things he wanted me to learn. Finally, I picked him up and held him out so I could gaze into one green and one blue eye.

"Talk to me." Since there was nothing else to do, I could at least listen. Salem yowled again, and I remembered him teaching me to meditate. What was it he'd said? Meditation allows the universe to flow through your conscious being and if you do it right, you can become one with the flow.

Still carrying him, I sank to the floor and tucked my legs into a crossed position. Anything was worth a try, so I concentrated on each breath. In and out, letting everything else float away until there was nothing left but the breath and Salem's bi-colored gaze.

"Stop looking for what is and try to find what isn't," Salem said in his man voice.

I popped out of the meditative state like a cork coming out of a bottle. What the spell did he mean by that? Look for what isn't.

"Not even a little helpful, Salem."

In answer, he snarled and took a swipe at me with one paw.

"Fine, I'll try." Setting the cat gently on the floor, I turned back to the fireplace and let my gaze rove over the flames again. Smoke curled up the chimney as the hot orange tongues devoured logs, bark and all. Nothing looked out of place to me. Nothing at all.

Look for what isn't. I let my eyes go slightly unfocused and nearly jumped out of my skin when I saw the anomaly. An actual hole in the source of the flames.

"Gran! Aunt Mag!" I called out. "You need to come in here, I think I've found something important."

It took a minute or two, some unladylike language, and finally, a rude hang-up before the two elder witches joined me in front of the Balefire. Mag caught my eye on the way in and held up the battery she'd removed from the back of the cordless receiver. There would be no more phone calls for a while.

"Look." I pointed to the negative space where the fire should be. "Do you see that? It looks like someone removed a piece of the flame and left it blank."

Silence grew while two sharp pairs of eyes scanned the flickering pattern and I wondered if I'd just made a giant fool out of myself.

"I'm sorry, It's probably nothing."

"Oh, it's something all right. I don't know how we missed it before. This fire has been meddled with." Gran agreed with me.

"But who? And when?"

"This place has been busier than a bee in a field of flowers lately." Mag started to list the possible culprits. "I think we can rule out everyone who currently lives here since we all have ready access and wouldn't need to steal fire for any reason."

"There's the coven, and I hate to mention it, but

Kin could have…"

"Kin would never do that." Hot anger flushed my face, and I interrupted my grandmother rudely.

Leave it to Mag to play the bad cop. "Now, Lexi, you have to admit he's had access."

"It wasn't Kin, so keep going with the list." My teeth ground together painfully when I clenched my jaw in anger as I rose to stalk out of the room. Back in the kitchen, I pulled a sheet from the magnetic grocery pad mounted on the door of the refrigerator and slashed out the names of the coven in bold strokes. My grandmother followed me but waited until I had filled one side of the sheet and flipped it over to continue the list before quietly suggesting more names. If I was hoping for an apology, it was clear none would be made.

Fine, but I had no plans to forgive the assumption, either, and I'll confess right now that I might have acted a little childish about the whole thing.

Okay, maybe more than a little.

Unfortunately, my snit was interrupted by the doorbell, and I never got to finish it properly because half of witchdom was standing on the porch. None were carrying pitchforks, but the mob mentality showed in the way they moved.

Clara nipped the rebellion in the bud with a few well-chosen words, and even though I wasn't her biggest fan at the moment, I couldn't help but admire the way she took charge. No wonder she'd become a high priestess. As usual, Mag practically faded into the wallpaper the minute the hallway started to fill, but I could see her appraising each witch passing by and I don't think she missed a twitch of the eye or a quirk of the lips. The woman could read body language better than I could read books.

When I could, I caught her eye and raised an eyebrow to question whether she'd picked up any nuance that would lead to the culprit. A barely perceptible shake of her head had me mentally crossing names off the list.

Surprisingly, Serena Snodgrass was among the first wave, and I didn't need Mag's eagle eye to see she was looking stronger. Either Gran had done as I asked or she'd had news of her mom. It couldn't have been anything to do with our previous conversation, and I wasn't going to say this to her, but I was happy to see the change.

Before I could approach the pair, the mob hit the refresh button on their diatribe.

"…been dealing with this for years while that granddaughter of yours…"

"…time for someone else to take over as Keeper…"

"…hoarding all the power for yourselves…"

"…dead children and our high priestess is missing…"

Fear-powered voices chattered and buzzed around

me to fling accusations at my family for being the source of all the rotten things that had happened lately. Gran opened her mouth several times to interject until finally the ruckus culminated into one pointed question.

"What exactly are you planning to do about it?"

"Oh, for the love of the Goddess, put on your big-girl witch hats and stop acting like a bunch of sissies." Mag's voice cut through the din like a machete through a mushroom, and a shocked silence fell over the room.

"Ever wonder why I don't see any use in congregating and electing leaders? It's this kind of idiocy. Where on earth did you get the idea this family owes you something for nothing? That you," an arthritic finger waved around the room pointing at the loudest complainers, one after the other, "or you, or you should be able to enjoy the perks of being a witch while the Balefires shoulder all the responsibility? Shame on you. Shame on you all for being such sniveling pansies."

Just because her insults were from the 70s, didn't mean they weren't warranted.

"Wake up and smell the potion, ladies. Flame feeds the witch, and that's all you can seem to grasp, but the other half of it is that the witch feeds the flame. What have you given to the flame lately, Millie? Or you, Winnie? How dare you come into our home and run your fat mouths as if you had a right to or deserved something for nothing? Serve you right if we shoved you out the door and washed our hands of the lot of you."

"She's right." A tiny voice spoke with more command than I would have thought possible, considering the source—Serena Snodgrass. The last person anyone had expected to speak on our behalf, and the one person who might be able to shut them all up. "None of them are responsible for the death of Tansy or the disappearance of my mother. I think I'd be the one to know, and I'm definitely the one who is going to report to your high priestess *when* she returns. It's up to you what I tell her: either get behind us or get out of our way."

Us? Serena considered herself part of us? Wrapping my mind around that one was going to take a circus-worthy bit of flexibility.

When Serena linked her arm with mine, I couldn't help wanting to cheer. White hair flying around her head like dandelion fluff, Mag winked at Serena, then shot her nose up in the air so she could look down its length. "What do you say, Clarie? Let them swing on their own rope?"

"Tempting as that might sound, I think we'd better put them to use instead." Clara joined her sister on one side and motioned me to take my place on the other. "If you're all done whining now, can we get on with the business at hand?"

Thoroughly cowed, the three-quarters of the coven who were currently crammed into the hallway nodded, and we stepped back to let them into the house proper.

Chapter 22

Clara

The only other time the Balefire burned this low was when Lexi failed to promptly reach magical maturity—and while I'd forgiven, I still hadn't forgotten my sister's part in that fiasco. My turn at being keeper hadn't been nearly as eventful, and I squashed the tiny, competitive voice inside me that wanted to crow about it.

Still, according to Lexi, it had never been as bad as this. Why? Because of the faeries. Poor girl had no idea what her godmothers had done, what they'd given up, to take care of her and to keep the flame going.

Tied to her charge on a magical level, that affinity meant Terra's cost was lower than the other two, and for Evian, to link with her polar opposite affinity must have been incredibly difficult. If I had to guess, I'd say Soleil would have paid the least, but she probably also shouldered the biggest burden. A remarkable effort for which I should remember to thank them as soon as the current emergency passed.

"Go get the faeries, please, dear girl. We're going to need them." Mag caught my eye, and we had one of those unspoken conversations sisters sometimes have. Her eyes widened, and I knew she understood what I meant to do. Maybe not all of it, but enough. "I hope it's not too late."

"Too late?" Lexi tossed the question over her shoulder and hurried to do as I asked while I stepped up onto the hearth to get a better view and turned to face my coven. Millie fidgeted under my scrutiny, and I wondered where her other half had gone to ground. It wasn't like Violet to miss out on anything noteworthy, and if I'd had the time, I might have given more than a moment's thought to her absence. As it was, worry would have to take a back seat.

"Okay, ladies. You know the situation, and it's not good. If we don't act now, we're sunk, so listen up. Every witch has a spark in their blood—the essence of magic that comes alive when we Awaken. Right now, that spark is all we have left, and we need to feed it to the Balefire. All of it, and I hope it's enough."

"Will it work?" Winnie's voice sounded stronger than I'd ever heard it. She must be one of those women who wimps along through life but thrives under pressure. Good for her. Maybe some of that pluck would rub off on Millie, who seemed to be going to pieces. "What will happen if it doesn't?"

"We all know what will happen if the Balefire goes out, don't we? That's why we carry the damnable flame all over the blasted world. Whether this plan will work or not is anyone's guess, but I don't see any other option. I assume none of you have a better idea?" I glanced around the room at faces carefully shuttered, "No? Okay, then."

"Gran?" Wings drooping, their bright colors fading to shades of gray, three faeries clung to Lexi with tiny hands gone pale enough to be almost translucent. They were running out of time. We all were.

"It's going to be okay." Please let it be okay.

"I think they're dying. Can faeries die?"

"Shh." It felt like we were the only two people in the room as I stepped down from the hearth and comforted my granddaughter by putting an arm around her as best I could and giving her a squeeze. The contact also gave me an excuse to brush up against each of the faeries and assess how much magic they still carried. Not as much as I hoped, but it would have to do. "Let Mag take them. I need you with me." When she hesitated, I gently helped make the transfer and pulled Lexi back to the fireplace.

Keeping my tone brusque to push back emotions that might otherwise overwhelm, I ordered my coven to do the one thing I never thought I would be called upon to do.

"Join hands everyone, and give me everything you've got." I reached for the witch nearest me and prepared myself to become the focus for all the magic we could pull together. Lexi, beginning with my sister who, I can freely admit, is the stronger of the two of us, did the same on her side of the room.

Hand joined to hand, and as each set of fingers entwined, magic grew from the smallest of sparks to a candle-sized flame that had better be big enough to rekindle the Balefire. When Millie and Winnie joined hands, they completed the chain that started with me and ended with Lexi, and I knew we were going to run short if I didn't strip the elementals of their connection to the Balefire.

I gave Mag the nod, watched as the faeries collapsed against her, and hoped I hadn't misjudged. Lexi would never forgive me if she lost her extended family. An oppressive silence fell over the room as if magic had taken a breath and left a vacuum in its wake, and then all spell broke loose.

The spark zipped toward Lexi, then reversed and raced down the line in my direction. If the situation hadn't been dire beyond the telling of it, I might have chuckled at the expressions I saw as the power traveled down the chain like an electric shock. Millie looked so flummoxed; I thought she might have peed her pants a little.

It wasn't as funny when the jolt hit me, and even less so when it arrowed back down the line leaving a trail of exclamations behind it. Until that moment, I'd have bet against Winsome Warner knowing any four letter words, much less daring to say one out loud.

"Gran, what should I do?" Lexi sounded panicked, and no wonder, the faeries clinging to Mag were losing consciousness. Should that be happening or should removing their connection have restored them? I could speculate later if they survived.

"I don't know. This isn't what I…" and then it hit me. The magic, searching for a focus, had sensed the presence of two keepers and was trying to choose between us. "It's seeking its master, Lexi. One of us needs to step up as Keeper. Permanently. It's time to decide."

Keeper was only part of what Lexi would be putting on the line. This decision had far-reaching consequences for her relationship with Kin. I'd wanted her to have more time to decide, but that's not how things work sometimes.

"Do it. You were here first. I'm the one who should let go. I want it to be you."

Now, Mag might have more divination skills than me, but I can spot a lie at fifty paces.

Did I want to be Keeper again? Lexi would end up with the job at some point anyway, so maybe she would appreciate a chance to leave home and see the world. Despite my boast in front of the coven, travel really wasn't my thing. At least, that's what I had thought. But now, faced with the choice I realized that twenty-five years of standing in one place had ignited a spark of curiosity. It *would* be nice to see something outside the confines of the eastern seaboard.

What? How come I didn't know that about myself before? Mag was the one who craved freedom, not me. Until now.

"Look at me." Of course, my granddaughter obeyed the order; she had grown into a lovely and respectful woman, no thanks to me. "Tell me true. Do you want the Balefire?" Wasting any of the precious magic on forcing her to speak her mind became unnecessary when eyes drenched with unshed tears met mine.

"Yes." That was all I needed to hear, and letting go of the duty I'd carried for many a year turned out to be as simple as willing it so. I pushed the crackling energy her way. It shot like a miniature rocket through her body and out the finger she pointed toward the fireplace. Sparks erupted with a blinding flash and noise that pulled at the eardrums. I heard buzzing and then cheering.

"It worked," Mag pointed toward the roaring blue flames and stated the obvious as she so often does. It's one of the things I love about her. Magic swelled, as did cheers from the coven. When I checked on them, the faeries were back in their larger forms, and Lexi ran from the room trailing sobs behind her.

"I'll be right back." I followed my heartbroken granddaughter out into the backyard, watching in fascination as it expanded and bloomed back to life. When this day was over, a painful conversation with Terra and her sisters about severing their connection to the Balefire rose to the top of my to do list. They'd served Lexi well—gone above and beyond anything I could ever have asked of them—but her conscience would never have given Lexi peace if I'd let anything happen to them. None of that negated the fact I should have asked their permission before I ripped away that connection.

I found her huddled in the hushed silence under the spreading canopy of a weeping willow. She flinched under the hand I laid gently on her shoulder.

"Lexi, what is it? Everything is all right now."

"No, it's not. I should have said no. I should have done the right thing, but I was selfish. Now you'll hate me and so will Kin."

"Come now, that's not true."

"Yes, it is. You should have been the one. Not me. The Balefire needs someone strong like you. Look at the mess I made of things. I took it away from you when I knew you wanted to be the Keeper. I should have stepped aside."

Silly child. I gave her a shake. "Did I say I wanted

to be the Keeper? You assume too much."

"I…what?"

"I don't want the job." Enunciating carefully and following each word with another shake, I talked sense into my granddaughter. "You try standing in one place for twenty-five years and see if you don't want a change of scenery at the end of that time. I love you with all my heart, and this will always be my home, but I've got a hankering to see the world."

"You do?"

"Are you certain you don't?" What we'd just done had repercussions for both of us. "Your young man seems to be going places, are you sure you wouldn't rather be completely free to follow him?"

"I'm a Balefire. Living up to my name is all I've ever wanted—even when I didn't have enough power to make a frog sneeze. This is where my work is, it's where I belong. You're sure? This is okay with you, too?"

Why does everything have to be a drama with this generation?

"I'd be happy to fire-sit from time to time, but I'm excited to see what freedom tastes like. Cross my heart and hope to fly."

Lexit's mouth dropped open. "You can do that? Fire-sit, I mean."

"Yes, of course. I might not be the reigning Balefire, but I'm still of the blood, and that's enough to let me be a substitute once in a while. What? You thought this was an all-or-nothing situation?" It wasn't magic, or the Balefire, or the demigod inside her that made Lexi's hugs feel like being blanketed with love, it was her heart.

"I love you, Lexi. To the moon, to the stars, to the bottom of the sea."

"To the top of the highest mountain and the edge of the universe," she added and it felt like we'd made a pact or a vow. The kind that can't be broken, even in death.

"We've got a house full of witches and another job ahead of us, are you ready to go back inside?" Keeping an arm around her shoulders, I led Lexi back toward the house. Mag's people skills were practically non-existent, so leaving her in charge of things was only good for the short term. Like ten minutes or less, and we were straining at the edges of the limit already.

Lexi

Aunt Mag does dirty looks almost as well as Terra, even if hers don't carry actual dust and grime.

"If you're finished fooling around with the touchy feelies, maybe we could concentrate on the bigger picture here? There's no telling how long the magic will last, so let's get moving."

"Yes, Aunt Mag. I'm sorry." Minor fib there. If Gran was happy with me being the official Keeper of the

Flame, I wasn't one bit sorry for how it came to happen. Okay, maybe telling Kin I had just tethered myself to the area semi-permanently wouldn't be a walk in the park, but if Gran agreed, I'd take a week with him in the middle of his tour. Sometime after Samhain.

"What's next?" About half my attention focused on making sure my faerie godmothers hadn't taken any permanent damage during the time without magic. The other half tuned in on the short but heated conversation between my grandmother and aunt, who talked in some kind of sisterly shorthand.

"We could…"

"Yes, but what about…"

"Then we'd better…"

"Okay, let's do it."

They seemed to have the situation well in hand even if I had no idea what the ends of any of those sentences might have been.

"Ladies, if you'd kindly follow us," Clara reached toward the handle concealed within the fireplace, and I think I was the only one who saw the split second of hesitation before she surrendered her fingers to the flame. Can't say I blame her for that. With the Balefire acting like it had a bad case of PMS, anyone with half a brain would be cautious.

The door to the sanctum opened smoothly, and if I felt a little bit like the fly entering the spider's web, it was only because the memory of those walls closing in around me was still crystal clear. Right down to the lump in my throat and the shiver in my hands.

Suck it up, Lexi. Witches are not wimps. Especially not Balefire witches.

"As you can see," Gran motioned to the alchemy lab and the long wooden table strewn with open volumes where we'd spent hours researching demonic symbols for the past several days, "we haven't been sitting around with our thumbs up our behinds. Mag, explain your findings to the coven, so everyone understands what we're dealing with here."

"Listen up, ladies, because what I think we're up against is something even I couldn't predict, and that's saying something. We found evidence of a demon presence at the scene of Tansy's murder, and there was a demon mark imprinted on her flesh—but it gets worse."

Mag had to hush the group as a flurry of gasps erupted, "We also isolated traces of Raythe essence, and the best we can assume is that the two are working together."

"But that's not possible…" Winnie practically shouted, an edge of hysteria creeping into her voice, "you assured us you had dispatched the last of them." Her eyes narrowed, and I prepared myself to battle more accusation and criticism.

"There are no absolutes, Winsome, and you know as well as I do that a new Raythe can be born anytime and the family might feel too ashamed to admit to loosing a scourge upon our world."

The simple truth shut Winnie right up and Aunt Mag continued.

"If a demon has tied himself to a Raythe, one summoning will kill two birds with one stone. Either woman up, or walk away. Your choice." Looked like Winnie was good for showing strength through one tragedy a day, and then it was back to normal.

Mag extracted a tiny bottle from a pocket deep within her robes and motioned for everyone to arrange themselves around the raised platform in the center of the sanctum, "You too, Terra, Evian, and Soleil. We're going to need every bit of juice we can squeeze."

"We wouldn't have it any other way." Terra's eyes met Mag's in an unspoken promise.

"Here goes nothing," Mag took a deep breath and exhaled slowly. Her eyes turned black and rolled backward as a stream of glittering red and black mist expelled from between her lips.

Rising power closed my throat and made my lips tingle until they itched. Gray smoke furled out of the pentagram in the center of the circle my great-grandmother, Tempest, had set into solid stone by magical means. If you tell my grandmother this, I'll haunt you when I die, but I squeezed my eyelids almost entirely closed and only peered through the tiniest of slits, and if I could have pinched my nostrils closed without anyone noticing, I would have done that, too.

I'd never seen a Raythe before; what if they steal a witch's soul through her eyes or her nose? Not a chance I wanted to take.

"You've got to be kidding me." Evian's disgusted exclamation popped my lids open, and I silently echoed her sentiment when I saw the three figures appear as the smoke wafted away.

Vaeta, Rhys, and Violet Bloodgood blinked and rubbed stinging eyes.

"It's not what you think."

Vaeta spoke at once, but Violet wasted no time stepping away from the center of the circle. Something about the look on her face when she lifted a surprisingly dainty—given the size of her other accouterments—foot over the rim of the circle betrayed strong emotions. She probably felt distaste at being in such close proximity to a demon. I know I always felt that way around Rhys.

"We summoned the demon who left the mark on Tansy and Rhys showed up. Am I missing something that might be construed differently?" Ice practically formed on Terra's tongue her tone was so cold.

"Yes. No. Terra, he never hurt that girl. He was trying to help. Why won't you listen to me?"

"I'd rather hear it from him," Grandmother spoke up. "And if he's lying, I'll know."

"Are you implying Vaeta isn't telling the truth? You know she's bound by…" Terra fell silent when the implication of her own protest hit her. "Vaeta can't lie."

"No, but she can believe a liar, and it's almost the same thing." Mag pointed out.

"It is not the same. It's totally different." Vaeta protested, her voice shrill. "And he's not lying."

"You would say that, wouldn't you?" Evian shoved in front of Mag and laid into her sister. "Airheaded twit. You wouldn't know a bad intention from a left-handed narwhal."

And there you go, name calling, the beginning salvo of every good faerie fight. The bad ones, too.

Instead of backing down, Vaeta snorted. "There's no such thing as a left-handed narwhal, everybody knows that."

"Enough." The command that shocked the argument into silence came from none other than Violet Bloodgood. Surprised me, because I didn't think she had it in her. "You stop it. Right now. It doesn't matter whether she's lying or not, or too dumb to see the truth. This demon is behind Tansy's death, and he needs to pay for what he's done. Margaret Balefire, weren't you bragging just last week about your exploits with demonic forces? Do what you're meant to do and take care of him. What are you waiting for?"

During the chaos that erupted, I forgot to wonder how Violet came to be summoned into the circle. Maybe that was what she wanted, but it was Serena Snodgrass who pushed things to the next level.

"Where is my mother?" She knocked Millie out of

her way and went toe to toe with Rhys. "If you've hurt her in any way, you can consider yourself a walking corpse. Killing you won't get me stoned since you're not a witch, and I'm pretty sure I'll have plenty of help."

"Shut up, Ms. Snot-in-the-grass. You're not much of a threat. What were you planning to do? Throw bubble gum at him?" There had been an incident between Serena and Vaeta and me that ended in a sticky mess. But that was before Serena had become a mother-to-be and everyone knows motherhood comes with a heightened desire to protect the young. I suspected Serena had more in her than she'd shown in the past.

Put a couple dozen keyed up witches in a room, add a few faeries and a demon to the mix, and you've got yourself a recipe for disaster. These women were out for demon blood and not especially interested in whether Rhys was guilty or innocent. Obviously, I didn't know Vaeta as well as her sisters, and I didn't like Rhys either, but she'd stood up for me on more than one occasion, and I'd heard her speak with great insight on people's character. Were the other godmothers selling her short?

No, it had to be Rhys. It was his mark on Tansy. There was demonic evidence left at the scene of her murder. So, why was Mag standing silently?

Salem once said everything you need to know about someone is in their eyes if you take the time to look.

Look. Not listen, not assume, but look.

Tuning out the buzz and chatter of angry voices, I locked in on Vaeta's gray gaze. What I saw there were an absolute certainty and trust in her own statements. My feet moved without me intentionally directing them, and Rhys fell under my scrutiny.

I got all up close and personal with him. Nose to nose, in fact.

One thing I know when I see it is love. It's my stock in trade, my heritage, the mythology my life is based around. Rhys loved Vaeta. Enough to be a better man if that was what she needed. Enough to allow for the nobility of purpose. Enough to act in un-demon-like ways.

Everything else fell away as I trained my gaze on his and asked the simple question. "Did you kill Tansy Blankenship?"

Silent up until now, he mouthed a single word, "No."

I believed him.

Sound returned to my world, but I knew it might be too late for the truth.

Clara

Violet, her voice shrill and strident, called for action, and the coven—my coven, witches I'd known for longer than a human lifetime or two, responded by showing all the signs of turning into an angry mob. Again.

A wave of women surged toward the edge of the summoning circle and would have penetrated its barrier if Mag hadn't thrown out her arms. This was her thing; the job she'd left home to do and my first chance to see her in action. All the secret missions, the ones that cost her youth; I was about to finally understand why she'd chosen the life she had. My sister was going to pull out the serious magics.

"Um, Mag, are you sure you want to do this here?"

Too late.

I felt the crackling heat as Mag drew strength from the earth, from the Balefire, from the living gold of the summoning circle itself. She pulled out her wand, a lovely tool made from black tourmaline-studded gorse wood and tipped with a double-terminated chunk of rainbow obsidian.

Without so much as a backward glance, my sister knelt to press her right hand firmly against where one point of the pentagram touched the outer edge of the spell ring and laid the crystal tip against her own chest.

Golden fire lit the ring, casting a glow over Mag. Her head fell back, her mouth dropped open, and a small cloud of vapor issued from between her lips. A figure outlined in blue light rose above her head. A demon's mark, the same one I'd last seen laid against Tansy's skin, grew out of the mist and Vaeta shrieked.

"It's not what you think. He's innocent."

"Shut up," Mag said without any particular emphasis. The job done, her hand clutched my arm. I helped my sister regain her feet and supported her until she steadied. Every witch watched the lighted sigil intently as it turned in the air. Bit by bit the mark evolved from a demon's signature to something else. "It's not him," she whispered in my ear, and we both went still.

A moment later, nothing remained but a fine, dark mist that seethed like a tiny storm cloud.

"Ostendium Nobis Cara!" The last time I heard a sound as pure as my sister's invocation was when we presented Lexi to the Balefire. The day when it accepted her with the blare of a thousand trumpets. Some notes, imbued with nothing more than their own nature, carry the power to change the course of events. Others, like this one, carried more. Power—yes. Power to spare, but something else as well; a sudden knowledge or maybe the knell of fate.

Once activated with the truth, the circle decided Rhys didn't fit the role of villain and ejected him without ceremony. Dragging Vaeta along by the hand, he flew out of there so fast his ever-present cowboy hat spun into the air behind him. The look on his face was priceless.

Skirting the now-empty ring, the cloud of mist fined down to a narrow finger and arrowed toward the last place in the room I would have expected it to go. Violet Bloodgood opened her mouth, took in the evil as though it were honey and nectar, licked her lips, and then looked back at me with a sardonically lifted brow.

"Didn't expect that, did you, Clara? Miss high and mighty Balefire."

Every one-sided conversation Violet had ever had with me during my passive years came back in a rush of clarity. I should have seen this coming. The veiled references to babies born on the wrong side of the sheets. I thought she'd been passing judgment on Sylvana, but she'd been talking about her own family.

Violet's mother must have had an affair with a null. Wrong side of the sheets? Wrong side of the bed, the house, the world. Learning Hester Bloodgood broke taboo to consort with a magic-less man-witch shocked, then illuminated. Odd rumors and half-heard conversations about scandalous liaisons made sense to me now. A null/witch relationship would make Romeo and Juliet look like puppy love. Oil and water, fire and ice, these things don't mix.

Not having read the entire genealogy of every witch family going back through the annals of time, I wasn't sure if there had ever been a witch/null match that resulted in anything other than a null baby and a Raythe. Leave it to Violet to flout convention by being born different.

Brains she lacked, but the power she had in spades.

So many things started to make sense.

My understanding must have shown on my face because Violet practically cackled. "You should have stayed in your place and let everyone think you were made of stone. Fooled me, you did. Fooled everyone, I suppose. Going to cost you now, though."

Buxom Barbie goes ballistic. Might be a good movie, but in real life, we had to put that witch away.

A snap of the fingers called Violet's Raythe out of the ether. Crouched at her side, the thing preened while she ran fingernails around its ears and the coven, almost as one, took a step back.

No taller than waist level to Violet, it resembled a muscular gargoyle and looked like it should have been perched atop the balustrade of a vampire's balcony.

"Your little pet looks like a half-breed to me. Not much of a threat," Mag tossed off a sneering remark that sent Violet into a thunderous rage.

"Half-breed or not, you old hag, Ravana is more than capable of defending herself," she screeched and faster than I could focus, the Raythe had my sister in her grasp.

Chapter 23

The primary use of a summoning circle is to contain that which has been called into its center. Violet had other ideas, and she didn't hesitate to pervert its strength to her advantage. Stepping back over the edge to join her hideous pet, and channeling power into the ring of living gold, she raised a curtain of magic around herself that even two Balefire witches couldn't cross.

Inside the circle, Mag's feet thrashed above the floor as she struggled to keep her soul contained and intact. I saw death in Violet's eyes. The evil scum wouldn't even trigger the ultimate payment for the crime since it would not be by her hand the deed was done. I could hate her for that alone, but if my sister died, Violet Bloodgood would be my ticket to a proper stoning, even if it took a hundred years to make good on the promise.

Lexi, bless her, took charge of the coven during the moment I hesitated. "Come on, let's pool our magic, just like before." The slapping of flesh, palm to palm rang out as determined witches joined together to save one of their own. *From* one of their own, which felt like a major betrayal.

Millie took up the other end of the chain, the stony expression on her face a testament to the fact she hadn't known anything about Violet's history or involvement. Maybe I could forgive her. Later, when this was all over.

"It's not going to work." Even if I added my power to the mix, I could see it wouldn't be enough. Not with the Balefire compromised. The Balefire. What if we put it out? No magic, no circle.

As if she read my mind, Violet shouted, "I wouldn't do that if I were you. Ravana's magic doesn't come from the Balefire, and if you hurt me, you'll just make her mad. She's quite protective."

Observing my expression, Violet grinned evilly and launched into a textbook example of when the bad guy in a movie has the upper hand and feels the need to gloat a little. Fine by me, while Violet focused on putting the rest of us in our place, Ravana took a break from trying to suck my sister's soul. I'd take whatever small mercies were on offer.

"You'll regret having been freed, Clara, and Tansy Blankenship should have minded her own business. Now you're going to pay in blood, just like she did."

"Are you going to slaughter the whole coven, Vi, and four elemental faeries while you're at it? Let Mag go, and we can talk this through."

"No way. She's chock full of Raythe essence, and once Ravana consumes her, we'll share in that power like we've always done."

Now we were getting somewhere. The seed of an idea began to grow, and I only hoped my witchy intuition had correctly picked up a helpful tidbit of information. "What's the problem, Violet, are you ashamed of your heritage, or just plain scared?" I goaded, knowing if I was wrong and didn't hit the sweet spot between confidence and self-preservation to keep Violet talking, Mag was done for.

Violet blanched, "*I* have nothing to be ashamed of. My mother might have fallen in love with a null, but you lot have been breeding with humans for centuries, and nobody seems to care. *I* have been blessed with power *and* a Raythe to do my bidding. No other null-born has ever been able to say that. Ravana does as I command, and what I want right now is to see all of you kneel while you watch your precious Balefires become Ravana's next meal."

If Violet was telling the truth, she shared an unprecedented connection with Ravana. Without a precursor, it was anyone's guess—including Violet's, I hoped—what might happen to one if the other were harmed. We might be able to use that connection to our advantage if we could only distract Violet long enough to formulate a plan.

"What did I ever do to you, Violet? Please, elaborate. Because all I remember is treating you with patience and kindness. What has Lexi ever done to you? Or Mag? Or Millie, your best friend? And Tansy. How did that poor soul get on your bad side?"

"Shows what you know, Clara! Millie's an idiot, just like the rest of you. I've had to hide what I am for fear of persecution since the day I Awakened. Ravana has been my only true friend and companion, and that meddling little Tansy poked around in the records. When she found out about my father, she showed up asking if a null-born could have magic. I only wanted to keep her quiet, but she wouldn't listen. Ravana knew what to do, and now I've got Tansy's soul and her power. There's nothing any of you can do to stop us!"

Lexi

"Lexi!" I heard my name and started to turn toward the source, somewhere just behind me and to the left.

"No, don't turn around. Act like you can't hear me." Evian's voice hissed, apparently from the mother of pearl barrette I'd used to clip my hair back earlier in the day. In a pinch, it seemed she could use any shell to communicate. Good to know.

"Vaeta has something to tell you."

"Rhys is…Well, it's complicated, but he's a

member of the Inter-Magical Alliance, and he's been tracking that Raythe for months, but he did something wrong, something you won't like, and he's very sorry, and he hopes you can forgive him, and me. I hope you can forgive me."

"Get to the point, Vaeta." I heard Evian hiss the words I was thinking. A tide of fury constricted my chest as it rose up and threatened to unleash the baser side of my powers. It wouldn't be the first time; Serena Snodgrass could bear witness to what happens when my magic goes dark. Violet wasn't worth risking my soul over, but Mag was family, and I would not let Ravana have her. Especially when it sounded like Violet's next move might be to sic the thing on Gran and me.

"Anyway, when Rhys found Tansy's body, he figured out the Raythe was attached to a witch, so he took some of the Balefire thinking he could take care of everything without anyone else getting hurt. It was wrong, and he's been trying to put it back, but someone kept showing up every time he got near the fireplace, and then there was the fight, and now he thinks giving it back is the only way you're going to be strong enough to take down that shield, but he doesn't dare to try in case Clara freaks out."

How she could talk so long without taking a breath was beyond me, but then again, Vaeta's element was air, so maybe she had more control over her use of it. And besides, what did she want me to do about it now? My face was practically pressed to the shield and Violet had her beady eyes on my every move.

I gave the tiniest shrug I could manage, barely a twitch of one shoulder, and then listened as a short argument raged in whispers. By slow degrees, I turned enough to see my godmothers, who appeared to be standing silently. Clearly they were using glamour to disguise their heated conversation, so couldn't they just do the same thing to keep Violet from seeing Rhys pass by? Or what about Soleil. Now that I knew how much they'd aligned themselves with the Balefire to keep it going during my—let's call it a dry spell—she must have some special affinity with it now. If the four of them, for once, could quit arguing, I'm sure they could figure out a way.

"…built like I am, people automatically think you're an idiot. Just because I have big boobs doesn't mean anything." I heard Violet say and nearly snorted. I was pretty sure her boobs were way bigger than her brains, but this wasn't the time for my stupid sense of humor to show itself.

It did give me an idea, though. Villains like it when you stroke their egos, so I took a chance. "Violet, it's obvious you're no disco bimbo," I said, putting a slight emphasis on disco. If the faeries were listening at all, they'd get the reference to that time when the clash between air, fire, and water ended up creating what I'd humorously dubbed the Faerie Disco Battle. Bubbles of water and air with a spark of Soleil's flame had been the good thing to come out of the fight and we liked them so much the light balls had become part of our celebrations.

Violet looked at me like I had two brain cells left.

"Oh. That might work." I heard Vaeta say in my ear. It took all of half a minute before they worked out a plan. Soleil manipulated the stolen Balefire to fit into a bubble made from Vaeta's air. Evian coated the bubble in water so clear it had a mirrored finish. As Vaeta gently wafted the enclosed Balefire toward the ceiling, Evian worked the surface, so it reflected whatever was above and behind it. You'd have to know it was there to see the mirage shimmer as it passed overhead.

Violet missed it, but then, she was focused on the sound of her own voice and the airing of petty grievances going back to childhood. Every witch in the room made her list; even my inability to mature at a time convenient to her was a problem. Like it was my fault.

"Everything would have been fine if your incompetent hellspawn had been able to keep the Balefire alive." Violet spat at my grandmother. "I might never have needed Ravana's power at all, but there it was, being offered to me on a silver platter. All of you have laughed behind my back, and all of you have paid the price for that whether you knew it or not. Winnie—why do you think you didn't get accepted to that summer program at Oxford even though you were more than qualified and your mother knew someone on the admissions board?"

Winnie's eyes widened as years' worth of wistful disappointment suddenly made sense. She bit her lip and glanced sideways at the Raythe, and I had a feeling she would have scratched Violet's eyes out if not for her menacing companion. "Why?" Winnie whispered.

"For all the times you used the term *null* like a racial slur. Think back, all of you, and I think you'll find I served karma well."

"Almost there," Evian whispered in my ear. Her voice sounded strained. "And we've figured out a plan to alert the others."

Only because I'd been watching the first stealth bubble attack were my eyes attuned enough to pick up the tiny blip—one of many—that circled in front of me and floated gently next to my left ear. I heard a pop and then a whisper.

"Missing Balefire restored in 10, 9…."

A ten count to be ready didn't leave a lot of time to get the jump on Violet. My limited history with the coven left me clueless about what to expect, and if I'm honest, most of them looked like bored housewives, not kick-butt witches with a lot of battle experience. Oh, who am I kidding? I'm not exactly a war-weary soldier either, and I had no idea what type of an attack to mount against Violet's energy field.

The faeries held little sway in what amounted to our inner sanctum. A stroke of luck for Violet because if this whole fracas had gone down outside, my godmothers would have set the elements against her and driven her into the ground before she ever had a chance to get the upper hand.

Mag looked like a wet dishcloth draped over a hook. She hung in the air between Violet and Ravana, her chin resting on the Raythe's razor claws, shoulders slumped forward, fighting to keep her eyes open. I prayed to Hecate promising everything short of my first born child as payment for her survival. Surely, I must be owed one tiny favor, gratis, but it didn't stop me from offering.

"6, 5, 4…"

I didn't hear the 3 because the Bow of Destiny chose that moment to play a little tune from its '80s collection. Thanks, but I already knew Vi was a cold hearted snake; I didn't need a musical reminder.

What I needed was a way to get inside the magic barrier. Or over it, since the shimmering curtain ended only three feet above my head. If Kin were here, he could use his basketball skills to lob a potion right over the top. If we had a potion to lob, the lack of which was another strike against us. I was the closest, so it felt like the burden of taking out Violet's protection rested on me.

Some witches carry an athame or a boline at all times, but my ritual knives lived in one of the drawers in the potions station, which was on the other side of the summoning ring. No help there. If only I had a weapon of some kind, something magical that would pierce her spell…oh, for the love of tiny pickles.

"2, 1. NOW!."

Evian released the water barrier around Vaeta's air pocket, and Balefire dropped out of the popped bubble with a hissing sound and then a roar. Luckily for me, the noise drew Violet's attention long enough for me to pull my father's bow, nock an arrow, and let a living gold tip with a razor point slice through the magic barrier. God trumps witch, and I didn't even need to call Miss Pinkeye to do it.

Maybe my subconscious aimed for the Raythe, or maybe it was simply instinct to act against the biggest threat. Living gold steeped in the strongest magic of all—love—thwacked into the hulking thing's chest (always aim for the heart) and quivered there.

I only meant to pierce the veil of protection and allow the coven a place to direct their defensive spells. The bow had other ideas and apparently required a living target. File that info away for the future.

Clara

In the middle of life and death situations, time does crazy things: slows down, speeds up. Every moment my sister edged closer to death seemed to rush past in a blur.

But, when I heard Evian's voice in my ear, her countdown dragged out long enough for me to formulate a plan. The flimsiest plan in the history of plans since I had no way of communicating with the rest of the coven and they were probably all doing the same.

Talk about lack of unity.

Then, when Evian shouted in my ear and the Balefire roared a welcome to its missing piece, time doubled in pace, and before I could act, Lexi set chaos in motion. Everyone says that history is doomed to repeat itself and I guess I can now agree. To a point, anyway. The Bow of Destiny is a weapon of love, not hate. Using it with the wrong intentions has consequences. I turned it on its owner and broke him with it, which makes me the poster girl for what not to do with the Bow of Destiny. After that, concern for Lexi took a backseat to the events of the moment, and I focused on saving the day.

Lexi's arrow turned out to be a blessing and a curse. On the plus side, the arrow did what it was meant to do and showed Ravana her truest heart. Fired with the right intentions, each arrow reveals a truth which its target has been unable or unwilling to see, and the focus is on love. Used in defense, the arrow pierces and lays bare the deepest desires and regrets of the soul.

When I fired on Lexi's father, I hadn't been aiming for him and had no idea what would happen. It's taken me twenty-five long years to come to terms with what I did to him, and I still haven't told Lexi that part. No one should be forced to experience the darkest places of their own psyche until they're ready to look.

As it turned out, Raythes don't exactly have a psyche, or a soul—hence the need to steal souls from witches. What they do have, though, is the desire to feed and to evolve. Violet's unique situation had spawned a Raythe with an abnormal set of desires—mainly to protect her. Once Lexi's arrow revealed to Ravana the depth of Violet's control, she shrugged it off, and the Raythe turned on her master.

Dangerous. Much more dangerous.

Suspended by wickedly-tipped claws around her neck, Mag dangled from Ravana's grasp, her face pale beyond the telling of it, and her feet barely moving. Always protective, Mag held her Raythe-defeating method close to the vest, a deep, dark secret which left me with little to go on but instinct.

Instinct said to use my strongest defense which, in this case, meant my best offensive spell.

"Weave and sew; bind our foe; loop and knit; her power omit."

Spellbindings—ropes born from soul magic, and tough enough to temporarily rob a witch of her freedom—formed between my outstretched hands. What they would do to Ravana was anyone's guess, but they were all I had. My best spell fed by the magic of my chant, my intentions, and my desperate need to protect my sister no matter the cost.

"Weave and sew; bind our foe; loop and knit; her power omit."

Joining her voice and her will to mine, Lexi repeated the invocation to double its power. As the last words of the chant echoed into silence, the bindings whipped toward the Raythe. Tongues of hot blue witchfire tasted Ravana's mottled flesh from wrist to shoulder, writhed like lightning-touched snakes from neck to waist and lower to bind both body and power. Claws retracting in a blur, Ravana freed my sister and focused her attention on that which held her. Time deceptively slowed to allow me the full experience of watching Mag's frail body fall toward the unforgiving stone.

Push back one threat and another steps up to take its place. Worse, the spell for making air pillows went out of my head so fast it left skid marks.

"Um. *Mullis polvinus? Molis pulvino?....*" My lungs and my magic would fall far short.

The wind tossed from a body in motion flung my hair in my face. Rhys used himself as a shield, grunting when Mag's weight slammed his head into the floor. Even as he rolled, he curved arms and legs around her for protection. Bruises bloomed on skin scraped by rough stone, but he caught my eye and nodded. Mag lived. Rhys scrambled to his feet, lifted my sister gently in his arms and, wobbling slightly from the blow to his head, carried her toward the corner where the faeries huddled.

I owed him an apology and myself a dinner of crow.

"Go with him. Help Mag, please Lexi!"

With Ravana tied up however briefly, it was time to put Violet Bloodgood in her place and damn the karmic cost.

Knowing she was the lesser of two evils and the linchpin in this crazy game, the rest of the coven had taken it upon themselves to give the rogue witch a taste of their collective ire. Ever seen a cat toy with a mouse? Then picture a clowder—the technical term for a group of cats—toying with a rat. A rat with big boobs and a penchant for tight skirts.

Winnie swiped first and came up with a fistful of blond curls and at least two broken nails, having foregone magic in favor of the traditional hair pulling and eye scratching. Millie hit Violet with her best engorgement charm, and Violet's skin began to swell and stretch until her fingers could no longer grasp her wand and it clattered to the floor.

Pansy Pinkerton joined hands with Lobelia Morningside and Serena, and the three of them sent a simple wall of energy at Violet, forcing her onto all fours.

Violet pulled all fifteen volumes of The History of Famous Nose Warts down on Serena, proving just how far over the edge she'd gone if a pregnant coven mate was considered collateral damage. The largest tome spun in the air and struck Serena's forearm spine-first, pulling a yell out of her when the bone snapped.

The pain seemed to spur Serena on because she never missed a beat and switched her wand from her left hand to her right. "Didn't count on me being ambidextrous, did you, Violet? It's not so easy when you pick on witches at your own level. Tell me what you did with my mother, or you'll be the one paying in blood. Mark my words."

Black fire formed at the end of her wand, and as much as Serena might need revenge, Violet wasn't worth dying over. It was time to shut this thing down.

Lexi

Everyone okay?" What a stupid question. Three paler-than-milk faeries, one battered demon, an unconscious witch, and Vaeta—looking robust compared to her sisters—occupied the most sheltered corner of the room.

Why the godmothers seemed so depleted was a mystery I didn't have time to unravel.

"Can you heal her?" I caught Terra's eye while laying a hand on Mag's forehead. Why? I have no idea, it's what you do when someone is sick.

"I'm sorry, I can't."

"Then I'll have to do it myself," I called up the memory of Salem listing the recipe for a healing potion in his most pedantic tone. If memory served, this one would take only a minute or two to make and while maybe not the most potent, should be better than nothing.

With one eye on Aunt Mag and the other on Gran's progress against Violet, I whipped up the concoction to the best of my ability. The godmothers helped me dump it down her throat.

"Ugh, I hate Echinacea," Mag grumbled as the color returned to her face. The bruising around her neck remained; she'd need more than a basic healing elixir for that. "Thanks, now get me on my feet."

"Tell me what to do, Auntie. You're not strong enough."

"That's ageist, and you know it." Regaining her feet with a little help from Rhys, Mag dusted off her hands and toddled back toward the fray with me trailing behind her.

We never made it, but we had a ringside seat for what happened next.

With their efforts focused on Violet, the rest of the coven ignored Ravana and Gran couldn't hold her alone. The Raythe gave a mighty shake that shredded the magical bonds to dust. I saw her pause and survey the room with beady eyes. I also saw the moment she made the decision that sealed her doom.

Ravana's eyes locked on Violet with a wild hunger.

"Get out of the way," I shrieked, but it was too late. The rampaging beast hit the coven like a bowling ball, scattering witches every which way, and before the last one hit the ground, Ravana had her master by the throat, lips locked on Violet's in a deadly imitation of a kiss.

There was nothing we could do but watch helplessly while Ravana feasted on her master's soul.

I've never watched anyone die before, and I hope I never do again. When the deed was done, Ravana triumphantly turned to the next closest witch and then the weirdest thing happened. She belched. A gusty, fetid burp that echoed off the far wall and spewed a faint, white shape in the same direction.

Ravana looked surprised, then dismayed. Or I think she did. Her expressions weren't that easy to read. She roared. She shivered. She fell to dust. Poof.

And she was gone.

Violet was dead. Not just dead, but thoroughly stoned. It must have happened while we were busy watching Ravana fall apart. How's that for karmic payback?

The fireplace slid open. Salem's eyes searched the room until they found me relatively unharmed, and I saw him sigh in relief. He tossed me a grin, then turned to help Millie Minkens to her feet. Pyewacket made a beeline for Gran, and the last to step inside was none other than Calypso Snodgrass.

White-faced, she raised her voice in as concerned a tone as I'd ever heard her speak, "Serena? Are you all right?"

"I'm okay." Serena, her arm already splinted and healing stepped out from behind the group. I can't remember the last time I'd seen a genuine smile on her face, and I admit to getting a little misty when I watched mother and daughter embrace.

"Never a dull moment, hey?" Leave it to Aunt Mag to boil a life and death situation down to a cliché.

Chapter 24

Kin showed up right before Calypso took charge of Violet's granite remains. An impressive flick of her wand sent the bulky statue floating.

"Where shall I put," her customary sneer reappeared, "this?"

"Put her next to a fire hydrant somewhere. One in a neighborhood with a lot of dogs." Simultaneous snorts went up from several sections of the room when Winnie offered her opinion.

Despite loss and injury, the mood was high, and I suspected Terra was about to see her Twinkleberry wine stash become severely diminished. She and her sisters had begun to regain their color and I'd had enough drama for one day.

Kin and I retired to my bedroom where I'd hoped to get a chance to shower off the day and cuddle in front of a good movie. One of his favorites since there was a good chance I'd fall asleep before the end. I felt like a Mack truck had run me over, backed up, and run me over again, but it turned out fate wasn't finished with me quite yet.

My phone blinked with a half dozen missed calls from Hannah, and I wondered what fresh hell might be waiting for me on the other end of the line. Good news didn't even cross my mind, and rightly so.

Without even checking my voicemail, I dialed Hannah's number and was surprised to hear Emily's voice on the other end of the line, "Hello? Who is this?"

"It's Lexi Balefire. We met at the farmer's market a few weeks ago."

"How do you happen to know my daughter?"

My heart leaped into my throat, but fortunately, I wasn't obligated to answer the question since Emily immediately launched into the more pressing reason for her call. "Hannah ran away, and her father and I are calling everyone in her phone log that might have information about where she went. You're the last person she called. Do you know where our daughter could have gone?"

I heard the fear in Emily's voice, and it broke my heart.

"I haven't spoken to Hannah since she called me a few days ago. Can you tell me what happened before she took off?"

Emily was silent for long enough I thought she'd

hung up. I'm sure she was wondering how much of her situation to reveal to a virtual stranger.

"Her father dropped her off at our house, and we got into an argument. We've been going through a separation, and Hannah hasn't been taking it very well."

My mind raced as I thought back over my conversations with Hannah, and I recalled her description of summer weekends at Coachman's Bluff. I'd bet my right arm that's where Hannah had gone, and dicey cell service out at the caves would explain why she hadn't taken her phone along with her.

The internal homing mechanism, now tied to the Bow of Destiny, kicked in to let me know I was correct.

"She did mention something once about Coachman's Bluff being her favorite place. Have you checked there? "

"Why didn't we think of that?" Emily rushed me off the phone, but even knowing Hannah's exact location wasn't enough to settle the jumpy feeling in the pit of my stomach.

"We have to get out to the caves at Coachman's Bluff. Can you drive?"

Kin nodded, his eyes wide with concern, and shrugged his sweatshirt back over his head, "I'm ready." He'd overheard my conversation and being a stand-up kind of guy was as worried about the lost child as I was.

Ten minutes later we were cruising down an unfrequented route out of the city, north toward an undeveloped section of coastline. The sun was just beginning its slow descent into the horizon, and we were quickly losing what remained of daylight. A sudden chill in the air left no doubt autumn was fully upon us, and as I rubbed my arms for warmth, I worried it would get frigid enough tonight to put Hannah in danger.

No way would I let it come to that. "Park over there, I bet that's the Aarons' SUV." I pointed toward a small clearing where a vehicle was parked beneath a low canopy of trees and hopped out before Kin put his car in park.

"Here, take this," Kin pulled a spare sweatshirt out from behind his seat and draped it over my shoulders. Then he hit the flashlight feature on his phone to illuminate an overgrown, boulder-strewn path. I heard leaves rustle in the woods to our right, and for once didn't stop to do the spider dance when I walked face-first into one of their webs.

"This is quite the hike to be doing in the dark," Kin commented quietly as he helped me through a particularly treacherous set of makeshift stepping stones. "Poor kid."

"It's this way, we're almost there." I led Kin a bit further, following the sound of voices punctuating the night.

"…Because I'm sick of you fighting, that's why." Anyone with ears could recognize the frustration in Hannah's shrill response. "I came here because it's the last place I remember being happy, and now you've ruined this for me, too."

"Come on, Lexi. She's been found, this isn't your problem anymore." Kin whispered and tugged on my arm, but I didn't budge.

"I think it might be. I made a mistake with Emily, and I think I'm the only one who can fix this for Hannah." How exactly to do that was still a mystery, and I didn't like the idea of invading their privacy, but I had to do something. My conscience wouldn't let me walk away.

I'm pretty sure the bow wouldn't either. Chiming like a chattering magpie, it berated me soundly. With sound. Hah, not funny.

"What do you need me to do?"

"Do you have any idea how much I love you? Not just because you're ready to jump in and help me help some girl you've never even met. Not just because I can admit I've screwed up epically and you don't judge. You shine."

I put everything I felt for him into a kiss that ended way too soon.

"I'm going to try something, can you just hold me?"

His arms tightened, "Forever."

I carried that word and traveled deep inside to where the goddess lived, and let her lead me into the cave. My first out-of-body experience.

Like three points of a triangle, the Aarons family

faced off. One look at Emily showed me the enormity of what I'd done. Hannah hadn't described the problem strongly enough. Everything about her was locked down tight. Her face, her emotions, her muscles clenched.

She and Matthew both carried the glowing symbol, but where his was bright and shining, Emily's looked tarnished and dark. The marks were the keys to this whole problem, I knew that with every morsel of my instinct. And yet, I had no idea how to interpret them.

If my arrow had taken something from Emily, though, maybe it was the only thing that could give it back. Oh, the bow liked that idea well enough to almost knock me out with sound.

All righty, then. Let's do this.

But on my terms.

I slid into the Goddess like a hand into a glove. Everything went pink. And bright. And I finally saw the symbols for what they were. Kissing lip emblems.

How dumb had I been? They were the symbol of true love's kiss. The verification of a match made that could not be broken from the outside. Stephanie's voice floated through my memory.

True love's kiss is not a guarantee. It's a promise that can be broken but only by the kissers. My interference had only caused more problems. This hadn't been a job for Lexi 2.0.

It wasn't Hannah's desire or my actions that would bring this couple together, it was their own choices. And now it was time to undo the damage I had done by trying to force the issue.

I fired the arrow this time. Me, Lexi. Not the Goddess, not the witch. Just me.

I cleaned up my mess and stayed a minute longer to see if I'd done the right thing.

Bit by bit, Emily changed. She relaxed, the pinched look went away. The symbol brightened, and she softened. Shadows cleared and she looked at her husband. Saw the tears in his eyes, the pain, the sorrow, and the love laid bare.

"You're crying."

"I thought we'd lost her, Em. I'd die if that happened. I already lost you, and I'm still not sure I'll survive it."

Emily turned her face away.

"No, Em. Look at me. I need you to see me. See my heart." Matthew closed the short distance while Hannah watched with hope. He took Emily's hand and pressed it to his chest. "Can't you feel it beating? It's for you, always you."

When Emily's other hand lifted to cover his, I knew Hannah would get her wish. It might take time, but my work here was done. Hannah's beaming smile was the last thing I saw as I let myself return to Kin's waiting arms.

Chapter 25

An emotional hangover followed me the entire next day, and I couldn't shake the niggling feeling that something frustrating was coming down the pike. You'd think I'd have learned to trust that gut feeling, considering I used it as a compass every day of my life when it came to being a Fate Weaver.

Alas, I was as surprised as anyone else when things took a turn for the worse, but what was bothering me now had nothing whatsoever to do with witches, the Balefire, or the balance of light and dark energy in the world.

It had to do with one thing: boy trouble.

I'd never put a family back together before. I'd been there for the beginnings of plenty of relationships, but fixing something that had been thought either lost or broken beyond repair was more fulfilling than a handful of newly-minted couples. Hannah wasn't some nebulous little person who would one day come into the world—she was already here, and for the first time, I could see the immediate effects of my power on a future generation. It was humbling and made me realize I had more work ahead of me than I'd ever imagined.

The problem is, that's not the only thing I was destined for. I was Keeper of the Balefire flame. It was part of my *name*. It was part of my history; my heritage, and it was *my* destiny. I spent so much time concerning myself with other people's fates, I'd almost forgotten I had one of my own. I wanted to tend the flame, wanted to host the Beltane celebration each year and follow in my family line.

But then there was Kin. I loved him, and it hurt my heart to think about him being away from me for an extended period of time. Would he wait for me? It was pretty clear that misunderstandings, anger, and resentment could throw even a fated couple off the rails. What if that happened to us? What if I looked back and wished I'd followed him to the edges of the earth—or at least to Chicago or Nashville? What if he got a record deal and never came back? There were too many what-ifs to think about, and none of them, in my heightened emotional state, ended well for LexiKin.

In the heat of the moment, I'd chosen to act as Keeper—and it seemed as though the Balefire itself was happy to now have only one master. And since I had taken the responsibility back from my grandmother, it was mine now. For keeps.

No extended vacations, no following my man to the ends of the earth. Now, I had to tell him I might be able to come along for a visit, but not the whole tour while making sure he made the life choices that were right for him. Even if that meant leaving me behind.

This adulting thing? Totally sucks.

When I finally arrived on Kin's front porch, I'd walked until my feet ached as much as my head did. I found him in an upstairs room lined with foam panels designed to muffle the thump of drums and bass. He had a pair of headphones strapped over his ears, and his eyes were closed as he lost himself in the rhythm and allowed his hands to move over the strings of his beloved guitar with an automatic ease.

I hung back and watched until he finished the song, a slow, lilting tune that conjured images of a country field on a warm summer's day. Tears welled in the corners of my eyes, and when he finally turned to face me, they'd begun to stream down my face leaving black mascara tracks and red blotches I'm sure were less than flattering.

"Babe, what's wrong?" He asked, striding over to wrap his arms around my shoulders and wiping the tears away from my cheek. It felt like the millionth time he'd had to ask me that same question during our short time together.

"It's the tour," I blubbered, crushing my face into

his chest, "I'm sorry, but I can't come with you, at least not full time."

I could hear his lungs deflate in a sigh as he pulled me closer. "Come sit down, dry your eyes, and let's talk." Kin led me downstairs and made a cup of tea while I cleaned myself up enough to speak coherently.

"Part of me would be happy to go. I could do my work—my Fate Weaving—while you're rehearsing; I could help more people, and I know we would have an amazing time together. But there's another part of me—the little orphan girl inside—that can't bear to leave my home now that it's finally filled with family. I made a commitment to be the Keeper of the Flame in the truest sense when we were trying to save the Balefire, and I can't go back on that now."

I'm pretty sure that last bit came out in fractured gibberish, now that the tears had begun to flow again. "Gran can hold down the fort for a few days, maybe a week, but no longer. I understand if you don't want to be tied down while you're away. I know long distance isn't what you had in mind, and I won't ask you to stay here for someone who might not ever be able to take the next step. Not for a tour and not to move in with you."

Kin sighed again and pulled me close. "Lexi Balefire, Daughter of Cupid, Keeper of the Flame, Fate Weaver Extraordinaire, you are *my* girl, and I'm not so crazy as to let you get away that easily. I've played clubs before; I've traveled this country, and never have I found another woman as beautiful and interesting and infuriating as you. You'll have to do a lot more than refuse to leave your home if you want to get rid of me."

On top of raccoon eyes, I gave him fish face. Eyes bugged out and mouth open in shock.

And he didn't run away. Wonder of wonders.

"Did you think this was some kind of ultimatum? Because it never was. It was an offer, and you're entitled to refuse it. You'll come for a week, and we'll figure out the living arrangements when I get back. And I will be back, you can count on it."

My heart slowly went back to its natural rhythm.

Chapter 26

Kin hadn't been gone two hours when Aunt Mag marched into the kitchen and announced she was leaving for Myrtle Beach.

"Come with me, Clarie. It'll be fun."

"Now? Lexi might need me."

"Clarabelle Doireann Neasa Balefire, that girl is a full grown adult, and there are four faeries living in the house, plus her familiar. I think she'll be fine if you take a week at the beach."

"Go, I'll be fine, just be back for Samhain because I'm flying to Nashville the day after. Unless I can talk Salem into teaching me to skim from place to place." I tossed him a look that was part question, part challenge. "Or maybe you could leave Pyewacket here, and she could show me." Putting his ego on the line almost ensured I'd be zipping like a big witch by the time I was supposed to board the flying metal tube of death.

After that, it didn't take much to convince Clara to pack a bag and go.

"I'll be gone for the next few weeks as well," Vaeta piped up. "Rhys has IMA business in Peru, and I said I'd go with him."

By the end of the day, we were down to five counting Salem. All the party planning boxes and bins marched—compliments of a nifty spell Mag taught me—out to the garage, and the house felt like it had doubled in size all of a sudden.

With little else to occupy my time over the next couple of weeks, I decided to dig in at FootSwept and get my business back in shape. I might have been using it as an excuse to try and learn more about how to use the bow, but I didn't see anything wrong with that plan.

Keeping myself busy filled the empty hours, and I threw myself into work with abandon.

When I ran into Mona Katz, and she had to wave a hand six inches from my face before I noticed her standing in front of me, I decided I'd better start trying to find that elusive balance again.

"Lexi, I haven't seen you in weeks. How are you doing?" Mona was a former client turned friend, not that I had been treating her like one lately.

I squeezed her shoulder as she wrapped me in an enthusiastic hug, and hoped she'd forgive me, "I'm so sorry, Mona. I've had some serious family drama to deal with, and now I'm trying to get back into the swing of things with work. How is Mark?"

"We're right in the middle of a debate about what size television I'll allow in our future living room—I'm merely suggesting it be smaller than one entire wall, but since I still have ten more months on my lease, he's got time to wear me down." Mona smiled that smile all women have when they think about the man they're hopelessly in love with, and I patted myself on the back for about the tenth time that week.

"Cave on the TV and then demand a gigantic whirlpool tub in the bathroom as compensation." I winked at Mona, and we dissolved into a fit of giggles that had more to do with missing one another's company than the actual conversation.

"I've got to get back to the shop. Your aunts have commissioned a giant Yoda-shaped groom's cake for a Star Wars theme wedding this weekend—it's not my first, believe it or not—and the ears are giving me trouble again. But let's get together after Kin gets back for a double date."

I agreed, watched Mona bustle off toward Crumb, where she had made a name for herself as one of the most creative pastry chefs in the city, and made a mental note to tell Kin I'd made us a couples date.

I recalled the details of Mona's journey to find Mark. I'd known from the second she walked into my office that this woman had a lot of love to give and that her mate was within a stone's throw from where we sat.

But rather than walking her down the street and introducing the two of them immediately, I'd done what I do best—prepared her for the big life change she was about to undergo. That's how I'd always operated. I'd get to know my clients, understand what it was they were looking for, and match them to the right person.

In my head, the happily ever after was a given. I mean, you put two soulmates together, and they stay that way, right? Stephanie had to be the exception to the rule, but her story had me curious, and I'd begun obsessing about checking in with all my former matches.

With that thought in mind, I decided to get Flix to show me how to access the database of clients he'd set up on the notebook computer. We'd made up a couple of days before and were still in our post-blowout honeymoon phase.

As I turned the corner onto State Street, I stopped short at the sight of a looming highway billboard framed in purple glitter and featuring a striking woman with a head of flowing auburn hair and a toothpaste-commercial smile.

"Let us find your diamond in the rough" read the tagline, right above a scrawled signature and a phone number. With the advent of online dating sites, traditional matchmakers were thin on the ground, except for me, that is.

Competition didn't scare me, especially considering I had the blessing of the gods on my side, but Diana

Diamond's face lacked the sincerity I knew contributed to my own success. Too flashy for my tastes, but then again, some people are attracted to shiny things.

And some things are only shiny on the outside, but pure evil on the inside.

-The End-

www.ingramcontent.com/pod-product-compliance
Lightning Source LLC
Chambersburg PA
CBHW061102190726
48286CB00006B/1845